Is this dese[illegible]

M[illegible]

Dr. Vivian Wei is juggling [illegible]ple life-changing events when her aging mother witnesses a violent death on the thirteenth tee. The only problem? There doesn't seem to be a crime to go along with the witness.

As an empath, Vivian knows her mother is telling the truth, but feelings aren't evidence of a murder. Can Vivian and her friends prove a killer is stalking the country club before he claims another victim?

MIRROR OBSCURE is the second book in the Vista de Lirio series, a new paranormal mystery series by Elizabeth Hunter, best-selling author of the Elemental Mysteries, the Glimmer Lake series, and The Irin Chronicles.

Praise for Elizabeth Hunter

Double Vision is a gem of a book that showcases how important female friendship is, even under the strangest of circumstances. Delightfully weird and definitely magical, it's the kind of book you want to grab when you are feeling the need for a quick and cozy escape.

— CAT BOWEN, ROMPER.COM

A fantastic cosy mystery, full of twists and a little spice.

— SASSAFRACK, GOODREADS

Elizabeth Hunter's books are delicious and addicting, like the best kind of chocolate. She hooked me from the first page, and her stories just keep getting better and better. Paranormal romance fans won't want to miss this exciting author!

— THEA HARRISON, NYT BESTSELLING AUTHOR

Developing compelling and unforgettable characters is a real Hunter strength.... Another amazing novel by a master storyteller!

— RT MAGAZINE

The bottom line: if you're not reading Elizabeth Hunter's novels, you should be!

— A TALE OF MANY BOOK REVIEWS

This book more than lived up to the expectations I had, in fact it blew them out of the water.

— THIS LITERARY LIFE

Elizabeth Hunter actually makes me look forward to growing older, especially if comes with these awesomely fun psychic perks. Her new paranormal women's fiction series is a truly fun, entertaining read!

— MICHELLE M. PILLOW, NYT BESTSELLING AUTHOR

Mirror Obscure

A VISTA DE LIRIO MYSTERY

ELIZABETH HUNTER

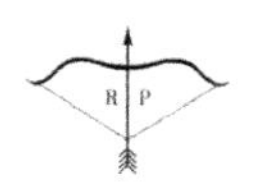

Mirror Obscure

ISBN: 978-1-941674-93-2

Paperback edition

Cover Designer: Karen Dimmick/Arcane Covers
Content Editor: Amy Cissell
Line Editor: Anne Victory/Victory Editing
Proofreader: Linda/Victory Editing

For more information, please visit ElizabethHunterWrites.com

Recurve Press, LLC
PO Box 4034
Visalia, CA 93278
USA

For the families we're born to
And the families we find

Chapter One

Her professional name had been Selene Beverly, discreet psychic to the stars and uncanny astrologer, but when she introduced herself to Vivian, she'd used her given name, Maud Peterson.

"Another deep breath in." Maud's soothing voice drifted over the cool morning air. "And out very slowly, letting any negativity—aaaaany friction or resistance—eeeeexit your body." Another deep breath, in and out. "Release it to the universe."

No need for professional names among peers according to Maud. Vivian was newly empathic. Her friend Julia, who was sitting directly in front of her, was a medium exchanging silent pointed looks with their friend Evy, the telepath of their small supernatural circle.

According to Maud, they all needed practice.

The more experienced touch-telepath happily agreed to join Morning Club two days a week to help Vivian and her friends with their "psychic workouts." At least that's what Maud called them. She was like a personal trainer if a personal trainer was more interested in your aura than your muscles and wore caftans for appointments.

"Another two breaths like that; then we'll start our meditation."

Vivian tried to focus on her breathing and not on the papaya-sized baby in her uterus who had decided to do backflips on her bladder that morning.

I don't have to pee. I don't have to pee. I don't have to— "Shit."

She'd whispered it, but when she opened her eyes, every gaze on the lawn that morning was directed toward her. Julia and Evy, Aunt Marie—the one who knew Maud in the first place—and half a dozen other Morning Club neighbors from Vista de Lirio, the weird and wonderful neighborhood that had become Vivian's second home.

"Sorry." Vivian awkwardly hoisted herself to her feet and pointed to her belly. "Need to pee again."

Maud nodded and waved her hands. "As we listen to our bodies and give them what they need—eyes forward please—we focus on centering our spines and connecting with the earth beneath us, the life around us, and the power within us."

Slowly everyone turned back, closed their eyes, and refocused their attention on Maud's guided meditation. Morning Club was a Vista de Lirio institution. No pregnant lady was going to trip it up.

Sergio Oliveira, their host that morning, shuffled over in a black T-shirt, a pair of grey sweatpants, and house slippers. His shoulder-length hair was tousled, and thick black stubble marked his jaw.

"What do you need, honey?" He blinked his dark bedroom eyes and yawned a little. "I can't ever sit still long enough for meditation. Can I get you some tea? No Bloody Marys or Mimosas for you these days, but I'll make you a virgin Screwdriver if you want." He squinted. "Maybe that's just orange juice. I'll get you an orange juice."

Good Lord, he looked like a movie star. It was at least the

hundredth time she'd thought it since Sergio had walked into her dental practice for a cleaning and she'd met the man who had started the string of unlikely events that had landed her where she was, newly psychic and pregnant at forty-two.

Okay, that was unfair. He was really only responsible for the psychic part.

"I'm fine." She brushed her hand over his arm and felt the happy wave of emotion that was Sergio. "I just need to use the bathroom. Again."

He yawned and waved at the house. "You know where it is. I'm going to make you some tea anyway."

"Thanks." Vivian walked to the bathroom in the sprawling 1930s mansion that Sergio shared with his husband, Dean; their two daughters; and Alula, their live-in nanny.

She sat down and did her business with great relief, then stood, wrestled her yoga pants over her ever-expanding belly, and tried to imagine life in three months.

Intellectually, Dr. Vivian Wei knew that her uterus would grow rapidly at this stage of pregnancy to keep up with the swiftly growing baby boy she was carrying. She knew that; she just couldn't imagine it. She was already feeling unwieldy and off-balance. Her feet were bigger. Her black hair was getting thicker every day, and she felt like sleeping constantly. Thank God she was in excellent shape and healthy for forty-two because she could not imagine doing this if she wasn't.

She washed her hands, walked out of the powder room and toward the sounds of life in the kitchen. Sergio was standing near the electric kettle with Dean, who was already dressed in a bright white shirt and linen jacket. Dean might be a commercial real estate broker, but it was August in Palm Springs. A suit and tie would be pure torture.

"Good morning, Vivian." Dean walked over and brushed a kiss on her temple. "How are you feeling?"

"Good, just distracted." She peered out the window at the

group on the lawn. "I have never been very good at sitting meditation."

"Same," Sergio said. "I'll join them in a half hour when tai chi gets going."

"That sounds like a plan." She tried to jump onto one of the half dozen barstools on the other side of the kitchen island before giving up and grabbing a chair in the breakfast nook. "At least the weather is nice."

"For another two hours, and then it's one hundred and eight today." Dean grimaced. "How are you doing?"

"Becoming a better swimmer every day." Vivian smiled. "And thanking the universe my grandparents' development has a pool." It wasn't technically her grandparents' development anymore; it was hers. She'd been living in Palm Springs full time for over a year now, but this was her first full summer. And her first summer pregnant.

What had she been thinking?

Oh right: time was of the essence.

Despite her single status, nothing about Vivian's pregnancy was unplanned. Nothing about her *life* was unplanned except for the jolt of psychic energy seven months before that had unlocked latent empathic power and turned her world on its head.

She had always known she wanted to be a mother. And she'd always had a plan to become one if she hadn't met the right partner by age forty. She had no qualms about scientific means of conception.

As far as Vivian was concerned, this mindset freed her from the pressure of finding "the right man" for a relationship and fatherhood. There was no deadline to settle for a subpar relationship when she knew that she could accomplish motherhood on her own. Now if she met someone, it would be for the right reasons, not because she was on a biological schedule.

Not that she was looking.

With a pregnancy nearing the last trimester, her parents' sudden and possibly permanent move to Palm Springs, and the unexpected ability to sense emotions when she shook hands with strangers, Vivian knew that any kind of romance was out of the question for the year. Maybe the decade.

At least she had fellow new psychics Julia and Evy to keep her company with the paranormal aspect of her life. And Maud. She had Maud.

"Here's your tea." Sergio sat across from her and blinked heavily. "I should probably at least try to meditate, right?" Dean barked a laugh and Sergio turned to him. "At least I try. What do you do for your mental well-being?"

Dean didn't even look up from the newspaper. "I kiss you and I golf."

Sergio looked back at Vivian. "See, what am I supposed to say to that?"

"Nothing." She patted his hand. "Come on. I'll finish my tea and we should get out there. If I don't keep practicing the tai chi, I'll start tipping onto patients when I look at their molars."

"YOU ARE SO MUCH BETTER AT TAI CHI THAN I AM." Evy wiped the glow of sweat from her forehead. It wasn't from exertion; it was because it was nearing ninety degrees already. "And you're pregnant. I really need to exercise more."

"Yes, you do." Julia took a long drink of the Paloma Sergio had made for her and leaned back in the patio chair. "Ladies, should I start looking for my own place?"

Evy looked around the shaded patio, the crystal-blue pool, and the rolling lawn where other members of Morning Club were chatting and sitting with their drinks while the weather was still bearable. "And move away from heaven?"

Vivian smiled. "I have to admit, your setup here is pretty sweet."

Julia was currently living in Dean and Sergio's pool house and had been for nearly a year. She was family though, so they refused to let her pay rent. And since Julia was a very successful real estate agent with homes in both Laguna Beach and Malibu, she had plenty of capital if she wanted to buy a house in Palm Springs.

"You're right. And half the time I'm house-sitting for Michael anyway," she said. "That is the benefit of having a part-time boyfriend."

Michael, Julia's new man, was a director and traveled a lot, so he was barely at his new house in Palm Springs, but at least Julia was enjoying it.

"You might need to start house hunting for me," Vivian said. "I'm starting to think my parents' move might be permanent."

"Oh, I knew it!" Julia smiled. "You *need* to move, Vivian. Living in Rancho Mirage is not for you. Why don't your parents stay there and you find your own place? Here. In Vista de Lirio."

"I thought your dad was helping at the practice?" Evy sipped her Bloody Mary. "Is it a little too much closeness?"

"It is, and he is. My dad is great, and my mom is so excited about the baby. They are definitely helping a lot, but I'm just used to having my own space." She waved a hand. "I'm sure it's just a transitional stage. I'll be grateful they're here when the baby comes. And I never have to cook anymore; that's so nice."

Plus she didn't have the budget Julia did. Vivian did well, but if she wanted to move, she'd need to sell the house her grandparents had left her, which was a house her parents loved. Her father could golf every day, and her mother had a mahjong club at the Jewish temple full of smack-talking old women, most of whom were fellow retired MDs.

In short: her parents were happy, enjoying the warm weather, and looking forward to spoiling a new grandbaby.

They were never moving.

"I CAN TELL THE MEDITATION CLASS IS WORKING." Joan Wei, MD, was serving dinner and filling in Vivian and her dad about her day. "Your color is good."

"This looks delicious, Mom."

Her mother was the first generation of her Chinese family born in the US, so she'd learned to cook all the traditional dishes Vivian's dad loved but also the varied dishes she'd grown up eating in Chicago. Italian, Mexican, and even Slavic dishes like the stuffed cabbage rolls she'd made that evening.

"I hope it's good. It's Marty's recipe and I liked it, but it needed some spice." She spooned a large helping of rice next to the cabbage rolls. "Hopefully it won't give you heartburn. It's just a little heat."

Vivian's mouth was burning with the first bite, but the flavor was delicious. "It's great." She nodded. "Perfect, Mom." *Tums, here I come.*

"There are more in the pan, so eat."

Despite the heat, it was a delicious meal. "Dad, how was your round of golf this morning? I hardly saw you at the office."

"It was good, but I'm not gambling with that Simon fellow again." Allan shook his head. "He's been golfing a lot longer than me; he wins every time."

"You lost to a ninety-year-old?" Joan asked.

"I told you." Allan nodded firmly. "Experience."

Vivian looked at her parents with a little bit of exasperation and a lot of love. They'd raised her and her sister to be successful adults but also raised them with so much love it threatened to make Vivian weepy.

Everything made her weepy lately.

Dammit, she was crying.

Joan's eyes went wide. "Vivian, what's wrong?"

"Nothing!" She smiled. "I was just thinking that this baby is so lucky to have such amazing grandparents." She reached out her hands. "Thank you for being here, Mom. Dad, I'm so glad you two are happy here."

They both reached out to grab her hand, and she felt their love and their worry. Pride and concern from her father, but her mother's emotions were so muddled Vivian wondered if they were too close to her own.

She wiped her eyes and smiled again. "Let's eat before it gets cold."

"You know, after dinner, we could watch the Desert Classic," Allan said. "I heard they were going to replay it on the Golf Channel."

Great. Awesome. Vivian stuffed the rest of the cabbage roll in her mouth. Just what she wanted to do on a Friday night, watch reruns on the Golf Channel.

VIVIAN WAS SOUND ASLEEP WHEN A MOVEMENT ON her bed jolted her awake.

"Vivian?" Her mother was sitting on the edge of her bed.

"Mom, what are you doing up here?" She'd moved to the upstairs guest room when her parents moved in because her mother's knees bothered her on the stairs. Why had her mother climbed to the second floor? "Is Dad okay?"

"He's fine." She opened her mouth, then closed it.

Vivian sat up and rubbed her eyes. She glanced at the clock and noticed the time. "Mom, what is going on? It's one in the morning; are you okay?"

"No." Her voice came in a whisper.

Vivian really looked at her mother. Her face was pale, and

she looked... scared? She leaned forward and grabbed her mother's hand.

Terror. Sheer terror.

"Mom, what's wrong?"

"I couldn't sleep," Joan started. "I... I have some tea that my mother used and I brought it from home, so I went to make it, and when I was waiting for it to steep, I looked out the window in the kitchen. You know the thirteenth tee is just over the fence line, and you can see the golfers when they're teeing up."

"Okay. Was there someone—?"

"He swung the golf club, and I didn't realize what was happening at first, but there was a light from somewhere and then I saw the club and then the man fell down." Her voice dropped to a whisper. "He hit him so many times, Vivian. There was blood and..." She looked up. "I think he's dead. Someone murdered that man."

Chapter Two

Vivian rubbed her eyes and wished so hard for coffee she nearly thought she'd manifested the warm Styrofoam cup someone pushed into her hand.

"You look exhausted." John Marcos, the chief of the Palm Springs Police Department, sat next to her. "Sheriff's deputy called me when you mentioned my name."

"Is this your jurisdiction?"

"No, but I work with Bernie, the commander here, a lot. He's a good guy."

"Does he know about the...?" Vivian tapped her temple.

They'd been lucky to meet Chief John Marcos months ago when Julia had found a dead body at one of her listings in Vista de Lirio. They'd come to find out that Chief Marcos was pretty open-minded about psychic powers, having worked with legitimate mediums and telepaths in the past.

Still, he was a cop, and cops were skeptical by nature.

"The psychic stuff?" John shrugged. "Bernie's a little more old-school. I'd probably leave that out of your statement if you want him to take you seriously."

"Me? I didn't see anything." She looked at the mug. "Is this tea?"

"Herbal. I didn't know if you're drinking caffeine these days. I did put some honey in it. That's how my sister likes hers."

"Thank you." She sipped it. "It's great, John."

"Do you want me to call anyone?"

She glanced at her mother and father, who were speaking with a sheriff's deputy. Well, her mother was talking and her father was holding her hand. "I don't think so. What did they find at the golf course?"

"I talked to the crime scene folks." John frowned. "That's kind of why I came over."

She cocked her head. "What's the problem?"

"Nothing." He shook his head. "I mean, Bernie asked me if you were a serious person—"

"Which I am."

"Obviously." He glanced at her parents. "And I know your parents must be too. But Vivian, they didn't find anything at the golf course."

She looked at the window. The sun had just barely come up. "You mean they didn't find a body?"

"I mean they didn't find *anything*." John shook his head. "No body. No golf clubs. No blood."

Vivian's eyes went wide. "Nothing?"

"Literally nothing out of the ordinary. The grass had just been cut and it was damp, but the sprinklers come on at night, so that's to be expected."

"So maybe the sprinklers washed the evidence away," Vivian said. "Maybe someone hid the body and they knew the sprinklers—"

"No blood at all?" John shook his head. "I mean, it's not very likely."

The attack her mother had described was vicious. Beating someone to death wouldn't have been a neat prospect; Vivian understood John's incredulity. "You're saying that there would be something. Some evidence."

"Blood for sure. With a beating like that, probably brain matter, hair, maybe torn fibers from clothes..."

Her love of murder podcasts confirmed that every word he said was true. Crime was a lot messier than TV shows usually depicted. "And there's nothing? What about the grass? Is it torn up? Does it look like someone was fighting?"

"The grass around the tee looks a little scruffy, but nothing out of the ordinary. There's a sand trap nearby, and they searched that too. Vivian, I'm telling you, there is no evidence that anything happened on that golf course last night."

She didn't know what to say. Her mother wasn't a fanciful person, and she'd *felt* her fear. Felt the terror radiating through her body. Nothing about what her mother had told her last night *felt* untrue. "I don't know what to tell you. She wasn't dreaming because she said she had insomnia. She was already awake. She was very lucid."

"She *is* seventy-five," John said gently. "Is there any history of dementia or... I don't know. Anything like that?"

"Please." Vivian nearly snorted. "This is my mother. She was a physician for thirty years, and she's still sharp as a tack. Does the *Chicago Tribune* crossword every morning—she wouldn't be caught dead with the *New York Times*—and she plays mahjong three times a week. She can beat me at any trivia game known to man."

"I'm just saying that she's getting older and it's possible—"

"I'm telling you it's not." She put a hand on John's arm and felt his worry and sincerity. It allowed her to stay kind and not storm off in irritation. "My mother has been living with me for two months; if there was something going on, if she was having problems like that, I'd have noticed it."

"I believe you," John said. "I just don't know how long the sheriff's department here is going to take her seriously."

"She saw a man killed behind our house!"

"I know." He raised his hand. "I know she thinks she saw it, but there's just no evidence that anything happened. They can't investigate a crime that doesn't seem to exist."

She motioned toward her mother and father. "She saw the man who was attacked. What about that? They said she could sit with a sketch artist. Did she already do that? Does it match any missing person reports? Someone must have noticed this man is gone."

"Um..." He frowned. "She did. She sat with a sketch artist, and they did get a really solid sketch from her. She said it was a very good representation of the man she saw last night."

"Okay, great. So that's something."

He raised a finger. "Give me a minute."

John rose, walked to an officer's desk, and grabbed a paper while he exchanged a few words with the tan-clad deputy and nodded at her parents nearby. Then he walked back to Vivian and sat next to her.

"This is a copy of the sketch. According to your mom, this is the man who was attacked behind your house last night." He handed Vivian the paper.

She held it up, and it took her a second to understand. "Oh."

"Yeah."

"Right." A heavy weight fell into her stomach, and it had nothing to do with the one-pound gymnast who was dancing on her bladder again.

It was a clear sketch. Very clear, in fact. And familiar.

Her mother had described the man in great detail, and the artist had captured him perfectly. Vivian could almost see the subjects famous blue eyes shining from the simple black-and-white sketch.

Because apparently, her mother had seen Robert Redford's murder.

"I KNOW WHAT I SAW!" JOAN SAID BEFORE SHE slammed the door in Vivian's and Allan's faces.

Vivian turned and faced her father. "What is going on?" She could feel his guilt from across the room without even touching him.

She was a daddy's girl, following her father around like a puppy as a child, following him into dentistry as an adult. She was his companion at baseball games, and he was her personal and professional sounding board. When she'd decided to have a baby, it wasn't her mother she'd called first—it was her father.

And now he was hiding something.

"It's just little things," he said. "Senior moments, you know? We all have them, Vivi." He pointed to her. "You'll get there too. Trust me. I'm making some tea. You upset your mother."

"Dad." She followed him to the kitchen and kept her voice low. "She said she saw Robert Redford being killed. I think we can be fairly certain if that man had disappeared, the news would be reporting it."

"Maybe he just looked like Robert Redford and her mind went there when she was describing him." Allan shrugged. "You know a lot of old white men look very similar."

"Dad!"

"I know your mother." Allan turned to Vivian. "If your mother said she saw something, she saw it. She can be harsh sometimes, but she never lies. You know this."

"If she is having..." Vivian measured her words carefully. "If she's having senior moments, then maybe it's more serious than you realize."

"Vivian, she's a doctor."

"And we both know that doctors are the worst about diagnosing themselves." When her mother had a lump in her breast,

Vivian's sister Debra had nearly come to blows with their mother, trying to get her into the doctor's office.

It had been a benign cyst, and Joan still reminded Debra and Vivian about their "useless worry" on holidays.

So Vivian knew she had to put her foot down. "Dad, we *have* to talk about this."

"What is there to talk about?" He turned to Vivian. "Do you not believe your mother?"

More measuring of words. "I believe she *thinks* she saw a man murdered."

"And why would she say she saw that if she didn't?" Allan was incredulous. "What kind of sick person would make up a story like that, Vivi? Your mother isn't you and your sister with the murder shows and the crime books. She doesn't think about those bad things even for entertainment. Why would that be in her head if she didn't see it?"

She crossed her arms over her chest. "Dad, I know you're hiding something. Maybe you're hiding it from yourself too. I don't know. But if there is something going on with Mom, we're not doing her any favors if we ignore it."

He'd already turned back to the water boiler on the counter and was staring at the glass teapot, waiting for her mother's tea to steep.

Their conversation was over.

VIVIAN POINTED THE FLASHLIGHT AROUND THE TEE area, examining grass that had been manicured until it barely resembled a living thing. It was smoother than the fake grass they sold at the outdoor garden center.

Evy cleared her throat. "So what are we doing out here again?"

Julia walked past both of them. "Just hanging out and seeing if anyone dead comes by."

Vivian glanced at them. "Thank you for not blowing me off when I called."

Julia frowned. "Vivian, it's your mom, and she witnessed a murder. The killer might have been good about cleaning the scene, but that doesn't mean it didn't happen."

She felt inordinately relieved. It was one thing for the police to question her mother, but Julia and Evy had gotten to know her parents. Julia and her boyfriend Michael had been over for multiple dinners. She felt relieved that they didn't doubt Vivian's faith.

"I know the sketch she gave the police looked like Robert Redford, but I just can't believe she could have imagined the whole thing."

"You know your mom," Julia said. "If you believe her, we believe her."

"Go through what happened last night," Evy said. "How much time are we talking about? Because I have to tell you, I'm not seeing much either. The police didn't miss anything obvious."

Vivian continued walking up and down the green while Julia strolled along the cart path feeling for ghosts and Evy kept an eye and a mental ear out for any living person approaching.

"Okay, so she came up to my room about one in the morning and she was terrified. I could feel it rolling off her without even touching her. Incredibly vivid fear. I asked her what had happened, and she said she'd been making some tea to help her sleep." Something about the tea. There was something about the tea that she'd missed before...

Evy was looking at her. "And?"

She'd have to think about the tea later. "Uh, she told me what she'd seen. You can see the thirteenth tee from the kitchen window and the back deck." She swung the flashlight around to her house. "That window right there. It's not that far away, and she said she saw someone being attacked with a golf club and she thought he was dead."

Julia strolled back. "Well, if there's a ghost hanging around here, they're being very shy. I don't know what to tell you." She shrugged. "Doesn't mean they're not here; I might not be sensing them."

"So after she wakes me up, I pop my head out the back door—"

"Vivian!" Evy's mouth dropped open. "Your mom just said she saw a murderer, and you pop your head out to say hello?"

"If there was someone clinging to life and I could give them CPR or something, I couldn't ignore him. But I didn't see anything, so I immediately called 911. The operator said she was sending a car over, and it felt like it took forever, but it probably wasn't that long."

"But they didn't find anything," Evy said. "Did they search the rest of the golf course? This is Oasis Springs. It's massive as hell. There are what? Two full courses?"

Vivian nodded. "It's one of the biggest in Rancho Mirage. There are thirty-six holes and a huge driving range. It's why my mom's parents bought a place here."

"That's a lot of places to hide a body though." Evy ticked it off on her fingers. "There'll be outbuildings and sand traps. Probably lots of green space, not to mention water hazards. There have to be two dozen ponds in this place at least."

Julia narrowed her eyes. "How long did they search the grounds?"

Vivian shook her head. "I have no idea. My mother and father took a shower after the first officer came and asked them to come down to the station for a statement. That took an hour or so. By the time we got down to the station, it was almost morning."

"And that's when they questioned your mom?" Julia asked.

"They took her statement, yeah. It looked like they asked a bunch of questions." Vivian turned her flashlight back to sweeping the grass. Was that a glint of something shiny in the long grass near a bunch of palmettos?

"And how was your mom?" Julia asked. "When the police questioned her, I mean. She had to be exhausted, and we know she was terrified."

Vivian walked slowly toward the area where she'd seen the glint. "She was exhausted, but this is still my mother. It's pretty hard to rattle her."

"The original Dr. Wei?"

Vivian smiled. "Yeah." There. There was something in the grass! "There's something here." She gently lowered herself to her knees because with this belly, squatting wasn't going to happen without tipping over.

Evy and Julia came running over.

"Do you need our help?" Julia asked.

"Viv, you should not be—"

"I told you, Evy. No Viv. My dad is the only one who can nickname me." She'd experienced too many irritating nicknames when she'd been a small, very bookish child with extremely thick glasses. "I've got it. I'm pregnant, but my knees still work."

So did her eyes. She reached for the mud-covered gold partially hidden in a clump of mud and grass that looked like it had been chucked from the tee. In a divot maybe?

"It's a ring." She picked it up with two fingers and examined it under her flashlight. "Looks like a man's wedding band maybe?"

It was heavy in her palm, a simple circle of yellow gold with no stones but a raised, rounded edge on both sides. Thick and cool, it looked like fourteen carat, which meant it likely belonged to an American, Latino, or European man and not one of the numerous Asian or African men who lived at or visited the resort. Like her mother and father, most of them wore higher-carat gold, which was a darker color.

"Looks like kind of a standard American-dude wedding band." Evy looked over Vivian's shoulder. "Is there anything engraved inside?"

"Oh right." Vivian angled it toward the light. "To T. Love always, M." She looked up. "That's a definite clue."

"Or it's a married guy who was planning on cheating with the beer-cart girl," Evy said. "Just saying, T could be a very alive asshole and not a murder victim."

Vivian rolled her eyes. "It's still a clue, Evy."

She smirked. "So we can't just pawn it to pay my electrical bill? Did your rates go up here in Rancho Mirage? Ours are insane this summer."

"We're not pawning it." Julia was scrounging in her purse. "I think I have a baggie in here. We have to give it to the sheriff's department."

"I don't know about that." Vivian reached a hand out, and Evy helped her to her feet. "They don't seem to think a crime took place. Maybe a better idea would be to hang on to it. We can ask around; find out if anyone with the initial T has been missing or is missing a ring."

Julia frowned. "You don't think we should turn it in to the sheriff?"

Vivian sighed and arched her back to stretch. "Listen, they already think my mom imagined a murder. If we go in throwing evidence at them, they're going to think we're imagining stuff too. I need them to take us seriously."

"Okay." Julia held the baggie out, and Vivian dropped the ring in. "We hold on to it for now. Who knows? Evy may be right. T may be alive, well, and screwing the beer girl."

Chapter Three

By the next Tuesday, Vivian was feeling more focused and less worried about her mother. She'd spent the weekend watching her mom's every move, searching for any of those "senior moments" her father had mentioned and trying to determine if her mother was acting out of the ordinary.

Was Joan onto her observation? Probably. Did she say anything? No, but there was a lot of side-eye.

She was finishing a phone call with her sister when she walked into her favorite coffee shop on Palm Canyon Drive. "I'm telling you, I watched her like a hawk all weekend. Nothing jumped out."

Her sister Debra was undeterred. "I'm just saying you should keep an eye on her. I had the same instinct as you do now before they left Chicago. I feel like there's something going on and Dad may be covering for her. You know how stubborn she is."

There was a line nearly to the door, but Vivian was happy to wait. There was no other place on Palm Canyon Drive that made decaf espresso as well as this café.

"I know, and I'll keep an eye on her and let you know. I may try to get her to the doctor just to deal with this sleep issue because it seems like insomnia is really becoming a thing and that's so unhealthy."

"Grandma was the same way, remember?"

"A little." Vivian glanced forward. The line was hardly moving, but they'd just brought on another person at the register. "Debra, I better go. I'll keep you updated if there's any news."

"Okay. You still feeling good?" Debra was an OB/GYN, so Vivian's pregnancy was really only two-thirds hers. Her sister was even nosier than a typical sibling.

"I'm good! Yeah, feeling great. Not as tired this month, so that's nice. And now Mom and Dad are keeping me on my toes." The line moved forward. "I really have to go."

"Call me after your next doctor's appointment, okay? Or sooner if you want to talk."

"Will do. Love you. Bye." She hung up and stared at the menu on the chalkboard above the baristas. She treated herself to a very fancy coffee once a week, and she usually tried whatever special they had posted. This week was a new one.

"Mexican-chocolate latte," she murmured. "Hmm."

"It's good," a voice behind her said.

Vivian turned and saw Richard Putnam standing in line behind her, and she couldn't stop her smile. "Richard! How are you?"

Vivian had met Richard at a gallery opening in the middle of the first murder mystery she'd been thrown into. He was a film producer, a good friend of Michael's, and a former murder suspect. Luckily, that had all been cleared up and he'd resumed normal life. Well, as normal as life got when you were ridiculously wealthy and somewhat famous.

"I'm doing well." Richard smiled. "I saw you pop in here, and it inspired me."

She smiled. "You got your own coffee craving?" She

motioned vaguely to her belly. "I usually bring coffee from home, but their decaf is surprisingly great, so I treat myself."

Just like the last time she'd seen him, he was tall, ridiculously handsome, and buttoned-up in an East Coast banker sort of way. His only nod to California casual was a white linen shirt open at the collar. Vivian wanted to mess up his carefully combed steel-grey hair in the worst way.

"I don't blame you." He glanced down. "I'd heard you were expecting. How are you feeling?"

Of course, now that she was finally free to ask Richard out, she was very pregnant and dealing with her newly aging parents. Of course. She'd wanted to ask him out last spring but was pretty sure getting involved with someone embroiled in a murder investigation was not a Good Life Choice.

"I'm feeling great, but I'll be happy for some cooler weather. I'm due around Thanksgiving."

"Should be cooler by then." The line moved forward. "And I do recommend the Mexican-chocolate latte if you like a little spice. I had it yesterday morning, and I was thinking I'd get it again."

You like a little spice, huh? Her pregnant-lady libido was in overdrive, which was superinconvenient because she did not have time to pursue anything with anyone these days.

"I'll try it then. I love spice." She looked toward the street. "Is your office around here?"

"It is. And your practice is right around the corner."

"You remember." She'd lured him into her office to check the crown that had been giving him trouble last spring, mostly as an excuse to question him and get him under her hands where she could read him.

Now she could read anyone's emotions if they were in close proximity, which was a blessing and a curse. At the moment, she was trying to ignore lots of distracted and stressed vibes from the rest of the coffee shop and focus on the nice warm glow she was sensing from Richard. She found herself wanting to curl up in it and purr like a happy cat.

Down, girl.

The line finally started moving. "So how are your teeth?"

He smiled. "They're great. You were right—that crown was a little bit loose, but I went to my regular dentist in LA and he fixed it right up."

"Excellent." She glanced at her watch. "My dad is in town, so he's been helping out with early appointments. Coming into the office this late, I better grab a coffee for him too."

"He came out to help while you're on maternity leave?"

"Honestly, I think he came out for the golf and the warm weather." She smiled. "But the new grandson and helping me out were the stated reason, yes."

"So it's a boy?" Richard's eyes were blue, but it was a warm, cheerful blue.

"Yep. Little boy. Haven't decided on any names yet though." She finally stepped forward, ordered the decaf Mexican-chocolate latte and a regular cappuccino for her father. Then she stepped over to the side to wait while Richard gave his order.

He joined her a few moments later. "So I was thinking..." He was fussing with his wallet, but he finally put it in his pocket. "We should— I mean, if you'd like to—"

Oh God, he was asking her out and it was the worst possible timing in the world. Six months pregnant. Parents possibly relocating. And a disappearing murder victim thrown on top of that.

"—I'd love to take you to lunch sometime," Richard finished. "Since our offices are so close."

He was nervous and it was adorable. Vivian wanted to say yes so badly.

Say yes.

Vivian fell silent as the full blown argument in her head raged.

Are you joking?

You were going to ask him out months ago.

That was before All The Things.

"That is" —Richard glanced at her belly again— "if you're single. I shouldn't assume."

"I'm single." She just couldn't decide which mental voice to listen to. "And I really want to say yes because you seem great."

He smiled, and she could feel his natural confidence return. "So say yes."

"I have so much going on in my life right now." She let out a shaky laugh. "It's... I mean, it's kind of ridiculous at this point. If a TV writer came to you with the pilot of my life at this moment, you'd say it's too unrealistic for television."

The corner of his mouth turned up. "I don't know. It's hard to imagine your life being crazier than mine was about six months ago." He leaned toward her a little, and she could smell his cologne. "It's just lunch, Vivian."

Damn, he smelled so good. And her name sounded amazing in his mouth.

Say yes.

You cannot be serious.

"I will say... yes. To just lunch." *Vivian, what are you doing???* "Just lunch!"

Richard shrugged. "You have to eat. Is Thursday a good day for you?"

"Yes?"

The barista called her name, and she walked to the counter to get her coffee. The young woman glanced behind her at Richard and whispered, "You guys are so cute."

"Oh." She shook her head. "We're not... together."

"Are you sure?" She raised an eyebrow. "You might want to rethink that. He's hot."

Vivian felt a little buzz of giddiness in her chest. "You are not helping." She stuffed a five-dollar bill in the tip jar. "Thanks though."

"Thank *you*." The young woman grinned. "Have a good one."

"Thanks."

She walked back to Richard with two coffees in her hands. "I better get to the office. About Thursday—"

"Why don't I swing by your office around noon and we can walk somewhere close?"

She'd been about to change her mind, but... "Okay. Sounds good."

And there was her libido, making commitments her brain wasn't fully on board with.

Vivian, get your shit together.

"I'll see you Thursday." She escaped the café before she committed to anything else that was probably not a Good Life Choice. At this point, Richard could ask her to run away to Brazil with him and she'd probably go along with it.

"It's a good thing you brought me coffee," the elder Dr. Wei said. "I had to deal with a biting kindergartener."

"Those little stinkers." She smiled and sipped her absolutely stellar coffee. Richard had been right. The Mexican-chocolate latte was amazing. "But at least you don't have to do that root canal in an hour. That's all mine."

"True." Allan Wei leaned back in the fabric-covered chair across from her desk. "You've got a really nice practice here, Vivi. You should be proud of yourself. Your techs are pros, and your office staff is on top of things. I'm impressed."

"Thank you." She might be forty-two, but compliments from her dad still thrilled her. "I can only take credit for about a third of it though. Dr. Sutton put together a great team, and I've just tried to maintain that. I'm still thinking about looking for a new associate though. We have the work for one."

"I would recommend it. You were struggling before I came, I think."

"Joel retired in May, and the first part of the summer was pretty hectic. Of course, I was in my first trimester too, so I was exhausted."

Her dad nodded thoughtfully. "An associate would be good."

"I think so." She paused while her dad finished his coffee. "So before I go into this root canal, what's really going on with Mom?"

He froze. "Vivi, I told you—"

"I think you've noticed something you're not telling me or Debra about. We talked this morning. She said she had the same feeling I have. Something is going on with her, but she's too stubborn to admit it."

Her dad set his coffee cup down. "Your mother is a very intelligent woman, and she knows her own mind."

"When was her last physical?"

"She went for her regular checkup with Grace just before we left."

"Dr. Mercer was her protégée, Dad."

"And she's an excellent doctor," Allan said. "Clearly. Your mother trained her."

"Okay." Vivian chose her words carefully. "And if you think Dr. Mercer noticed something about Mom's cognitive health that she was concerned about, do you think she'd say something to her? Or would she feel awkward bringing it up with a woman who was her mentor?"

Allan opened his mouth, then closed it. "Something is different with you. Why are you so skeptical about your mother? Have you seen something to make you concerned?"

"Not necessarily." *But I can tell when you're lying now.* "I'm the same person, Dad, but I am worried about Mom, so yes, I'm being pushy. If it's something like Alzheimer's—"

"No one in our family has a history of that."

"Or something else." She sighed. "It's not always genetic, Dad. If she's acting out of character these days or having gaps, it could be early onset of something neurological, or it could be something else. Confusion can be a symptom of any number of things."

"People get forgetful when they get older, Vivian." He stood. "Mothers get emotional when they're pregnant. Hormones are powerful things, and I think yours are causing you to worry when you don't have to."

If it were anyone other than her father, she would have torn into them, but Vivian held her tongue.

Her dad walked over and kissed the top of her head. "We are so thrilled about the new baby, but don't let your imagination run away with you. Your mother and I are healthy, Vivian. Worry about finding a new associate to take some of the stress off your shoulders with the practice. I'll take care of your mother."

"And what about what she saw on the golf course last week?"

"The police are investigating." He walked to the door. "I fix teeth, so I'll let them solve crimes, okay? I'm sure the sheriffs know what they're doing; they'll find out the truth of what happened that night."

Chapter Four

Vivian had nearly forgotten about the ring in her relief that her mother seemed to be acting normally and not overly traumatized by whatever she'd seen, but by Wednesday morning, the band of gold in the small plastic baggie was staring at her from the top of her dresser.

She'd taken it out and taken lots of pictures. Should she fingerprint it? That probably wouldn't be useful, especially since she wasn't an official of any kind. She didn't see any fingerprints on it, but who knew what was visible to professionals?

You should take it to the sheriff.

And tell them what? That she'd found it near the tee on the golf course where there was no body and no evidence of any crime? It was probably nothing, and they would write her off like they'd written off her mother.

She'd take it to the club. After all, chances were there was a completely innocent explanation and this had nothing to do with the attack her mother had seen. People lost rings all the time.

She popped the ring in her purse and went downstairs to

find her mother puttering in the kitchen. "Hey, Mom! How are you this morning? Did you sleep all right last night?"

"Yes." She held her arm out, and Vivian gave her a side hug. "The tea works. I slept very well. How about you? I slept so soundly when I was pregnant with Debra, but with you? I was up all night with your gymnastics."

There was something in her mother's emotions that felt off. Joan was one of the most upbeat people Vivian knew. She wasn't always cheerful—she was too realistic for that—but she was always directed. She was never idle and always found a purpose or a plan.

This morning... Something about her mom felt wistful, maybe a little sad, and scattered.

"You okay?"

"Of course I am." She patted Vivian's belly. "What about the little man?"

Vivian only took belly pats from her mother. "That roast you made last night must have lulled him into sleep because he didn't start jumping as soon as I lay down last night." She reached for a travel mug and a packet of tea. "So I slept really well."

"Good." Joan turned to the oven and cracked it open. "I'm making egg-muffin bakes. Do you want one before you go to work?"

"I'm going to grab a yogurt and granola, but thank you."

"That's not real food."

Vivian smiled. "But it's the only thing that doesn't upset my stomach this early." She listened for her father. "Is Dad on the course?"

"He and Andy Carpenter were playing nine this morning." She glanced at Vivian. "I think he's going to buy a golf cart."

Vivian grimaced. "The garage is already packed. Where is he going to put it?"

"Don't ask me." Joan lifted her hands. "He's wanted one for

years. I think they're ridiculous, but he always complains about the ones the club has to borrow."

Buying a golf cart was yet another indication that her parents were here long term. "Hmm." She poured hot water over her tea and glanced out the window at the pair of women teeing off in the distance. "Mom?"

"Yes, honey?"

She looked at her mother and phrased her words carefully. "What do you want to do about what you saw the other night?"

Joan straightened from checking the oven and frowned a little. "I thought you didn't believe me."

"What?" Vivian shook her head. "Of course I believe you. I know you're telling the truth about what you saw. That's just the police. And... I mean, I can't say I blame them, I guess. Hard to justify investigating a crime when you can't find any evidence."

"Your father says I should drop it." Joan pursed her lips. "I don't know."

Her mother didn't want to drop it; that much was clear to Vivian. "You know, I don't know anyone at the sheriff's department, but I do know the chief of police in Palm Springs a little bit."

"Are they different?"

"Yes. Palm Springs maintains their own police department, but most of the other towns here in the valley fall under the sheriff's jurisdiction. I'm sure it can get a little complicated, but what if I called John—he's the chief of police I know—and see if you could look at missing person reports? He can probably access ones from the whole area."

Joan perked up immediately. "I'd recognize the man I saw getting attacked. I'll never forget his face."

Especially if it's Robert Redford's.

Vivian didn't say that, but she did nod. "Okay, I'll call him this morning and find out when we can do that. We'll probably have to go down to the police department in Palm Springs."

"I don't mind. Just remember I have bridge today around noon."

"I won't be free until..." She tried to think. "Probably about three. I'll see if that works for John. Maybe I'll call Julia. She knows him too." She added a little honey to her tea and sipped it. "And don't forget I'm having dinner with friends tonight."

"I know, but I'll make enough for you," her mom assured her. "That way if the food's not good, you can just leave it and eat at home."

The sad funk had lifted from Joan's emotions, leaving Vivian feeling much better about taking off for work. She walked over, kissed her mother on the cheek, and said, "I'll call you after I talk to John."

"Sounds good, honey." Joan patted Vivian's belly again. "Don't work too hard."

THE OASIS SPRINGS CLUBHOUSE WAS A SPRAWLING, modern building built to mimic Santa Fe architecture in the California desert. Since the house came with club membership, she and her parents were members by default. It was something her parents loved and Vivian resented every time she had to pay fees.

At least the gym and the dining room were good.

She walked into the lobby and searched for the office. She'd never had to visit before, but she figured it would be clearly marked. It was.

"Hello?" She poked her head into a cozy front office decorated with Georgia O'Keeffe prints. "Is anyone here?

"Just a minute!" a voice called from the back office. She heard a few more murmured words; then a pretty woman probably in her twenties walked out, shut the door, and moved to the empty desk in front. "Sorry about that. How can I help you? Are you inquiring about membership? Currently we're not taking new applications, but—"

"I'm already a member." Vivian interrupted her sales spiel. "Vivian Wei?"

"Oh! Dr. Wei's daughter." The woman smiled. "I'm Mindy Davenport, the secretary here at the club. Your father is so sweet. I saw him heading out this morning while I was walking in. He always makes me smile."

"Then he asked if you flossed?"

Mindy nodded. "Yep."

"We're dentists, so..." Her dad charmed any and all women he ran into. Then he told them to floss so they kept their beautiful smiles.

It was excellent advice that most people ignored.

Mindy's emotions were exactly as she presented. There was an open, bubbly happiness that told Vivian she was completely sincere in her admiration for Vivian's dad. She also either really enjoyed her job or was just having an exceptionally great morning.

The secretary sat at her desk. "So what can I help you with today? Did you have a question about your account?"

"Oh no. I'm here because I found something around the thirteenth tee—"

"North or south?"

"Oh, south. Sorry."

"No problem." Mindy grimaced. "The unluckiest tee on the course."

Vivian froze. "Is it?"

"It's the tee of drama." Mindy lowered her voice. "I mean, someone reported something to the police last week that turned out to be nothing, but we had to shut the entire course down for like six hours. It was a mess, and Ethan" —she nodded toward the closed door that read CLUB PRESIDENT'S OFFICE— "Mr. Wainwright was having a slight meltdown."

"I'm sure it was awkward."

"We straightened it out. Had to give out a few free rounds for missed tee times, but it's fine." She held out her hand. "You said you found something? Ring maybe? We get a lot of those."

"Yes." She reached in her purse. "As a matter of fact, it is one."

"A lot of guys take them off when they're golfing because of the gloves."

Or at least that was what they say to their wives. Vivian didn't question her. "So has anyone reported one missing?" She handed the baggie to Mindy.

Mindy looked at it, narrowed her eyes, then smiled. "I know exactly which one this is. He loses it at least once a month." She reached for the phone on her desk.

Vivian blinked. "That seems like a lot."

"It's Trent's. Trent Everett. He's the club pro." She dialed a few numbers on the phone. "I'm just surprised you found it. I think it's the third one his wife's bought him since he started working here. I don't know why he doesn't just keep it in his desk, you know? He said he was going to start doing that the last time he lost it."

"Right." Vivian was late to work, and it seemed like there was a reasonable explanation for the ring being found. Everything Mindy had said made sense. "Okay. Well, if you're sure it's his, I'm going to—"

"Oh!" Mindy raised a finger in a "give me a minute" gesture, so Vivian waited. "Trent? Yes, someone found your ring again." She paused. "I will. It's in the office." She hung up the phone and glanced at the closed door, then back at Vivian. "Do you have a few minutes?"

"Probably?"

"I hate to ask for more of your time." She held the baggie out to Vivian. "But do you mind taking this back, pretending you didn't turn it in to me just now, and giving it to Trent when he comes in a couple of minutes? If you officially turn it in, there are all these forms I have to file and I have to take pictures of everything and—"

"Oh!" Vivian didn't mind sparing someone a little paperwork. God knew it was the bane of her existence at her own office. "No problem. I completely get it."

"Thank you so much." Mindy smiled. "So you're a dentist like your dad, right?"

"I am. And my mom is a doctor and my sister is one too. We like tradition in the family."

"That's so cute."

Cute? Vivian didn't frown, but she kind of wanted to. "So have you worked long here at the club? I'm so busy I rarely come in, so I'm terrible about recognizing people."

"I've been working here about five years now. I started as a beer-cart girl in college." Mindy flashed the smile that had probably gotten her a small fortune in tips. "And then I worked in the events department. Now here. I'd like to eventually get back to events, but this was a promotion, so..."

"I get it." Vivian nodded.

Mindy was eyeing Vivian's belly and she was dying to ask something, but she kept her lips pressed shut. She was probably curious—like many people were—why an unmarried professional woman was having a baby. Vivian hadn't thought her pregnancy would stoke that much curiosity, but apparently it did.

It *really* did.

A set of heavy footsteps approached the office, and both Mindy and Vivian turned to watch the door. A tan, golden-haired man entered the room in a pair of khaki pants and a crisp white golf shirt with the Oasis Springs logo on the pocket. If Vivian had a mental picture of what a "golf pro" looked like, it was completely confirmed by the man she assumed was Trent Everett.

He looked at Mindy, then at Vivian. "Hey! Ring?"

"I have it." Vivian held out the baggie. "I'm just glad Mindy could identify it."

"I have been missing that since last week." He smiled. "Where was it this time?"

"Over on the thirteenth tee on the south course." Vivian watched Trent Everett's eyes go from relief to panic in the space of a heartbeat.

"Over on thirteen. Right." His heart was beating in his throat. She could see it fluttering, and while he tried to hide it behind an unwavering white smile, she could feel the jolt of panic coming off him. "I, uh, I think I changed my gloves on that one. Must have fallen out of my bag."

Vivian continued. "I was walking the cart paths a few evenings ago, and I saw it in the grass."

"Excellent." Trent's smile only grew wider as his fingers closed around the ring. "Thanks. I really appreciate you bringing it in."

Vivian forced a smile. "Just happy to find the..." *Killer*. He was the killer. She was sure of it. "...the owner." She nodded and turned to Mindy. "Thanks, Mindy. I'll see you later." She glanced back at Trent. "Have a great day."

"Better now!" He was feeling more assured. His panic was swiftly floating away the closer she got to the door.

Vivian sped out of the office, walked to her car, and slammed the door shut with her heart in her throat. She locked the doors and fumbled for her mobile phone, then messaged Julia and Evy on their group text.

So we may not know who was killed last week, but I'm pretty sure I just found his murderer.

Chapter Five

She sat across from John Marcos's desk at the Palm Springs police station and tried to remember everything she could about her brief interaction with Trent Everett. "I know he was terrified. Maybe *terrified* isn't the right word. My mom was terrified when she saw the murder."

"Alleged murder," John interrupted.

"Fine." Vivian sighed. "Alleged murder. What Trent was feeling was closer to panic. His emotions were more scattered than focused."

"But he didn't say anything incriminating?"

"No." She shook her head. "He said thanks for finding it. Mentioned he lost it last week."

"Which is..." John spread his hands. "...a completely reasonable explanation. I've seen the guy when I play at the course. He's a fixture."

"What's his story?" She glanced over her shoulder to where her mother and Julia were looking over a binder of missing persons reported in the Coachella Valley. "Mindy mentioned the police searching the course last week, but she didn't mention my mom. Is her name public knowledge? Could this

Trent guy find out who the *alleged* witness is and come after her?"

"I don't think you need to be worried about Trent." John squinted. "Honestly... I gotta tell you, Vivian, I just don't see the guy murdering anyone."

"He definitely looks strong enough. And he has access to the course. Obviously he has golf clubs, so he has access to the murder weapon."

"Of a murder victim who has never been found."

"John, I believe my mom. Now more than ever after meeting this guy."

"And I completely understand why, but I'm not going to get any traction investigating Trent Everett for a crime that no one can even prove happened." John folded his hands and took a deep breath. "Did you notice any bruises? Any cuts? Anything that might indicate he'd been in a fight?"

"No." Vivian's heart sank when she felt John's confidence in her flicker. "I know you don't believe he did it."

"I do not doubt your read on him, but I also don't think Trent Everett is capable of violently beating someone to death."

Vivian waited, hoping John had more to base his assurance on than just his gut.

"I know the guy, okay? We weren't friends in high school, but we knew each other a little bit. He's part of the Desert Prep crowd."

"The school where Sergio and Dean's girls go?"

"It's the one where all the rich kids go if their parents are connected. I went on a football scholarship, which of course made me the subject of pity." He rolled his eyes. "Whatever. There are some good kids who go there and some assholes like everywhere else."

"Which was Trent Everett?" Vivian was betting asshole.

"He was kind of a blank, to be honest. He followed whatever the popular crowd was doing. I'd say he was pretty self-centered.

Played a lot of sports—I guess that was his claim to fame. Had a lot of expensive hobbies. His dad flies planes—I think he does too—but golf is Trent's thing; I'm pretty sure he played in college. Went to Yale or Princeton or something like that. But I don't remember him being any kind of bully."

Vivian chewed on the knowledge, trying to fit it with the image of Trent she'd been building in her mind. "So if he's a rich kid, why is he a golf pro at Desert Oasis now?"

"I mean, probably because of his father. His dad has money, but he doesn't really have a business or anything for Trent to take over like a lot of them. Colonel Jack Everett is retired military, and he made a bunch of money in Hollywood being a consultant and stuff."

"Which is why he has so many expensive hobbies?"

John grimaced. "I remember Trent's dad. That guy seemed like an asshole."

"Interesting." So Trent grew up rich and ended up being a golf pro at a country club. Pampered layabout or family disappointment? It was hard to tell. "But he's married now. Does *she* have money?"

"I think so, and her family is also right in that Desert Prep alumni crowd. I'm sure their kids go there." John shook his head. "I don't know, Vivian. I'm not doubting your abilities at all. If you say he was panicked, I believe it. But isn't it possible he could have been panicked because he'd been cheating on his wife or something?"

She glanced at her mother again, who was carefully paging through the binder of missing people's faces, looking at each one and examining it with keen eyes. "She saw something, John. And it was on the tee where I found Trent Everett's ring. Maybe it's a coincidence, but I can't ignore it."

"Ask Dean and Sergio," John said. "Like I said, his kids go to the same school. Maybe they know him better than I do." He glanced at her belly, which was taking up more room in front of her by the day. "I have to say, I don't love you going freelance on this stuff right now."

"Because I'm six months pregnant?"

"Yeah."

"Pregnant chicks can do stuff, John." She picked up her purse and braced herself to stand up from the surprisingly comfy chair in his office. "I'm growing an entirely new human." She motioned to her belly. "I literally feel like a superhero right now."

"Yeah, you're also a superhero who tends to charge into dangerous situations with your friends without even an alpaca to back you up."

"That was one time." She stood. It wasn't graceful, but it wasn't her worst moment. "And to tell you the truth, I don't think that Paco would have helped if we'd brought him along. He acts like a jerk, but really he's a sensitive soul."

John moved to the door to open it so she could join her mom. "Just please don't rush into any life-threatening situations without calling me this time. I don't want to have to explain myself to Sergio if you ladies get hurt."

"You know, with Evy's telepathy now, there's very little we don't see coming."

John looked a little uncomfortable. "Yeah, how is that? She really can hear just... anything now? From anyone?"

"She still kind of has to focus to really tune in on people. Right now she's pretty stressed out. Learning how to tune out the background static of people's thoughts is pretty difficult. According to our psychic coach though, it can be done."

"Good. That's good." He cleared his throat, and Vivian felt a distinct and very low-key sense of embarrassment.

Vivian raised eyebrow. "Just what thoughts have you been having around Evy, Chief Marcos?"

He narrowed his eyes. "I think I'm changing my mind about being friends with you three."

Vivian let go of a burst of laughter. "Talk about incriminating thoughts."

HER MOM KEPT GLANCING AT HER ON THE DRIVE home.

"What?" Vivian asked.

"You were laughing with that nice policeman. Do you like him?"

"Yes. He's a good guy. And he was respectful to you; that matters to me."

"No, Vivian. I mean do you *like* him?" She raised her eyebrows.

"Oh!" She hadn't been expecting that one. "Not like that, Mom."

"I'm just saying he seems like a nice man. He's handsome. Has a good profession. I didn't see a wedding ring." Joan shrugged. "It's something to think about."

This was so far from what Vivian had been expecting she didn't know what to think. "Are you saying I should ask John out when I'm six months pregnant, you and Dad have just moved in, and I'm still trying to find an associate to assist in my dental practice?"

Joan waved a hand. "You're my daughter; you know how to multitask. And that's why your father wanted to come out here; so you could have some personal time."

"To date?"

You just made a date with Richard.

That wasn't a date; it was... lunch. And her mother didn't need to know about it.

"There's no rule that single pregnant women can't date."

"Mom, I don't—"

"I don't like the thought of you raising a baby alone," her mother blurted out.

Vivian could only blink. She stared at the road and tried to ignore the burning sense of embarrassment in her chest. It was one thing to flout the expectations of mainstream culture, but it was entirely different to feel that she was disappointing her mother.

"I'm thrilled about the baby," Joan said. "Please don't think I don't understand why you made this choice. It is utterly sensible, and I know you put a lot of thought and consideration into it."

"But you don't think I can do it on my own." Vivian pressed her lips together so she wouldn't say something she'd regret.

Her mother's own feelings were bouncing all over the car, and the most dominant one was regret. For what, Vivian couldn't be sure.

"I know you're capable of raising a baby on your own," Joan said. "You are my daughter, and you are the hardest working woman I know. Do not take this the wrong way. I'm only saying that it's hard. I had your father and your nǎinai watching you every day while I was at work, and I still felt the pressure."

"And I have you and Dad," Vivian said carefully. "I have a good support system here, and excellent staff at my practice. I'll start interviewing nannies soon, but until I find one, all the girls in the office are excited for me to bring the baby in."

In fact, the women at her office were over the moon about her son and already had an entire corner of baby things they'd brought in from their own nurseries.

Vivian hadn't even looked at cribs yet.

"It's not just the work things." Her mother clasped her hands together. "It's the good things too. When you or Debra did something wonderful, the first person I told was your father, and when he was excited, it made my own happiness even more. It's sharing the work but sharing the joy too."

"I have friends, Mom. I have you and Dad. Maybe that's not a traditional family, but are you saying you're not going to share all that joy with me? That it's going to be less somehow because it doesn't look the same as Debra's family?"

"Please don't think that's what I'm saying." Her mother reached over and touched her shoulder lightly. "You are so lovely, and I want you to find someone who appreciates you."

Vivian tried to see past her own hurt to her mother's heart. She knew her parents worried about her, just like her sister did. Debra had been more blunt, but blunt honesty was what sisters were for. Debra's exact words when she found out Vivian was pregnant? *I think you're fucking nuts, but if anyone can make this work, it's you.*

Her parents had only been supportive, but apparently that just meant they were smothering their worry, not that they weren't feeling it.

Vivian took a measured breath, then let it out slowly. "I am not going to lie—I always thought I would meet someone earlier in my life and we would have a family the traditional way, but that didn't happen. Like you said, I will be able to make this work, and..." She felt herself get weepy. "I'm really glad you and Dad are here. Trust me, this baby is going to get so much attention and love. I don't want you to worry, okay?"

"Just promise me that you won't get so focused on taking care of work and the baby that you neglect making time for *yourself.* And don't close yourself off to meeting someone because you think you're too busy," Joan said. "The right relationship will add to your life, not be an obligation."

Vivian's mind wandered back to her "just lunch" with Richard Putnam on Thursday. The timing was... Well, it was horrible. She was hormonal, exhausted, and juggling more balls than a circus clown.

But she'd still said yes.

"I won't close myself off to meeting someone," Vivian said.

"I promise. But I'm telling you now, John is not for me. I think he might like Evy in fact."

"Your friend the comedian?" Joan nodded. "That would be an interesting match."

The telepath and the police chief?

Vivian shook her head. "You have no idea."

Chapter Six

Vivian lay on a lounger by Sergio and Dean's pool, fresh from her dip in the water as the early evening sun slanted toward the horizon. Most of her friends were inside the large kitchen and dining room preparing dinner, but she was enjoying the quiet of the silent yard. As long as she kept getting in and out of the pool, she didn't overheat.

"Vivian?" Dean called her name from the kitchen door.

"By the pool." She draped a sarong over herself and sat up a little. "Here." She waved from the shade.

He walked over with a smile and a bright pink drink dripping with condensation. Dean Steward was a tall, regal man in his early fifties with silver hair trimmed short around his aristocratic head. He was East Coast prep transplanted to the California desert, and he had the tan to prove it.

He set the drink down on the small table beside Vivian's lounger. "I'm going to gush like Sergio for just a minute because you are so damn cute in your bathing suit with your belly." He pulled over a chair and sat next to her. "I made you an alcohol-free sunset, which is very sweet, so tell me if you want something else."

"You are the *best.*" Vivian sipped the drink through her striped green straw. The combination of pineapple, orange, and cherry *was* sweet, but with enough of a sour kick to make her mouth pucker. "This is great; thank you."

Dean smiled wistfully at her belly. "I'm remembering when Sergio's sister was carrying the girls—she was our surrogate—and she and her husband and their two kids basically lived here for the second half of her pregnancy. It was such a special time. We were so stressed, but she made us laugh every day."

"Oh, that's so sweet." Vivian's heart melted. "I love that you have that memory. Sergio's family sounds amazing."

"They are... an experience." He laughed. "When she agreed to carry our babies, she'd already had two of her own, so we were fortunate. She felt confident about carrying twins, which is a huge concern, of course. It's very intense."

"I can't imagine carrying two." Vivian sat up, enjoying the pregnancy gossip. "I mean, I feel like my symptoms are overwhelming most days, and I only have one. I know this has been an easy pregnancy, but it's still a lot."

"Any nausea anymore?"

"No, thank God. Cravings are mostly under control too. My mom is here, and I think she makes hot-and-sour soup for me at least three times a week."

"With the girls, Serena craved sweets. Constantly sweets."

Vivian shook her head. "Sour or salty for me. I can tell the swelling is going to get bad in the next couple of months though. I'll be ready for cooler weather."

"Anytime you need a pool, come here. I know the Oasis Springs ones are communal, and some days you may not want to hang with other people. Even if they are all sweet retired folks." He grinned. "Better than the too-cool young ones, right?"

"All my neighbors are so considerate, but yes, very chatty." Vivian sipped more of her drink. "Can I tell you that it's kind of hilarious to me that my two best girlfriends here in Palm Springs have like, zero interest in hearing about pregnancy stuff? You and Sergio are the only ones I talk to other than my sister."

Dean waved a hand. "Julia and Evy have never been baby people. Julia is the best aunt in the world, but when the girls were babies? She kind of poked at them and told us to call her when they could talk." He grinned. "I love the teenage years with Aurelia and Juliana—I'm a sadist, I guess—but I cannot lie, I am so excited to have another baby around."

His excitement soothed the sore heart her mother had inflicted that afternoon. Intentional or not, Joan's doubts had fueled the worry train building speed in Vivian's head for months.

"I question myself constantly," she said. "So it's a relief to hear you excited." She laughed and blinked away tears that had surprised her eyes. "My mom was... Well, she was being a mom today, I guess. Worried about me. Worried about me tackling motherhood alone."

"Don't be ridiculous." Dean stretched his legs and crossed them at the ankles. "You're kidding yourself if you think you're going to be alone. Sergio and I just wish you lived closer."

"I think your husband would be sleeping on my couch if I lived closer."

Dean smiled a little. "You're probably not wrong."

"Has he bought me any more baby clothes this week?"

"All bright yellow and orange to avoid gender stereotypes, of course. Nothing off-white for my man." Dean stood. "And he has a list of nanny leads; he said you mentioned it."

"I did." Vivian held out her hand, and Dean helped her to her feet. "Is dinner almost ready?"

"It is. Grilled chicken with greek salad."

"That sounds amazing." She remembered her meeting with John earlier. "Did Julia and Evy tell you about the ring we found on the golf course?"

"They did. Said it belonged to Trent Everett?"

She nodded. "I gave it to him myself, and trust me, that man is guilty of something."

Dean nodded. "Come on inside and we'll talk. I don't know Trent except by reputation—I sold his parents their current house—but Sergio might know more."

"I MEAN..." SERGIO SHRUGGED OVER HIS WINE. "WEAK character. That's all I'll say. He strikes me as very wishy-washy. Quite boring. I can't really see him killing anyone; he's not daring enough. Of course, I've only spent time with him at school events; he's part of the Booster Club crowd."

Aurelia, one of Dean and Sergio's fourteen-year-old daughters, dropped her fork on her plate. It clattered loudly, halting conversation as every eye swung toward her. Aurelia had complemented her Goth style that week with a new hair color that mimicked the red wine in Sergio's glass.

"If he's in the Booster Club, he's capable of anything." The pronouncement was spoken in an ominous tone.

Dean rolled his eyes. "Not this again."

Vivian turned to Aurelia. "Not what again?"

Juliana, Aurelia's twin, was identical and yet completely opposite in style. If she'd decided to don a string of pearls for dinner, Vivian wouldn't have been surprised.

"The Booster Club," Juliana began, "is a criminal enterprise with possible ties to the Freemasons and Skull and Bones. If this man is in the Booster Club..." She dropped her voice to mirror her sister. "Aurelia is right; he's capable of anything."

Sergio set his wineglass down. "Just because the school decided to pull money from the library expansion to start a lacrosse club does not mean the Booster Club is evil."

Aurelia picked up her fork. "So you say."

"Agree to disagree." Juliana pointedly looked at Vivian. "*Don't* discount him as a murder suspect."

Julia was watching her nieces, an amused expression on her face. "The Freemasons?"

Dean tried to smother a smile, but it wasn't working. "Trent Everett's father-in-law actually is in the Masons."

Sergio turned to his husband. "Don't fuel this nonsense."

"See?" Juliana pursed her lips in disapproval. "We're not wrong."

"Okay, okay." Evy held out her hands. "But what evidence do we actually have against the man? Vivian felt him panicking about his ring. I still say he could be a cheating husband or something like that. Or he lost it on a bet. Or... I don't know. But it doesn't necessarily mean that the man is guilty of a murder."

"It doesn't *not* mean he's guilty of a murder either," Aurelia said. "Have they found the body yet?"

"No." Vivian shook her head. "They haven't found anything, and I'm starting..." She sighed. "I'm starting to wonder if my mother really saw what she thinks she saw." Vivian groaned. "I hate saying it, but I'm having doubts now too."

Julia raised an eyebrow. "Seriously?"

"I don't think she's making it up, but she's been having insomnia. What if this was some kind of... I don't know. A waking nightmare or something like that." She looked at Evy. "You're right. I felt Trent Everett's panic, but maybe that was about infidelity. Or cheating at golf. Or any number of things. John said the same thing to me at the police station today, and he's a trained investigator. I just don't know anymore."

Sergio narrowed his eyes. "Are waking nightmares a thing?"

Aurelia raised her hand briefly. "You told me my room was a waking nightmare once."

"That was a metaphor." Sergio stood and walked to the bar. "I think the house rule should be that if we're talking about murder conspiracies, we have to be drinking wine."

Evy pressed her fingers to her temple. "I think the house rule is that we go outside to continue any conversations after dinner. I don't even care how hot it is anymore."

"Sun's down, so it should be cooler." Vivian frowned. "The blocking not working well?"

"I'm starting the antianxiety meds next week," Evy said quietly. "If Maud is correct, that should help. But yeah." She ran her fingers through her asymmetrical bob. "Sitting in here with all of you is kind of like trying to have a conversation in a heavy metal club. Outside is better."

"Outside it is then." Dean stood and pointed to the girls. "Dishes before phones."

The girls exchanged an inscrutable look.

"Deal," Juliana said.

"It wasn't a negotiation." Dean kissed the top of both their heads, then helped Vivian pull out the massive dining room chair. "And you do not breathe a word of any of this at school."

Juliana looked up with a cool gaze. "Our campaign to expose the Booster Club will not be deterred."

"Fine, but leave the murder speculation at home."

VIVIAN HAD NEARLY FORGOTTEN ABOUT HER LUNCH date by the time Richard knocked on her office door. "A minute!" She quickly shuffled a pile of files and closed her computer browser, which had been open to an entire page of automatic breast pumps.

Because that's the kind of supersexy vixen that she was.

"Come in." She'd worn a pair of fitted grey slacks that morning and a flowing top that didn't hide her belly but didn't emphasize it either. She was standing to grab her purse when Richard opened the door.

"I hope I'm not intruding."

She smiled. "Just finishing up. I was going to meet you out front."

"Sorry." He smiled, which didn't look sorry at all. "It's pretty warm outside."

"Of course." She waved a hand and hooked her handbag over her shoulder. "No need to wait out in the heat because I was running late."

And now my entire office staff can gossip about our lunch date.

"Do you mind walking?" He waited at the door and let her lead the way. "It's a scorcher today."

"I really don't mind."

Vivian offered her wide-eyed secretaries and dental assistants a brief wave before she walked outside with Richard. The blast of heat hit her like opening an oven door.

"You're probably going to think I'm nuts," she said. "But I enjoy heat like this, especially if it's in the middle of the day when I've been sitting in my office. The girls tend to keep the air conditioner very low because that front door opens and closes a lot, but it makes my office a freezer."

He walked next to her, occasionally touching the small of her back as they crossed streets or a car sped by. "So I'm guessing you don't miss the snowy winters in Chicago then."

"Never." Vivian stepped to avoid a manhole cover. "People who are sentimental about snow usually haven't lived in it all their lives." She nodded toward a Thai restaurant. "That place has great noodles if you're game, but they do make their food spicy."

"You know I like some heat." Richard opened the door and ushered her into a brightly decorated modern Thai place that she and her father often visited. "Is there anything you can't eat right now?"

"Sushi of course." Vivian sat at the table the hostess led them to, thankful she didn't have to explain why a booth wasn't going to work for her. "And I don't eat much red meat, but I love the shrimp here."

"I'll keep that in mind." Richard opened the menu. "So I feel the need to inform you that this may be just lunch, but I mentioned it to my daughter and she told me I'm still allowed to pick up the bill."

Vivian smiled. "She seems sweet." In addition to his very public divorce two years before and the murder scandal last year when he was exonerated, Richard Putnam had also discovered he had a daughter he'd never known from an affair when he was young. According to Julia's boyfriend Michael, Richard had been thrilled to meet her.

"So how is that going?" Vivian asked. "With Maddy. She's living in the guest house at your place, right?"

Richard nodded. "She is, and I think it's going well." He raised his shoulders. "They don't really make a parenting manual for when you become a father to a twenty-nine-year-old."

Vivian couldn't stop her laugh. "Yeah, I think *What to Expect* has been sleeping on that market."

"To be fair, it's not a huge one." He smiled, and his subtle amusement was devastating. "We're taking it month by month, but I think it's going well."

Her eyes caught on his perfect smile, his surprisingly full lips, and Vivian had to remind herself this was a first date and it would be more than a little forward to invite him back to her place.

Where her parents were now living.

Also, she was over six months pregnant.

While that hadn't killed her libido in the slightest, she also wasn't feeling the most confident about her body even if Sergio and Dean gushed over how "adorable" she was.

The waitress took their orders, and Richard picked a chicken dish that the chef recommended while Vivian got her favorite spicy shrimp. He added spring rolls for the table and two tall waters while she handed over her menu.

Richard Putnam was confident and friendly. Respectful of the waitress and curious about her favorites. She was charmed. More than that, she was deeply attracted to him. There was something about him that made her brain buzz.

Chemistry. Pure chemistry.

"Thank you for lunch," Vivian said. "And... I don't know if this is all just being friendly—"

"I'd say my interest is slightly more than friendly." Richard didn't hesitate in the slightest. "I will confess that I've never dated a pregnant woman before, but as long as you're single, I don't see it as any kind of impediment." He held a hand out. "If you're comfortable, of course. I understand that dating might not be your biggest priority at the moment."

"I was planning to ask you out last spring." Vivian sipped the water that the waitress brought. "I'm sure you can understand why...."

"You decided against it?" Richard's smile was a little stiff. "I confess it was a surprise to be arrested like that. As you probably guessed, I've not had many run-ins with the police."

"That does not shock me in the least."

"I'm lucky I had an alibi that night, to be honest. When I'm not working, I tend to be a homebody." He mirrored her and took a drink. "How about you?"

"I like being home," Vivian said. "But I like having people around. Does that make sense? I love going over to Sergio and Dean's because their place is very relaxed and homey, but there's always something going on."

The corner of his mouth tilted up. "And all the animals."

"So many!" She smiled. "I mean, they have what? Three golden retrievers? At least two birds, I think. Aurelia has all her reptiles."

"And don't forget Paco," Richard said. "That alpaca has chased me across the lawn more than once."

She took a sip of water. "I can't believe I missed that."

"It was a few years ago when they first got him." Richard shook his head. "They're great, those two. If they've adopted you, you're in good hands."

"I kind of feel like they have." She smiled. "And now my parents are here from Chicago, so being alone is not a problem for me these days."

"Well..." His dark blue eyes met hers. "Maybe you can take pity on a newly single me then."

Damn. Just... damn.

Vivian felt her heart skip double-time. No, taking pity on Richard wasn't the problem. Staying away from him might be.

Chapter Seven

"Details!" Julia crowed from the kitchen in her boyfriend's glass-walled house, which he'd bought five months before. "I'm making dinner—you have to entertain me."

Vivian groaned and lowered herself to a plush couch. Julia's boyfriend Michael was on location in Australia for a new project, but he'd be back next week for a month.

"Don't groan; I want details." Julia chopped peppers for the veggie tacos she was throwing together for dinner. "I told Michael you two were going out for lunch today; you know he's going to want to gossip when he calls tomorrow morning."

"I'm not sure I want you and Michael gossiping about me and Rich."

She wiggled her eyebrows. "So you're already calling him Rich, huh?"

"Well, he is. Extremely so." Vivian shook her head. "I mean, he's not pretentious, but there are moments when you catch something that throws you off, like him casually mentioning Maddy joining him for Christmas at the family compound in

Bermuda." She rolled her eyes. "I mean, who has a family compound in Bermuda?"

Julia slowly raised her hand. "I don't have one, but I want one? Maybe I can convince my parents to chip in."

Vivian laughed. "At least he's not from New York, though I don't know if my parents will think Boston is much better."

"What's so bad about New York?"

"Oh my God, do you know how sick people from Chicago get of comparisons to New York? I mean... I'm not going to say that's the reason I moved away, but it was a tiny factor. Mostly it was the weather, but I don't miss New Yorkers coming to the city and being surprised we eat more than beef."

"I don't miss assumptions about Southerners either. It's probably the reason I was determined to lose my accent so quickly." Julia threw a handful of peppers and onions in a pan and steam rose as they sizzled. "So lunch was great. Richard is rich—in many ways—and the big question is, are you going out again?"

Vivian winced. "I kind of left it open-ended? He asked when I was available for lunch next week and if I'd like to go, but I told him I would need to check my schedule and I'd call him."

"And? Nothing wrong with that. Are you put off by the big family-money thing? Or the minor-celebrity thing? I have to tell you, so far it's not really an issue with Michael. Granted, there haven't been any movie premiers or anything like that for him lately, but mostly it feels like a job. I imagine producing—"

"Do you really think I should be dating someone when I'm pregnant?" Vivian blurted out the question that had been circling her brain. "Isn't that weird? I mean, shouldn't I be focusing on becoming a mother?" She closed her eyes. "I don't know; I feel weird. The timing on this is awful."

"I'd say the timing is better now than when you have a newborn," Julia said. "Just saying. You're really not going to have any time then. Let me think about this."

Vivian waited while Julia mulled. It was one of the things she liked most about her friend. Evy was the charge-ahead, nothing-can-stop-you encourager, but Julia was a realist and very practical.

"I think your concern about timing is completely rational." Julia tossed a couple of corn tortillas in another pan while she watched the peppers fry. "If you weren't worried at all, I'd say you weren't very serious about dating Richard. But I also think that he's a mature man, and he obviously knows you're pregnant and have a lot on your mind. He wouldn't have asked you out if he expected your undivided attention."

"What do you think about my parents?"

"I think your parents are also adults, and they came here to be helpful not because they needed a ton of care." Julia shrugged. "I mean, if one of them needed a full-time caregiver, you'd be juggling a baby, a new relationship, and aging parents." She frowned. "Okay, when you put it that way—"

"It's a lot!" Vivian stood and walked to the counter. "Most mornings I don't even want to get out of bed, Julia. And it's not because I'm depressed, it's because my bed is comfortable and I want to sleep while I can."

Julia's eyebrows went up. "But you're getting a night nurse, right?"

"I am, but do I really need to add anything else to my life right now?"

"Hmmm." Julia flipped the tortillas and stared at the cast-iron pan. "Do you *need* to? Absolutely not. You don't have to do anything you don't want to do. I would say that if the idea of dating Richard makes you happy, you should do it. Think about it like self-care."

"Get a massage, have a hot cup of tea, date a wealthy Hollywood producer?"

"Everyone needs stress relief, Vivian. *Especially* expecting mothers."

Vivian laughed. "I guess I like the idea of it; I'm not sure I'm prepared for the reality. I worry a new relationship would just be adding more work on top of the obligations I already have."

"Dating Michael doesn't feel like work, but I know what you mean. Any new relationship needs time and attention." Julia set down the tongs she was using to flip the tortillas. "I do think you may be worrying about things that aren't actually a problem yet."

"I like to plan ahead."

"For problems that may not even be problems?"

"You think a wealthy, attractive man like Richard Putnam is going to be content coming... not even second, but maybe third or fourth in my life?"

Julia shrugged. "I mean, if he isn't, then you know he's not the right man for you. As long as you're up-front with him about your commitments, I say go for it and let him decide."

VIVIAN KEPT THINKING ABOUT JULIA'S ADVICE AS SHE drove back to Rancho Mirage. Julia was right. Richard was a grown man, and he knew she would be busy. And she was wrong. Richard was a father, but he'd missed his daughter's childhood through no fault of his own. He probably had no idea how absorbing babies could be.

But mostly Julia was right. If nothing else, Richard deserved at least one more lunch after the wonderful time they'd had that afternoon. Vivian would lay out how much she had going on in her life, probably exaggerate how busy she was, and then he could decide if he wanted to spend time with her.

More than likely, he'd run away screaming—internally, of course, he was a gentleman—and she'd be sad, but she'd completely understand.

She pulled into her driveway, parked next to her parents' Acura, and got out her phone to text Richard.

Lunch next Wednesday?

She saw him start texting almost immediately but was saved from staring at her phone by a polite tap on the hood of her car. She looked up to see Oscar, the landscaping manager who worked on their section of the development, waving at her from the passenger side.

Vivian smiled and grabbed her purse before she opened her door, shifting her weight to get out. Before she could stand, Oscar ran around to help her out.

"Thank you." She smiled and accepted the hand, even though it brought her a shot of Oscar's emotions. "You are so thoughtful."

He was a mix of tired and amused but mostly cheerful with a shot of sentimental sadness thrown in. "No problem, Dr. Wei."

"Please, *please* call me Vivian." She waved at the house. "There are so many Dr. Weis around here right now, I'll never know if you're talking to me."

Oscar grinned. "You got it."

"And thank you." She motioned to the car. "I'm worried I might need a hoist in a couple of months." She laughed a little.

"My wife had our third about four months ago, so I've got experience helping ladies out of cars." Oscar smiled. He was a stocky man of medium height, just a little taller than Vivian. He'd been working at Desert Oasis long before she came here to live, and his naturally dark complexion was even darker for all the time he spent in the sun.

Vivian looked around the yard. "Well, it looks gorgeous around here, just like always." The association paid for the front yard landscaping, but Vivian added the service for her small backyard as well. "Was there a problem in the back or anything?"

"Oh no." He shook his head. "But you know I help out with building maintenance too, right? I was going to ask when I saw you pull in, with your parents here now, is there anything that we can do to help out?"

She frowned. "What do you mean?"

"Ramps. Walkways. Any kind of uneven ground that needs smoothing out. You know, stuff like that. You can imagine we get a lot of older people who are..." He shrugged. "You know, their needs change, so we like to make sure everyone is comfortable in their yard and garden. No one should feel trapped inside, you know?"

"Oh my gosh, you are so thoughtful." She put a hand over her heart. "Thank you so much, but I think we're good right now. My mom's knee does bother her, but we're nowhere near needing accommodations like that. Dad is still golfing three or four times a week." She felt a well of gratitude and had to force back tears. "Thank you, Oscar."

Damn you, hormones!

Oscar smiled. "Hey, I see your dad out there! He's a real friendly guy. That's the way to be, right? Keep active." He flexed his arm. "I admire that. Okay, well if there are any changes, you just call the maintenance department and ask for me. I'll get a crew out here, help out with whatever you need."

She pointed at the car. "Is there a crane to get pregnant ladies out of the car that I can borrow?"

Oscar laughed. "You know, I don't know if you've noticed, but there aren't too many pregnant ladies living in Desert Oasis."

Vivian smiled. "I've noticed." A thought popped into her head. "Hey, Oscar?"

He'd started to walk away, but he turned. "What's up, Doc... uh, Vivian?"

"You were around last week, right?" She dropped her voice. "When the police came out because someone saw...?"

"Oh damn—" He covered his mouth. "Pardon my language. That was you?"

"No, it was my mom." She kept her voice low and stepped closer. "I know the police are looking into it, but I've been... Well, it's my mom, you know? So I've been trying to keep track of what's going on."

"The police haven't told us anything," he said. "They were here for most of the day, shut down a lot of the course. Mr. Wainwright and Mr. Everett, they were both real mad. Uh..." He scratched his head. "But I don't think they like, took anything. As far as I heard, they think your mom must have seen something else. Maybe just a fight or something."

That was a possibility, but Vivian didn't think Trent Everett was feeling that kind of panic over a fistfight. "What about you guys in landscaping and maintenance?"

"You know, they questioned us a lot about the watering schedule, took a bunch of notes, but they didn't hassle any of my guys." He nodded at the men loading clippers, leaf blowers, and mowers in the back of a shiny green pickup. "They're all good."

"That's a relief, but I guess I was wondering more if you'd noticed anything unusual that day. Or maybe even before then. If you'd seen anyone out of the ordinary or someone you think wasn't familiar with the club. Anything like that?"

Oscar frowned. "I don't think so. It was a pretty normal week. We had a local tournament on Friday morning for charity and a bunch of part-time residents were out here, so it would be hard to say that I didn't see *anyone* new 'cause I don't always remember the part-time people. There were news crews and everything out from the local stations. I didn't notice anything unusual. That kind of event happens pretty regularly."

Vivian felt her heart sink; she'd been hoping for some kind of lead. Maybe she could find the local news footage of the event. That was a poss—

"You know what?" Oscar snapped his fingers. "I didn't think of it because we didn't notice until Sunday when we were scheduled to do some routine stuff on the traps in the north course, but there was a theft. It's possible it happened that week. No one had checked that storage shed since the week before, I don't think."

"A theft?" Vivian leaned forward. "What was it?"

"Sand," Oscar said. "I know it sounds weird, but that's actually one of the top things we have stolen. It's real pretty sand, so if you had a landscaping thing or a sandbox for your kids, you could use it for that."

"How much?" Vivian wondered if the sand the golf course ordered came in bulk. That would make it hard to track.

"Not too much," Oscar said. "About two bags is all, and another one broke while they were taking it. It was probably kids or something."

Or something. It could also have been a murderer looking to hide a body in a sand trap. Would two bags of sand be enough for that? Could one man even carry them?

Vivian asked, "How heavy are those bags?"

Oscar thought for a moment. "Probably about a hundred pounds or so. I tell the guys to always load them in pairs on the trucks, but the younger ones like to show off."

"Two hundred pounds of sand." Vivian frowned. Was it enough to cover a body?

Or possibly... Vivian's eyes drifted to the pond beside her house where a dancing fountain sent streams of water shooting into the desert air.

Two hundred pounds of sand might not be enough to cover a dead body, but it would be more than enough to weigh one down.

Chapter Eight

Vivian was enjoying one of the best dreams she'd had in a long time. She was lying naked in the sun, and a soft ocean breeze brushed her body. She felt the hands on her back, slowly smoothing something cool over her bare skin while his fingers played along the tops of her thighs, the edges of her breasts, and the sensitive line of her spine.

Mmmm, more.

Vivian?

Richard.

"Who's Richard?"

She rolled over, pulling up the covers as her eyes flew open. "Dad?"

Her father was frowning at her as he stood next to her bed. "I didn't want to wake you up, but then I heard you talking and I thought you were already awake."

Okay, she was going to have to lock her doors at night because this was ridiculous. She felt a twinge in her side from rolling to her back so suddenly, and she rubbed the aching muscle. Maybe one of those bellybands was a good idea after all.

Vivian blinked her eyes and sat up in bed. “Dad, I know you’re living here now, but it is not okay—”

“I can’t find your mom.”

Vivian’s heart skipped a beat. “What?”

His eyes were wide and frightened. “She’s not in the house. The car is here. Her keys and her purse are here, but the french doors are open in the back and I think the golf course gate is open.”

“Oh my God.” Her mother had gone for a walk at... She glanced at the clock. “She decided to go for a walk on the course at three in the morning?”

“Should we call the police?”

Vivian hesitated. They already thought her mother was a senile old woman; this wouldn’t help that impression. “Let’s just get dressed and go look for her. You know she loves that spot by the duck pond where the benches are. Maybe she just wanted some fresh air.”

“It’s been so hot lately,” her father muttered. “She hasn’t been able to walk by the lake. Maybe she’s missing home.”

“Dad, just...” She waved at the door. “Let me get dressed. I’ll meet you downstairs.”

Vivian threw a cardigan over her pajama top and quickly changed to a pair of leggings and slipped on her old Vans. She left her hair in its braid and rushed downstairs to find her father already out in the backyard.

She grabbed a flashlight from the emergency drawer in the kitchen and shoved her phone in her pocket before she walked out to join him. “Come on.”

Every residential garden in Desert Oasis had a gate that led from the garden to the golf course. Residents were encouraged to walk the cart paths in the morning and evening. Many of them used the golf courses as their own private park, and it wasn’t unusual to see picnics or groups of friends having cocktails as they drove golf carts around the artificial hills, ponds, and fountains of the private club.

Tonight Vivian wished her father had given in to the temptation to get the cart. There were too many paths and too many places her mom could wander off, not to mention the fear that neither of them spoke: there was still a murderer loose in Desert Oasis.

"Do you see anything?" Vivian asked her dad.

"No." He pointed to the right. "The pond she likes with the benches is this direction."

It was a good thing one of them knew where they were going. Vivian followed her father as he nearly jogged down a cart path lined by bunches of Mexican fan palms. She could hear water in the distance and suddenly remembered the pond her father was talking about.

Most of the water hazards in Desert Oasis were man-made, but there were a few natural springs that gave the resort its name. This was one of the large ponds the golf course had been built around. Tall grasses and graceful palms lined the oasis, and a few picnic tables and benches had been installed for residents to enjoy. The pond was deep enough that they held fishing tournaments in the fall, and it was home to a year-round wild-duck population, a pair of swans, and some migrating waterfowl.

As they rounded the corner and the trees grew thicker overhead, Vivian could hear the low chatter of ducks drifting in the night. The pond came into view, and she sighed in relief. Her mother was sitting at a picnic table, and a few birds were milling around her, clearly confused why a human had intruded on their nighttime peace.

"Mom?" Vivian tried not to yell, but she was so relieved.

Her mother looked in their direction, and as they came closer, Vivian could feel a cascade of emotions.

Fear. Relief. Confusion. More relief. Anger.

Allan knelt down next to Joan. "Honey, what are you doing out here? You scared me to death."

Joan looked at her husband, and her face mirrored the feelings she was broadcasting to Vivian. "I don't know."

"What do you mean?" Vivian stood with her hands in her pockets.

There was something about the tea...

Joan looked at Vivian, and she remembered.

The tea her mother had made the night she saw the murder. The insomnia tea from her Chinese doctor back in Chicago. It wasn't just for insomnia—Vivian remembered now—it was the same tea her grandmother had started to take when her memory began to falter.

"It's more than just senior moments, isn't it, Mom?" Vivian's heart sank.

Joan took a deep breath and let it out slowly. "I don't remember how I got here. It's like I woke up and I was sitting at the pond."

With a murderer on the loose.

As her father helped her mother to her feet and put his arm around her waist, Vivian watched them carefully. She needed to call her sister in a few hours. She'd need to find a Chinese doctor out here or in LA to complement whatever treatment the Western doctor found. She'd definitely need to find an acupuncturist.

Vivian followed behind her parents as her father led them back to the house. "We're calling your doctor in the morning," she said. "Ask her for a referral out here. The medical center here is excellent."

Joan sighed. "I know."

She knew. The whole time, her mother had known that her memory was a problem and she hadn't told Vivian.

SHE WAS EXHAUSTED BY AFTERNOON AND TOOK OFF work early so she could run by Jensen's Market. The large grocery store in Rancho Mirage was nice, but Jensen's made a cake that her mother loved, and Vivian felt like everyone in their house needed cake tonight.

So many phone calls, so many notes in her appointment calendar.

She looked longingly at the wine section as she passed by, not realizing she'd been staring until she heard a light chuckle.

Vivian turned her head to see Richard standing by the cheese counter.

He raised his hands. "I'd be the same way with my whiskey cabinet; no judgment."

At least he made her smile. "It's been a day."

"I'm sure you deserve a glass or two." He glanced at her belly. "But I'm sure he also appreciates your self-control."

"I hope so." She pushed her cart over. "So how are you?"

"Looking forward to a lunch date I have on Wednesday." A smile flirted at the corner of his beautiful mouth. "How about you?"

Oh God. Lunch. She couldn't do lunch on Wednesday, could she? Her mother had a doctor's appointment that afternoon. It wasn't until two, but—

"What's wrong?" Richard was frowning. "You're not happy."

Happy? She didn't even know how to see happiness from where she was standing in the middle of the deli section at Jensen's, staring at the wine, mentally juggling neurologist and obstetrician appointments and trying to figure out what to make for dinner.

Vivian started to sniff, and she waved a hand. "Richard, I need to—"

"Are you okay?"

"I'm not..." She couldn't speak because she was going to

start crying. Forget the cake—she started toward the door. "I need to go. I need to—"

"Allow me?" He scooped the few items in her cart, including her mother's cake, into his, maneuvered his grocery cart with one hand, and put his other hand at the small of her back. Within minutes, he'd checked them out and was standing in the parking lot. "Where's your Tesla?"

"I can't fit in it anymore." She sniffed and her eyes started to water. "I had to borrow my dad's car." She pointed toward the Acura, and Richard grabbed the keys that were in her hand.

"Nice." He walked over, loaded the groceries in the back, and then started the car to turn on the air conditioner. "This is a nice car."

She was seconds from breaking down. "Richard, I don't think I can have lunch with you on Wednesday."

"Okay." He helped her into the car and knelt down. "What's going on? I refuse to think you're this upset because you have to break a lunch date. I know we're just getting to know each other, but this doesn't seem like you."

"I'm ridiculous and hormonal." She waved at the back of the car. "I'll pay you back for the groceries; thank you for keeping me from having a breakdown in the middle of Jensen's."

"What is going on?" His quiet voice undid her.

She lost it, bursting into tears as the weight of the morning finally crashed down.

Richard gently pulled her up from the driver's seat of the car and folded her in a secure embrace. She felt enveloped in heat, both from the summer afternoon and his warm arms.

"My mom wandered onto the golf course last night in her nightgown. We found her by the duck ponds, and she couldn't remember how she got there. And I'm hot and uncomfortable; my feet hurt all the time. I'm crying in a parking lot and I hate crying. I don't do this."

"Damn." He pressed her closer, and she thought he might

have kissed the top of her head. "I'm so sorry about your mom. That's really frightening."

"I know that logically, her confusion and memory interruptions could be any number of things that are treatable, but my grandmother had dementia, and I'm so scared—"

"My mother has Alzheimer's." He said it quietly. "I completely understand. Are they expecting you at home right away?"

Vivian shook her head and sniffed. "She insisted on going to her mahjong game today. Said she was feeling fine and my dad could drive her." She groaned. "I look like a mess now. I was going to surprise her with the cake. It'll melt in the car if I don't—"

"My house is five minutes away." He hugged her closer. "Come over for a cold drink. Cool down. Calm down. Put the cake in my fridge and relax a little before you go home, okay?"

His house, Casa de Lirio, the famed estate where Julia had found a body last year and a murderer had held her and her friends at gunpoint.

Richard remembered when she did. "I just realized that my house might not be that relaxing for you."

"It's fine." She took his hand and squeezed it. "I promise. I went over with Julia and Evy after it happened, and I don't have any phobias about it."

He pulled back and looked her in the eye. "Come over for a drink?"

She nodded. "That sounds great."

VIVIAN FOLLOWED RICHARD'S LAND ROVER THROUGH the twisting streets of Vista de Lirio to the house that had established the neighborhood, Casa de Lirio, a three-acre estate that overlooked the mountain slopes on one side and the Coachella Valley on the other.

It was also home to a spiritual portal that attracted ghosts, but Richard probably didn't know about that.

As she pulled her father's Acura into a parking spot near the garage, she saw Richard's daughter Maddy come out of the pool house to greet him. He said something to her quietly, then walked to Vivian's car and opened the driver's side door.

"Maddy is going to make some tea. She loves the stuff; reminds me of my mother."

Vivian took his hand and maneuvered out of her father's car, which was slightly more comfortable than her own, but not by much. "I'm going to have to sell the Tesla."

"Why?"

She pointed to the baby. "Car seat won't fit in back. I'm going to have to get a new car. Just another thing I have to do in the next two and a half months." Along with getting a diagnosis for her mother, finding a nanny, decorating a nursery. "Richard, I really like you, but there is just no way—"

"Hold that thought." He took her by the hand and grabbed the bag of groceries with the cake from the back. "Hold the 'I like you, Richard' thought and just sit with that while Maddy and I make you some tea."

He led her around to the back of the house where a breeze off the mountains rustled the palm trees and a fountain trickled in a courtyard. The pool gleamed blue under the desert sky, and the sun cast its shadow behind the mountain, immediately cooling the backyard from scorching to tolerable.

"I'm going to turn the misters on and put your cake in the refrigerator." Richard led her to a table and pulled out a chair for her. "So just sit and watch the view and take a few deep breaths, okay?"

He was relishing this, and Vivian didn't even mind. Richard was clearly a man who liked to play the knight in shining armor, and while sometimes that annoyed her, this afternoon it felt like a breath of fresh air.

He came back with a white towel. "I soaked it in the sink. Cold water. Do you want it for your neck?"

She blinked. "You are really good at this."

"I have three sisters, and they all have at least three children. I'm actually not that inexperienced with pregnant women."

She smiled and took the towel, setting it against her neck and immediately feeling relief. "You know, I really do like the heat. Most of the time."

He took the seat next to her. "The incident with your mom happened last night?"

"Technically this morning. Three o'clock or so."

He nodded. "So you've had a really long day."

"A very long day." She sniffed and pressed the heels of her palms to her eyes so she didn't start crying again. "I'm not usually a crier, but I think my hormones are in overdrive."

"It's understandable," he said. "Your body is doing what it needs to right now, but I imagine that makes everything feel way more extreme."

"Yes." She dropped her hands. "I'm usually very good at multitasking, but I'm starting to get overwhelmed. My sister wants my parents to come home, but my dad insists that he needs to help me with the practice out here."

"Does he?"

"Honestly?" She nodded. "I was counting on him to cover the gap when I go on maternity leave until I can find another associate."

He nodded. "So they stay here. There are fabulous doctors in Palm Springs. Your mom will get amazing care. Does she like it out here? Is she happy?"

"Very. She loves it. Her parents had the house here, so she's spent a lot of time in the area and she has a lot of friends. I don't worry about her having a support system or anything."

Except that she did. Vivian felt selfish as hell, but the thought of having her mom decline while she was juggling her dental practice and a newborn made her want to run away and hide.

"What are you thinking right now?" Richard was staring at her.

"I'm feeling selfish." She took a long breath.

"For?"

"Having a baby."

"Vivian." He reached across and took her hand. "Life doesn't stop because your parent has a health scare. You are not selfish for wanting to be a mother."

She looked at him and his fine, aristocratic face, his kind eyes, and his highly kissable mouth. "I talked to Julia about you."

He smiled a little. "What did Julia think? I like her for Michael. They get along well."

"I told her that I didn't have time to date anyone even though I like you so much. And she said you were a grown man who could decide if you were fine with not having my undivided attention."

"Julia is a smart woman." He frowned. "What adult goes into a relationship at our age thinking they're going to have a person's undivided attention? That's ridiculous. We all have careers and families and commitments. If someone gave me their undivided attention, I'd probably think they had no life."

"Richard." She turned toward him. "I like you so much, but I really have a lot on my plate. I don't know if dating right now is very responsible."

The corner of his mouth tilted up. "Then we won't call it dating. We'll call it two new friends spending time with each other when they can. You still spend time with your friends, right?"

"Yes."

"And you let your friends help you when you need it, correct?"

She narrowed her eyes. "Why do I feel like you're looking for an open door to be intrusive?"

"Helping friends is not intrusive." His eyes were soft. "Especially when that friend has a lot going on in her life."

"Richard—"

"I know you're busy, but Julia was right: I'm an adult, and I know what I want." He squeezed her hand. "I'd rather have a fraction of your attention than the whole of someone else's."

Damn it. Forget keeping away from Richard Putnam. Vivian was going to have to do everything in her power to keep from falling in love with him.

Chapter Nine

Vivian's week was a whirl of doctor's appointments, making future appointments, furious calls to dentist friends and peers to find a younger dentist who was looking for a foot into an established practice, and more phone calls.

Her sister was talking about flying out to Palm Springs, her mother insisted she knew the early signs of dementia and she did not have it, and her father was playing the stern referee with both of them.

And Vivian was grateful.

Allan Wei was the world's happiest, most cheerful dentist and dad, but when things got serious, he could put his foot down with her very strong-willed mother. He was in full dad-organization mode, and Vivian could only be relieved.

He was also adamant that everyone stop speculating about his wife until actual tests had been run, which was easier said than done. Both Vivian and her sister remembered her grandmother's slow decline and knew it had been incredibly stressful on their mom. Vivian was feeling her own fear, but also her mother's and father's, though they would never admit it.

But on Friday night, Vivian shoved all that to the back of her mind while she donned a dress she'd ordered a month ago when Julia first invited her to the Desert Prep Annual Benefit Gala. Julia and Dean's real estate company were corporate sponsors, and Evy was the master of ceremonies for the event. At the time, she'd been so excited at the prospect of dressing up and going out with her friends that she hadn't even thought about saying no when they offered her a ticket.

She slipped on the burgundy dress and strappy black flats, hoping she'd make it through the night without heartburn or foot pain.

When she walked down the stairs, her parents looked up from the tournament on the Golf Channel.

"Oh, Vivian, you look so beautiful." Her mom's face glowed. "What a stunning dress."

It was a column dress that gathered just under her bust to drape over her belly. Vivian had ordered it because she really didn't know how big she'd be by the time she wore it, and the cut of the dress made it adaptable.

She touched her hair self-consciously. "I was going to do something more with my hair, but I didn't have time to go to the salon."

"It's perfect the way it is." Joan looked from side to side. "You know, I wasn't sure about the bangs when you cut them, but they frame your eyes beautifully."

"Thanks, Mom."

Her dad got up too. "Wow." He put his arm around Joan. "Did we raise an elegant lady or what, Dr. Wei?"

Joan's cheeks went a little pink. "I believe we did, Dr. Wei."

Her dad put a hand on the side of her belly and leaned down. "Okay, little man. Not too much partying tonight. Be good for your mother."

The wave of love and pride from her father was so big Vivian blinked hard to keep from spoiling her eye makeup. "You are going to have so much fun with him."

Joan beamed. "He already bought a putter. The smallest one he could find. It's in the garage."

"Dad!"

"It's fine." Allan waved. "He's going to love golf. As long as he's not a lefty, then I might have to return it."

There was a knock on the door, and Vivian hurried to grab the clutch she'd packed earlier. "That's my ride. Julia said she'd send a car for me since driving is getting a little difficult."

She opened the door to see Richard standing on the other side in a crisp tuxedo.

Oh my God. That just wasn't fair.

"Richard. I didn't know... Julia said she was sending a car, I thought—"

"She called me up and asked me what service I would recommend, and I offered." He smiled. "I hope you don't mind."

She heard her father behind her. "Did she say Richard?"

Alarms blared in her mind, and she immediately nudged him out and started closing the door. "Thank you, that's so thoughtful, I really appreciate it." She called over her shoulder. "Bye, Mom! Bye, Dad. I'll see you tomorrow morning. Don't forget you have an early appointment, Mom." Then she shut the door and started walking toward the car.

Richard was still standing on the doorstep. "Should I—?"

"Nope." She reached back and grabbed his hand. "That meeting will eat up an hour at least, and we are not going there tonight."

He chuckled under his breath. "Don't want me to meet your parents, huh?"

"I don't want you to meet my parents *right now*. There's a difference." Vivian stood at the car door and waited for him to open it. He walked over, reached for the handle, and paused. "What's wrong?"

"Nothing." He leaned closer. "You look stunning. Absolutely ravishing."

Not. Fair.

"Richard, if you think I'm going to kiss you standing in the driveway of my house when my nosy parents are spying out the window, you are kidding yourself."

"I don't think you are," he said quietly. "But I'm glad you were thinking about it."

She felt the heat rush to her cheeks as he opened the door. "I wasn't thinking about it. You were."

"I was." He helped her into the sleek black sedan. "But so were you."

THE DESERT PREP ANNUAL GALA WAS ONE OF THE BIG social events of the valley, with rich parents mingling and competing to bring the most famous guests. There was a band, a silent auction that regularly raised over a million dollars in a single evening, a gourmet dinner, and dancing. The hosted bar probably helped with the dancing. A professional photographer was taking pictures inside the event, and there was an actual red carpet leading into the country club where it was hosted.

And Vivian walked into the room with her arm in Richard's.

"Oh." She felt eyes swing toward them. "This is going to be a thing, isn't it?"

"I should have warned you about the gossip." He sounded regretful. "Damn photographers. I apologize, Vivian. It didn't occur to me—"

"Don't." She looked up and smiled. "We're friends, right? Let them talk. It'll probably be good for business."

He smiled down at her, and the corners of his eyes crinkled. "Let's find our table, shall we?"

"Are you sitting with Dean and Sergio?"

"I am. I was going to skip it this year, to be honest. It felt strange after everything that happened, but Maddy is teaching here, of course. She encouraged me to come. Then Julia and Michael called and said you'd be here."

"Did you come because of me?"

"It helped." He kept her arm tucked firmly in his as they wound through the crowd. "I don't see them, do you?"

"You're asking me? You're like a foot taller than I am. So you just happened to have a tuxedo handy?"

He glanced down, and she saw a company smile fixed firmly in place. "I've owned a tuxedo since I was sixteen. In my family, it's part of the wardrobe."

"You are rich in a way I do not understand."

"Trust me—I don't really understand it either." He waved and guided her to the right. "Found them."

"We're sitting pretty close to the front."

"The better to see Evy light up the room, right?"

"She's going to have to be on her best behavior with this crowd." In fact, Vivian had no idea how Evy was going to host an event this large with her telepathy turned up to eleven. Maybe she'd been having private lessons with Maud.

"Richard!"

Vivian turned toward Sergio's voice and saw Sergio, Dean, Julia, and Michael all at a table. Next to Michael was Genevieve de Winter wearing a zebra-striped turban and giant black sunglasses, a spectacularly tall and handsome Black man at her side. He had closely cropped hair, a vivid blue cape, and a gold earring dripping to his shoulder.

Julia looked chic in a formal off-white suit. Michael looked vaguely uncomfortable in formal navy blue.

Dean and Sergio were both in tuxedos, though Sergio had lent his a more casual air with a shirt open at the neck and a brilliant green ascot.

Yes, this was definitely the table where she wanted to sit.

"Vivian!" Julia walked over to her. "You look amazing." She hugged her and whispered, "And oh my God, you and Richard are stunning together."

"I know you set this up. Calling Richard to ask about a car service?"

Julia kissed her cheek. "What are you talking about? He's a very knowledgeable man."

"Cute." Vivian tried to suppress her smile, but she could feel how pleased Julia was. "We making new friends tonight?"

"Maybe." She glanced over her shoulder. "I sat us right next to the infamous Booster Club crowd. Recognize anyone you know?"

"I see Trent Everett and a bunch of Trent Everett clones." The tuxedos definitely weren't helping because nearly all the men at Trent's table wore either a tuxedo or a plain black suit. "Are there five couples? Everyone looks the same," she hissed.

Julia took Vivian's arm and guided her back to the table, whispering in her ear. "Sergio only knows the actual Booster Club members. Trent and his wife. Trace Mitchell and a date—he and his wife are getting divorced."

"Trent and Trace?" Country-club parents really needed to get a baby-name book with some better options. All *T* names were officially out of the running for her son.

"Then there's the ringleader of the group, according to Sergio. The tall blond one with the blue eyes."

Vivian scanned the table and spotted him immediately. "He's definitely more noticeable than the rest. He looks familiar."

"I thought the same thing, but I don't know why. That's West Barrett, or Archer Weston Barrett IV, that is. I've been watching them a little, and everyone at the table does seem to take their cue from him."

"Archer Weston Barrett IV?" Vivian's eyes went wide. "Goodness, that smells like old money, doesn't it?"

"Very old, very wealthy. Oil people from Los Angeles, and West is the ringleader of the group according to Sergio and my nieces."

"Is he the Skull and Bones connection?"

"He graduated from Harvard not Yale, but who knows?" Julia flashed someone a smile and a wave, then turned back to Vivian. "Then there're the ladies in the Club, Ashley Gates—no relation to Bill—and Pippa Stanford."

"Who names their daughter Pippa?"

"Rich people, Vivian." Julia smiled and walked to her chair, pulling out the one next to her for Vivian to sit.

She noticed that Richard was already sitting on her left, which left Genevieve—Julia's odd neighbor—and her tall companion across the table from her.

Genevieve de Winter was a tiny retired woman who lived on an estate guarded by two Savannah cats and a three-legged standard poodle named Gaston. She had worked in art, fashion, or something glamorous at one point but moved to Vista de Lirio with her third or fourth husband. Vivian found her fascinating yet somewhat terrifying.

Genevieve pointed an empty cigarette holder at Vivian. "You're Sergio's psychic friend, are you not?"

"Uh..." Vivian glanced at Richard, who frowned.

Sergio jumped in. "Darling, Vivian and Julia are *both* psychic. Julia is the one who sees ghosts, and Vivian is an empath."

Genevieve immediately turned to the man on her left and broke into a long stream of French that had the man nodding thoughtfully, though he didn't say a word.

Richard cleared his throat. "I missed... Are you really?"

"Psychic?" Vivian shrugged. "You might say that. I'd say that I'm... very perceptive in unusual areas."

"Right." He felt confusion and a little fear. "Can you read my thoughts?"

"No." Vivian shook her head. "Not at all. That's Evy."

His eyes went wide. "What?"

"I sense emotions, which isn't nearly as intrusive, though it does make me a very good judge of character." She dropped her voice. "And I can pretty much always tell if someone is lying, so there's that."

The band started playing entry music, and a few second later, Evy strode out onto the stage to a hearty greeting of applause.

"Welcome, ladies and gentlemen!" Evy wore a fitted tuxedo that showed off her model-like stature and a brilliant, shining top hat. "I want to thank you for coming tonight; I'm your hostess and mistress of ceremonies—" The sound of a cracking whip echoed through the sound system, and the room laughed. "Not that kind of mistress, Mr. Rutledge." She winked at a man in the crowd. "Don't get excited."

Mr. Rutledge's table roared in laughter, and Vivian laughed along, feeling a swell of pride for her friend. When EV Lane turned on the charm, she could captivate a room. Her smile alone was incandescent.

"I wanted to greet all of you and introduce myself before the lovely servers you see hovering begin to bring out your dinner." She nodded at the band, who began to play a low, jazzy number. "Thank you for your generosity. Just by being here tonight, you've helped support the Desert Prep Alumni Association and Booster Club, who sponsored this event."

Vivian turned to the Booster Club table and saw the five members exchanging smug looks as people applauded for them. She decided to keep her hands in her lap.

"More importantly," Evy continued, "you're supporting the students, teachers, and coaches of Desert Preparatory Academy, the pride of the valley, in the work that they do to educate, illuminate, and excel."

Julia grabbed her hand under the table and squeezed it

tightly. She felt a jolt of panic and a bright flash of recognition from her friend. "Vivian."

Vivian turned to her. "What's wrong? What do you see?"

Julia stared at the Booster Club table as West Barrett stood. Someone walked over and handed the tall man a microphone; he began perfunctory thanks and acknowledgment of the organizers as dinner servers began to move through the room.

And Julia couldn't take her eyes off him.

"Julia, what is going on?"

"The man your mother saw on the golf course that night." Julia turned away from West. "The victim she described to the police. Do you remember what he looked like?"

Vivian rolled her eyes. "How could I forget? She described Robert Redford to a tee."

"Well, I don't think she was confused." Julia leaned toward her. "A ghost just arrived at the Booster Club table, and he could be Robert Redford's twin."

Chapter Ten

Vivian begged off a second dance with Sergio and went looking for Evy the second she saw her friend leave the stage. She ducked into a hallway to the left of the stage and looked for anything that seemed like it would be a green room or staging area.

She heard voices behind one door that read STAFF ONLY, so she opened it and saw Evy sitting at a dressing table with her feet up on a chair, talking to a man in shirtsleeves.

"Vivian!" Evy's face lit up. "Oh my God, you look gorgeous. I love that dress." She waved her over. "Come sit with me and Paul. He's one of the guys doing sound tonight, but he's taking a break with me while the band does their thing."

Evy looked so relieved, Vivian hated to spoil her calm.

"Do you have a minute to talk alone?" Vivian asked. "If you don't, I completely—"

"It's cool." Paul rose from the couch and walked to the door. "I was going to grab a smoke before we went back on."

Vivian walked over and sat in a chair, worried getting up from the couch would be too complicated. "Hey, I am so sorry to spoil your break. You have been amazing all night. How are you doing it?"

"The antianxiety meds combined with a very carefully dosed edible are doing wonders, my friend." Evy cracked a smile. "I think I might finally be able to function. And oddly enough, it's actually easier to block everyone out when I'm hyperfocused on performing a set. As long as I keep my mouth moving, I don't really hear anyone's thoughts."

"Julia saw the same man my mother did."

Evy frowned. "The guy from the golf course? He's here?"

"No. You don't understand. Only *Julia* saw him."

"Oh." Evy grimaced. "So the dead kind of here."

"Yeah." She shifted in the metal folding chair. "He's standing at the Booster Club table, and we don't know why."

"Wait, you mean the Booster Club is actually a criminal organization?"

"That's probably stretching it, but they definitely have at least one criminal at the table. The problem is, the one the ghost is focused on isn't Trent Everett but the main guy in the group. West something."

"Oh." Evy made a face. "West Barrett. He and his father are complete assholes. They hired me to do an event for their company once, then tried to get out of paying me even though they have more money than God."

"That's gross." Vivian arched her back to stretch it. "What else do you know about him?"

"West Barrett?" Evy frowned. "I mean, other than my experience with him, mostly it's all gossip. He cheats on his wife regularly with his friends' wives, but no one says anything about it. He's the one running the family investment firm now, but his father refuses to give up the reins officially, which has led to all kinds of drama. They have houses in Pasadena and Malibu. A place in Manhattan. They're friends with all sorts of money people back in New York." She tapped Vivian's shoulder. "You know who'd know more about business stuff is Richard. He and Archie Barrett—that's West's dad—run in the same circles."

Vivian nodded. "Okay, I'll ask him. Oh! Apparently, Rich hadn't caught on to the whole psychic thing about me."

Evy's eyebrows went up. "Oh. Awkward?"

"Quiet for him. We've danced a lot, but it's not the most conducive place for a conversation, you know? I feel like he's holding back about a million questions right now."

"That's okay, I have about a million questions, and I'm one of the psychic ones." Evy's eyes looked tired. "As long as I sleep well tonight, I'll be fine."

"I've been missing Morning Club. Are you still working with Maud?"

"Roughly three times a week, yeah." Evy shrugged. "She comes by the house."

"Good." Vivian reached over and squeezed Evy's hand. "Well, you look amazing. Like a dark-haired Cate Blanchett in a tuxedo."

"Oooh, I'll take that!" Evy smiled. "And you look like you. Beautiful, graceful, and all put together."

"Then the facade worked." Vivian stood. "Do you need anything? Drink? Food? More edibles?"

Evy shook her head and nodded to a table where a silver dome covered a tray. "I'm going to eat a little something in just a minute. I don't like working on a full stomach, but they're taking good care of me for now."

"If you need me or Julia, just text."

Evy gave her a thumbs-up, and Vivian walked to the door.

"Oh!" She turned before she opened it. "Julia and I are going to head to John Marcos's office tomorrow and fill him in on the ghost showing up; then we were thinking we'd do another walk-through of the golf course tomorrow evening. Not at night this time, but around sunset. Julia says that's a good time for activity. See if anyone new shows up."

"Count me in for a ghost walk, but I'll pass on Marcos's office." She made a face. "No Landa is going to willingly spend time with police."

"Because you come from a family of crooks and conmen?"

Evy spread her hands. "We like to call ourselves inventive entrepreneurs. Don't judge."

Vivian laughed and walked back out to the party, only to nearly bump into Julia as she exited the hallway.

"Oh!" Julia looked over Vivian's shoulder. "Did you find Evy?"

"I did, and I filled her in. What's up?"

Julia looked like someone had put Pop Rocks in her champagne. "I found him, the ghost."

"Isn't he here?"

"No, I found out who he is!" She grabbed Vivian's arm and led her back toward the table. "I did some online snooping about West Barrett and it jumped out at me."

When they reached the table, Julia grabbed her phone, opened it, and showed the screen to her before she could say a word.

"Oh." Vivian blinked. "Yeah, he really does look like Robert Redford. No wonder my mom got confused."

John Marcos was incredulous. "Archie Barrett is the murder victim? West Barrett's father? CEO of Barrett Investment Group and Barrett Energy?"

Julia held up the same picture. "Tell me this man doesn't look like Robert Redford."

John opened his mouth. Closed it. Sighed. "Okay, he does look like the sketch your mom gave the sheriff, but this is Archie Barrett. If he was murdered or missing, we would have heard about it by now. The man is a prominent businessman and a fairly public figure."

"Who lives in two or maybe three places according to everyone I talked to last night," Vivian said. "What if he hasn't been reported missing because everyone thinks he's somewhere else?"

John leaned back in his chair. "That's actually not a stretch to imagine."

"His ghost was at the benefit last night, hovering around his son," Julia said. "And his son is friends with Trent Everett, whose ring was found on the same green where Joan Wei said she saw a man fitting Archie Barrett's description being beaten to death."

"Okay. One, there is still no body. Two, what possible motive would Trent have to kill his friend's dad?"

"I don't know," Julia said, "but don't you think it's worth questioning him about?"

Vivian asked, "Did you get my message about the sand? The sheriff's deputies searched the course, but I don't think they searched all the ponds. Maybe the body was weighed down with sand and sank."

John looked tired. "Vivian, do you know how expensive water searches are? The sheriff doesn't have those kinds of resources."

"Which is exactly why the killer might choose that method to hide the body."

Julia leaned both hands on John's desk. "Do you believe me about seeing Archie Barrett's ghost?"

John shrugged. "I have no reason to doubt you."

Other than the whole matter of seeing ghosts in the first place. Vivian was very aware they were incredibly lucky to know a police chief like John Marcos.

"Okay," Julia continued, "then at least call the man's office. Find out where he's supposed to be. Because I guarantee you, when people start asking, he's not going to be found."

THIS TIME THEY WALKED THE COURSE AT SUNSET, which both felt safer and meant they weren't completely alone. While all the golfers were finishing their rounds and the crack of golf balls could still be heard in the distance, Vivian, Julia, and Evy were far from the only people walking the course.

"See, I think my mom should get her mahjong group out here to walk like those ladies. One of them is in a wheelchair, but it's motorized and the cart paths are smooth. She's not getting enough exercise. Otis?"

She was debating names with her friends and not her parents, because in that direction, frustration was inevitable.

"Otis feels kind of hipsterish." Evy turned her face to the setting sun and held out her arms. The breeze lifted her loose cotton shirt, billowing it out behind her. "I'm glad it's finally getting cooler when the sun goes down."

"Does Otis sound good with Allan? Otis Allan Wei?" Vivian shook her head. "No, you're right. Not good."

"I'm not a fan of Otis either, but I'm relieved about the weather." Julia kept her eyes sweeping the landscape. "I can't lie —my first full summer here was a lot."

"You get used to it," Vivian said. "I'll be glad when it's cooler though. Fredrick? Fredrick Allan Wei. I like that."

"He'll be a Fred or Freddy though. Do you like Fred?" Julia asked.

"I can only think of *Five Nights at Freddy's*," Evy said.

Vivian sighed. "So that's a no."

Julia said, "You could go the Latin route like Sergio and Dean. Call your son Augustus or Caesar."

"I want simple and classic," Vivian said. "I don't like trendy names. And something to go with Allan obviously." Her father only had granddaughters so far, and she wanted to use his name for a middle name.

"Fredrick isn't trendy, but it is a bit much for a little tiny baby," Evy said. "What about Louis?"

"Louis Allan?" Vivian nodded. "Not bad. George?"

"George Allan sounds like a furniture shop," Julia said.

"That's Ethan Allan." Evy laughed.

"Ethan Allan is a definite no." Vivian stopped in her tracks as a name dropped into the front of her mind. "Henry."

Julia and Evy looked at each other, then at her. They were both smiling.

"I love Henry," Evy said. "Henry Allan Wei."

"*Doctor* Henry Allan Wei," Julia said. "I mean, let's be honest, the chances are better than average in your family."

"I love Henry." Vivian put a hand on the side of her belly and felt a swell of happiness. "Hey, little dude." The baby in her belly flipped at the sound of her voice. "Is your name Henry?" She looked down with a smile and saw a faint movement. "I think it might be."

"Oh my God." Julia was blinking and she had her phone out, holding it toward Vivian. "You look so beautiful right now."

Vivian began to laugh. "I don't know about that, but I feel good."

"No." Evy blinked hard. "You look amazing, Vivian. You look so happy."

Vivian held out her arms, and Julia and Evy went to her embrace. She held them for a long time, blinking back tears. These two women who had barged so unexpectedly into her life and changed... well, everything.

"I can't believe I let my mom's fears about my raising a baby alone get to me so much." She let Julia and Evy go and wiped her eyes. "I have so many people here. You know, on the surface, I knew so many more people in Chicago, but I wasn't close to anyone but my sister. Not like with you two or Dean and Sergio."

"And now Richard?" Evy wiggled her eyebrows. "What are the odds that you find Mr. Right when you're six months pregnant, huh?"

Vivian shook her head. "Almost seven months now, and let's not get ahead of ourselves, okay?" She pointed at the path ahead. "Come on, we have a ghost to find."

They walked past the pond where Vivian's mother had wandered, listening to the ducks quack as the sun went down and watching the birds settle in to roost.

"Nothing?" Vivian looked at Julia.

Julia shook her head. "I don't even get the sense that a spirit is here and hiding. It's completely quiet."

"Damn, I thought maybe there was a reason my mom wandered over here."

Evy raised a curious eyebrow. "You think your mom may have a gift we don't know about?"

She took a deep breath and let it out slowly as they started walking on the path that led to the clubhouse. "I don't know; she's always been really intuitive. I thought maybe..."

"It's not a bad thought." Julia motioned toward a line of condos bordering the golf course. "These places are going for a fortune. Golf course properties are skyrocketing right now."

"That many people love golf?" Evy asked.

"It's the space," Julia said. "The lifestyle." They walked a little farther along the path. "Vivian, have you thought any more about moving? I know you've held off on looking for another house because you own the place here, but if your parents are moving permanently, maybe it's time. The house here is perfect for them."

And not so much for you.

Julia didn't have to say that part out loud. Desert Oasis wasn't strictly a retirement community, but Julia was by far the youngest person in the homeowners' association. It would be nice to be in a neighborhood with more younger people, especially after the baby was born.

Henry. Henry Allan Wei. Henry would want to be in a neighborhood where there were other kids. Where she had a yard and maybe even a swing in the garden. Where there were quiet streets to ride a bike.

Vivian still had money stashed away from the sale of her condo in Chicago, and she knew it would be more than enough for a down payment on a small place, but she hesitated.

"I need to have a conversation with my parents. Them being out here for a month or two for a visit is one thing, but if they're thinking this move might be permanent—which wouldn't be a bad thing—then it may be time to look. I love them, but I want my own place."

She was forty-two and didn't love the idea of sleeping in her guest room permanently. The third bedroom at her current place was, at best, big enough for a home office and not ideal for a nursery.

"Maybe that's why I've been hesitating to get the third bedroom ready for a baby. Well, that and my sister keeps telling me that the baby will probably be happier in my room for the first few months."

"If you want me to put out some feelers in Vista de Lirio, I will. I suspect a couple of properties might be ready to move in the next few months."

Henry would probably love growing up in Vista de Lirio where Aurelia and Juliana would be the coolest babysitters around, he could run over to swim in Sergio and Dean's pool, or ride his bike to Auntie Julia's.

They turned the corner to the clubhouse, and Vivian nearly tripped over Julia when she stopped dead in her tracks.

"Julia?"

"Ghost." She was blinking. "Hello?"

It was always weird to watch Julia have a conversation with

the dead because she genuinely looked like she was just talking to thin air.

"No, I don't know..." Julia frowned. "What are you saying?" She reached her hands out, and Vivian and Evy grabbed them on either side.

"Is it Archer Barrett?" Evy whispered. "Do you see him?"

Julia said nothing, but she kept staring into a shadowed corner between two bunches of palm trees.

Evy looked at Vivian, but Vivian felt nothing from Julia except intense curiosity.

"Can you hear anything from...?" Vivian pointed her to her temple.

"No. You two are usually muffled, but right now her brain is a brick wall."

Julia's grip on Vivian's hand eased. "Sorry. We should head back to Vivian's, but I have a feeling he might follow me now."

"Is it Archer Barrett?"

"No, and this just got way more complicated." Julia looked over her shoulder. "He's following me but keeping a distance. He's very confused."

"Who is it?" In a place like Desert Oasis, a recently deceased resident wasn't unexpected. "Did he die here?"

"He didn't die here; I think Desert Oasis was just his favorite place. He said his name is Fisher Gates and that everyone thinks he died of a heart attack." Julia glanced over her shoulder again. "The problem is, Mr. Gates doesn't think he had a heart attack; he thinks he was murdered."

Chapter Eleven

"Fisher Gates was not murdered." John Marcos set his coffee mug down with a decided thunk. "Julia, I'm not doubting you, I'm just saying that the ghost of a dead banker with an obsessive need to control his entire family is not the best witness about his own death. I'm sure it pissed him off, but Gates died from a heart attack."

Vivian and Evy exchanged a look. They were all gathered for Sunday brunch at Sergio and Dean's: Julia, Evy, and Vivian, John Marcos and Michael. Aurelia and Juliana were sitting at their own table playing a card game while they waited for breakfast.

"Fisher Gates is the father of Ashley Gates-Bradley," Aurelia said ominously.

"She's in the Booster Club," Juliana added.

John turned to the girls. "So are about twenty other people, girls. That doesn't mean anything."

Aurelia shrugged. "Not on the board. There are only five on the board."

Dean had invited Richard to brunch, but he'd had a

previous commitment and Vivian felt relieved. It was one thing to date the man; it was another to have her friends couple her up in a neat package to fit their social plans.

"It sounds from your description," Evy said, "that Fisher Gates might not have been the most popular guy at the club. Isn't it possible someone wanted him dead?"

"It's very possible. In fact, over the years, I've probably overhead half a dozen people threaten to kill the man. That doesn't mean they did."

"It's possible the medical examiner missed something," Julia said. "That's what Mr. Gates says. Or his ghost says."

John looked annoyed. "Is he hanging around here still?"

"He and Mrs. Griffin are chatting by the gazebo."

John turned toward the gazebo decorating the front lawn and yelled, "Fisher, you died of a heart attack! Get over it; you weren't going to live forever."

Vivian turned to Julia and kept her voice low. "Is his ghost actually over there?"

"Yes, but he is not listening to us. I think he and Mrs. G might be kindred spirits."

Juliana piped up from the card table. "I imagine with the correct medications, it would be possible to fake a heart attack." Juliana looked at her aunt. "Right, Auntie Julia?"

"You're asking me? I *take* heart medication; I don't use it to murder people."

Vivian attempted to refocus the conversation. The girls were experts at sidetracking the adults. "Why are you so certain Fisher Gates was not murdered?"

"Because he was eighty-nine, had already survived three other heart attacks, and was on something like a dozen different medications. That the man made it to eighty-nine is a medical miracle considering how high-strung he was."

Sergio walked out to the table, holding a tray of pastries.

"Can confirm. Fisher was a character, and he was a heart attack waiting to happen. He had the patience of a gnat. I told him to relax once and I thought he'd come after me with his cane."

"So he was an asshole," Julia said. "That doesn't mean he wasn't a murder victim. In fact, that makes him way more likely to be a murder victim."

"True," John said. "Except Gates did die in my jurisdiction, and I can tell you there was no evidence that he was murdered."

"Did you look for any?" Juliana adjusted her tortoiseshell sunglasses. "If you thought he died of natural causes, there would be no need to look for evidence of foul play."

"We don't actually say 'foul play' in law enforcement. That's just on TV."

"It's an excellent expression," Juliana said. "You *should* use it."

There was a snorting sound from the edge of the patio, and Vivian turned to see Paco the rescue alpaca staring at the girls from the lawn.

Aurelia turned to the animal and said in a firm voice: "Absolutely not."

Paco huffed, turned his nose up, and trotted off toward the gazebo and the ghosts.

"What was that about?" Sergio asked.

Aurelia and Juliana exchanged a look. "We've discovered that Paco has a taste for champagne," Aurelia said. "It's inappropriate. He's only three, which even in alpaca years makes him underage."

Sergio blinked. "How has he developed a taste for…?" He held up a hand. "You know what? I don't want to know."

"Probably my fault," Julia whispered to Vivian.

Vivian was in Sergio's camp. She really didn't want to know.

"What about Archie Barrett?" Vivian asked. "Has anyone spoken to him yet?"

"Okay, there are some questions there." John took another

sip of coffee. "I followed up with his office here and can confirm he's not in Palm Springs. But he was here for the golf tournament at Desert Oasis the Friday that Vivian's mother witnessed the attack."

Vivian sat up straight. "And no one has seen him since?"

"He told his son he was driving back to LA that night, so we're following up with his office in Pasadena."

"It's been three weeks," Evy said. "His son hasn't talked to him in three weeks and he thought that was normal? I thought they worked together."

"According to West Barrett, his father is mostly retired and it's not out of the ordinary for him to go weeks without contact. His father's more interested in charity and Barrett Family Foundation work these days, and West handles the day-to-day. So..." John shrugged. "I guess it's not that unusual. West has a business, three kids, and a lot of social commitments here in the valley. I could see how time could get away from him."

Vivian thought it was weird, but then again, she didn't go a week without talking to her parents ever. She talked to her sister every few days, and when her parents were in Chicago, Debra saw them every other day at least.

"I know not all families are close," Vivian said. "But that doesn't strike you as a long time? Especially for two men who are in business together? Maybe a week or two, but three?"

John nodded. "I admit that it raised a few questions for me too, but West volunteered an alibi for the night the attack happened, and it's way too public to be a lie."

"What was his alibi?" Julia asked. "Don't tell me it was his friends, because that would be too convenient."

"Friends, but also staff at the Desert Oasis clubhouse. There was a party that night, and employees confirm that West Barrett was there the entire time, holding court with his buddies. They were there until at least two in the morning."

Her mother had seen the attack happen a little bit before one a.m. Vivian let out a slow breath. "Okay, so maybe Archie's ghost is haunting his son because... I mean, maybe he just had unfinished business or something like that."

Julia nodded. "That can happen. It doesn't mean his son had anything to do with his death."

"But we still don't know where Archie Barrett is," Evy said.

John's phone picked that moment to ring, right when Dean walked out to the table, bearing individual quiches and a fruit salad. "Breakfast is ready."

John answered his phone and walked away.

Dean raised an eyebrow. "Not a quiche fan?"

"Count me in for quiche." Julia reached for one and put it on her plate. "Vivian?"

"Yes please. My reach is significantly shorter these days." She waited patiently while Julia served her a steaming mushroom-dotted quiche and a hearty helping of salad.

Food was passed around the table, but John still hadn't returned when people started eating.

Sergio looked at their friend, who was pacing the flagstones at the other end of the pool. "Something must have happened."

"And lucky us, we get to hear it first." Evy raised her champagne glass. "More Mimosa please?"

"Just promise you won't give any to Paco." Sergio refilled her glass as John walked back to the patio. "What's the story, Chief Marcos?"

John's handsome tan face looked paler than normal. "That was the sheriff's deputy over in Rancho."

Every eye turned to him.

John looked at the full table. "Um... I hate to spoil breakfast, but it sounds like they probably found a body at Desert Oasis."

"*Probably* found a body?" Vivian was already standing up to get her phone and call her parents. "What does that mean?"

"It means they found a hand floating in the duck pond," John said. "They're sending diving crews out as we speak."

JOAN ASKED FOR VIVIAN TO STAY WITH HER WHEN THE sheriff's deputy questioned her, and Vivian asked John to sit in.

"The coroner is pretty sure it's Archie Barrett based on the jewelry the body was wearing," Deputy Sheriff Bernie Hightower said. "Mrs. Wei—"

"Dr. Wei," Vivian said quietly.

Deputy Hightower glanced at her. "Dr. Wei, thank you again for coming forward that night and making a statement. If we were skeptical at the time... Well, I'm sure you can understand why."

"You said you have more questions for me?" Joan seemed uninterested in the deputy's attempts at explanation.

"Did you know Archie Barrett?" the deputy asked. "Had you seen him around the club before maybe?"

Joan leaned back in the couch. "I don't know. I don't think so. Was he a member here?"

"No, I believe he was a member of Monte Verde, but he did golf here regularly according to the club president."

Vivian glanced at John. Monte Verde was Sergio and Dean's club. Richard's too. John nodded slightly.

Vivian's mother continued. "It's possible we crossed paths, but my daughter is the one who lives here full time. My husband and I have visited Desert Oasis for years—my parents originally bought this place—but it was a seasonal thing. I might have run into Mr. Barrett at the clubhouse or crossed paths with him at an event of some kind, but I don't think we were ever introduced."

Deputy Hightower scribbled in his notebook. "And you, Dr. Wei?"

Vivian turned her attention from her mother to the sheriff's deputy. "Do you mean me?"

"Yes."

"I don't think so." Vivian took her mother's hand. "I don't

go to many events at the clubhouse, and Mr. Barrett and I didn't know each other socially."

"But you know his son West."

Vivian frowned. "I'm not sure why you would think that."

"Oh, I just remember seeing your picture in the paper a few days ago," Hightower said. "Saw West Barrett's picture too."

Joan perked up. "You were in the newspaper, Vivian?"

"I didn't know I was."

The deputy tapped his pencil on his notebook. "You were at the event he chaired, right?"

"Yes, it was a school benefit. I was there, but I went with friends. I saw West Barrett, but we weren't introduced. I don't know him socially. If our pictures were next to each other in the newspaper, that's purely coincidence. There were probably three or four hundred people there."

"Interesting." Hightower glanced between John and Vivian. "I understand you're the one who suggested that Chief Marcos call Archie Barrett's office the other day."

John interjected. "You got a snitch in my department, Bernie?"

Hightower leaned back. "You know how things go with the grapevine around here. I'm just curious why you all were asking around about Archie Barrett when his own family didn't think he was missing until his body turned up."

Vivian held a hand out when John leaned forward. "It's okay, John."

"Don't love the tone, Bernie. Dr. Wei and her mother are concerned citizens and friends of mine."

"Come on, John, I gotta ask."

Vivian said, "I believed my mother, Deputy." She held the man's gaze. "That's why I spoke to John about the incident she saw. I knew people weren't taking her seriously, but I was with her the night she saw Mr. Barrett attacked and I knew she wasn't imagining things. When I saw West Barrett at the event last week, I heard someone remark that he looked like a young Robert Redford." She unfolded a copy of the sketch the police artist had made. "It piqued my interest. It's not difficult to find pictures of West's father online; he's a prominent man. I think the resemblance is striking, don't you?"

Deputy Hightower watched her with eyes that said he knew she was hiding something but he didn't know why. It didn't matter—Vivian knew her explanation was completely logical.

"I think it's strange that the man's own family didn't realize he was missing for over three weeks," Vivian added. "Don't you think that's odd?"

"I think a lot of things are odd about this case, Dr. Wei." He glanced at his notebook again, tapping his pencil eraser along the edge. "You turned in a ring to the clubhouse the week after your mother saw Mr. Barrett attacked."

"I did."

"Do you golf?"

"No." Vivian gestured to the rolling hills of the golf course visible through the windows to her left. "One of the benefits of living in Desert Oasis is that I have a very large backyard." She smiled. "I often go walking on the cart paths in the evenings. It's a great place to relax."

"And you found the ring near the thirteenth tee."

"I did. I noticed it in the grass."

"On the same tee where your mother saw a man attacked." He glanced at her. "You didn't think to turn that ring in to my office?"

Vivian narrowed her eyes. "According to your office, no crime had been committed. There was no body found. Why would I have turned the ring over to you? I took it to the club-house, and the secretary recognized it."

"She said it belonged to Trent Everett?"

"Yes. I believe he's the club pro."

Joan added, "Oh, that makes sense. Your father has lost two rings because he takes them off to play and they fall out of his bag. I tell him to just leave it at home, but he forgets."

Deputy Hightower looked at Vivian. "Is that what Mr. Everett said? That he dropped it at tee thirteen?"

"I believe he said something about changing his gloves." Vivian flashed back to the intense panic she'd felt from Trent Everett that morning. He had to be involved. He just had to be. "Have you asked him?"

"Not yet, but I will." Deputy Hightower closed his notebook. "I think that's all for right now, Dr. Wei." He looked at Joan. "And Dr. Wei." He smiled politely at Joan. "Again, thank you very much for coming forward. We're going to do our best to make sure whoever killed Mr. Barrett is arrested."

"Do you think my mother has any reason to be concerned about her safety?" Vivian asked.

"I don't think so, but I'll make sure to increase the public-safety patrols on your street while all this is going on." He stood and reached into his pocket, pulled out a business card, and handed it to Joan. "And Dr. Wei, if you remember anything else or see anything else, you call me directly, okay?"

Joan glanced at Vivian, then at John. "Okay." She smiled at Deputy Hightower. "Thank you, Detective."

"Oh, it's..." He smiled. "You're welcome." He glanced at John. "John, I'll give you a call later."

John stood and walked with Bernie Hightower toward the door. "Let me know if there's anything you need."

Vivian sat with her mother, holding her hand and staring out the window as another group of four golfers pulled their carts up to the thirteenth tee.

Her mother squeezed her hand. "I guess they know I'm not a crazy old lady now, don't they?"

Vivian looked at her mother, who looked sad and tired. "I'm sure they'll find whoever killed that man, Mom. Don't worry."

"What if he thinks I saw more than the man he attacked, Vivian?" Her mother's forehead was furrowed with worry. "What if the killer thinks I saw his face too?"

Chapter Twelve

"I don't blame her for being worried." Evy pinned pictures to the large corkboard in the front room of her house. What had once been her aunt Marie's crafting space had been turned into a meditation room that also housed a large corkboard they'd used the last time a murder had interrupted their lives.

Murder and meditation. Yes, that sounded like Vivian's life now.

The pictures of Justin Worthy and his twisted social circle were being replaced by society pictures of Archie Barrett at various events, West Barrett, and Trent Everett along with a map of Desert Oasis Evy had found online.

"I don't know how widely it's known that she's the one who witnessed the murder," Vivian said. "But I don't like it. I'm tempted to bully them onto a plane back to Chicago."

Julia was sitting on Evy's green couch, sipping a Coke. "That's not a bad idea."

"I don't think they would go." Vivian had dragged in one of the chairs from the dining room. Evy's couch was too low; if she sat in it, she'd need a small crane to hoist her up. "I feel like a whale."

"What?"

"You've got to be joking."

"What are you even talking about?"

"Where is this coming from?"

The reassurances came fast and furious, but Vivian waved them away.

"I'm not talking about my weight or anything. My OB says I'm right on track for where I should be. I feel healthy, I just..." She framed her belly with both hands. "Have you ever seen a beached whale? They're out of their element. Unwieldy. I physically do not feel like this is my body anymore; it's bizarre and there's absolutely nothing I can do about it. I'm stuck like this until I give birth."

"And you're going to get bigger," Evy whispered.

"Don't remind me." Vivian sat in the hard-backed chair. "It's just a very weird thing to feel like your body isn't yours anymore."

Julia stood and walked behind her to rub her shoulders. "I think you need some self-care days. You've been tense ever since your mom witnessed the murder—and there's no way to avoid that because it was horrible and traumatic—but is there any way you could take some time off work? Maybe get a massage?"

Evy said, "You could boink Richard."

Vivian snorted. "No."

Julia's hands stopped massaging her shoulders. "Did you just say *boink*?"

"I would normally say *fuck*, but that seems a little crude for pregnant-lady sex, you know?"

Vivian started laughing, and she couldn't stop. Tears came to her eyes. "Oh my God, I'm going to pee."

"What?" Evy started laughing too. "You could *fuck* Richard. Is that better? I hope my aunt didn't hear me say that."

Julia snorted; then she started to giggle too. "I don't think I've heard anyone say *boink* since I was in high school."

Vivian's side was aching, but she couldn't stop laughing.

"*Boink* seems bouncier than *fuck*," Evy said. "And you know, she's got the belly now, her boobs are bigger, she's carrying a little extra junk in the trunk. Bouncy, fun sex is probably the way to go."

"Stop!" Vivian really was worried about peeing. "I didn't bring extra pants with me."

"I've heard that you can be extra horny when you're pregnant," Julia said. "Is that true?"

Vivian took a deep breath and let it out slowly. "If I weren't carrying a baby the size of a small melon, I would definitely fuck Richard." She wiped at her eyes. "But I am, and I just told you both I feel like a beached whale. Why on earth do you think I'd want to have sex with anyone?"

"You didn't say beached whale first, you said *whale*. And whales in their natural environment are graceful and elegant," Evy said. "Maybe your natural environment is Richard Putnam's bed. Have you considered that possibility?"

Vivian covered her eyes and wished the mental picture was less tempting.

Julia tapped her shoulder. "Evy's right; that's just logic. I think you need to test this hypothesis by boinking Richard. For science."

Vivian bit her lip so she didn't start laughing again. "I love you both, but this conversation needs to head in a different direction. Can we get back to talking about murdered millionaires please?"

"I still think you should have sex with Richard." Evy turned back to the board. "His life was a roller coaster when he was married to Lily; he's probably ready for someone normal like you."

"Thank you for flattering me and yet somehow also making

me sound boring." Vivian crossed her arms over her newly giant boobs. "Who are all these other people?"

"Okay." Evy turned and spread her arms out. "Julia, I know your nieces are prone to hyperbole—"

"They're dramatic fourteen-year-olds; where is this going?"

"But!" Evy raised a finger and held up a picture of an elegant woman in a pantsuit. "This is Ashley Gates-Bradley. Graduated with honors from Brown. Former art dealer and professional wife to a very rich man. She graduated from Desert Prep the same year as Trent and West."

"And?"

"Her father is Fisher Gates" —Evy held up another picture — "the ghost Julia met at Desert Oasis who claims he was murdered." Evy stuck the two pictures to the corkboard.

Vivian saw where this was going. "So Ashley Gates is friends with West and Trent, her father is recently deceased by—we'll say —questionable circumstances, though John is convinced that Fisher Gates's death was purely natural causes."

"And!" Evy held out a paper. "I looked online, so this is all public information, but guess who's the treasurer of the Desert Prep Booster Club?"

Julia reached for the paper and held it out so Vivian could read it too. "President West Barrett. Secretary Trent Everett. Treasurer... Ashley Gates-Bradley."

"I know it seems crazy," Evy said, "but I think your nieces are right. Desert Prep Booster Club might actually be a criminal organization."

By the time Vivian got home, dinner was long finished and her parents were watching a golf tournament on the television, her dad in his favorite easy chair and her mom on the overstuffed sofa.

"Hey, guys." Vivian hung her purse by the door and set her keys on the entry table. "Mom, how are you feeling?"

"I'm feeling great, honey."

"Good." Vivian picked up the mail and started paging through what was mostly junk. So many mailers for Medicare insurance supplements. Her new membership card to AARP. And of course, *Prevention Magazine*. A complete waste of trees.

"So irritating," she muttered.

The television switched off. "Hey, kiddo," her dad said. "Come sit with us."

Vivian looked up from the mail with a frown. Something was wrong. "What's up?"

"Come sit." Joan patted the couch. "Your dad and I need to talk to you about the house."

"Oh God, is it the downstairs bathroom again?" Vivian sighed. "I know. There's something going on with the shower drain. I'll call a plumber tomorrow."

Allan chuckled. "That's not the issue. The shower is fine. It just needed a little caustic soda. I already unclogged it."

She frowned and sat next to her mom. "Okay, so what's up?"

Joan took her hand. "When we came out to California this time, we told you we wanted to help you out the last months of your pregnancy and Dad wanted to help out at the practice while you were looking for a new associate."

"Yes." She put her hand on top of her mother's, enjoying the warm, affectionate glow that she only felt from her mother. Other people loved her, but no one loved her like her mom. "And I am so appreciative. I know I need to be more on top of the nursery stuff too; I've just been busy."

"There's plenty of time for all that," Joan said. "Now I'm having these little... episodes, and we need to get those checked out. I suspect I may have had a small stroke or a series of ministrokes, which aren't always evident until you check for them—"

"Strokes?" Vivian held on to her mother's emotional signature, which felt cool, calm, and steady. "You think you had a stroke?"

"I'm speculating because we're still waiting for tests," Joan said. "Don't jump to conclusions. It wouldn't be uncommon for someone my age."

"You're thinking you want to go back to Chicago." Vivian squeezed her mother's hand. "You want to deal with doctors you know. Mom, I completely understand. Do not feel like you have to stay out here for me. You've met my friends; I have wonderful support here."

"I can see that, but no, that's not what I'm feeling at all," Joan said. "Hannah—from my mahjong group—has already recommended two specialists that she helped train when she was teaching at the hospital here. They're local, both in private practice now, and she says either one would be very good. I'll send my scans and bloodwork to my doctor back in Chicago, but I think it might be good to have a fresh perspective."

"That's great." Vivian had never been more grateful that her mother was a doctor. She rarely overreacted to any health scare. "I want to be sure you're comfortable though. Is there anything I can do to help? Is that what you wanted to talk about?"

Her dad spoke up. "We need to talk about the house, Vivi. Before when we came, we were just here for visits. We never felt bad taking your room for a month or a few weeks. But now—"

"You're having a baby," Joan said. "You need to decorate a nursery. Make a space that works for your new life as a young mother."

Well, not *that* young, but Vivian saw where this was going. "Are you guys thinking about getting your own place?" She knew that someday, she or her sister might have her parents living with them, but right now Joan and Allan were still young, active, and independent. They would want their own space.

"We've been looking for a couple of weeks now," Allan said.

"We want something with a couple of extra rooms for when your sister or our friends from the city come to visit, but we want to be on the course. That's part of the appeal of moving out here. We've talked about this before."

"You have."

Joan continued, "Unfortunately, there's not much available right now, even with our budget, that's actually *on* the golf course."

Her parents owned a beautiful condo on the waterfront that would likely sell for millions if they wanted to offload it. And it had always seemed obvious to Vivian that when her parents were ready to move, they would find a place similar to this one, but if none were available...

"Wait." She frowned. "Are you saying you want to buy my house?"

Joan held up both hands. "It's completely up to you, honey. A move right now would be a lot of work and we know that. We're in no rush, but we thought that if you were maybe looking for a different neighborhood...?"

"One with more kids and fewer old people." Her dad smiled a little. "I know your grandparents wanted you to have this place because you loved the desert, but it's not exactly a house for someone with an active social life."

"And definitely not one for a young family," her mother said.

The fact that her parents had almost mirrored her thoughts about Desert Oasis wasn't lost on her, but the idea of a move two months before her due date made her feel a little panicky.

"I don't know what to say."

Yes. Say yes. The same internal voice that told her to say yes to Richard Putnam's invitation was telling her this was exactly what she wanted. Timing be damned.

"Take your time and think about it. There's no reason to rush. We would insist on paying market rate though," Allan said.

"We don't want any favors because you're our daughter; this is your inheritance from your grandparents."

That was true, but it was also true she could afford the down payment on another house and mortgage payments. She'd sold her place in Chicago for a nice profit.

"Like your father said, there's no rush." Joan patted her hand.

"Of course," Vivian said. "No rush for you either. I mean, you should think about whether you want to make this permanent when you know what's happening with your health."

"Oh, we know we want to move out here," Joan said. "The winters were getting to be too much for both of us."

Allan said, "If I never shovel another snowy driveway, I'll be a happy man."

"I thought the maintenance department of your building shoveled the sidewalk?"

"And I felt guilty every time I walked past them," Allan said.

"Okay, but..."

But what? Her parents wanted her house, and she wanted a new place anyway. This was exactly what she had wanted, but she was feeling panicky about the timing.

Not unlike Richard...

No. No, this was good.

"It's just an idea, sweetheart." Joan patted her hand again. "If you don't want to deal with moving—"

"It's a good idea." Vivian smiled. "Trust me, I've been thinking about this too. Julia has been bugging me for months that I need to be in a different house."

"So your friends agree!" Joan smiled. "Good. Julia is a very smart girl. She'll find the perfect place for you and the baby."

"I love this house; I love the memories here." She took a deep breath. "But you're right. Henry and I should have a neighborhood with a few more friends for him to play with."

Joan's face lit up, and she put her hand on Vivian's belly.

"Henry? I *love* that." She turned to Vivian's dad. "Allan, did you hear that? Henry."

Allan smiled. "That's a fine name, Vivi."

"Henry Allan Wei," Vivian said. "It's not for certain until I actually meet the little guy, but I'm pretty happy with the idea."

Allan had tears in his eyes. "Oh wow."

"*Doctor* Henry Wei." Joan nodded. "Yes. That's good."

Vivian and Allan both laughed.

"What?" Joan said. "In this family, the chances are pretty good."

Chapter Thirteen

"So you're moving to Vista de Lirio, right?" Richard's daughter Maddy looked delighted. "I love that for you. It sounds like you have a lot of friends here."

Richard was also feeling quietly happy, though Vivian knew he was holding back from offering an opinion.

"Absolutely." Vivian sat on the back patio of Casa de Lirio, watching the sky light up as the sun slipped below the horizon. "And I feel like there's a transition going on right now. On the way over here, I saw two new KIDS PLAYING signs on the road."

"You're right." Richard poured a glass of red wine for himself and handed another to Maddy. "What do you think? The neighborhood still filled with the olds?"

Richard's daughter laughed. "I have never said that. Ever." The young woman sipped her wine and tucked a strand of her sandy-blond hair behind her ear. "But I do know what you mean. There are a lot of new people moving in, and most of them are quite a bit younger."

"Luckily, they don't all seem to be cookie-cutter rich people," Richard said.

"Says the wealthy East Coast financier?" Vivian raised an eyebrow.

Maddy bit her lip and nodded, her eyes dancing with laughter.

"Hey, I will have you know that I'm actually the one who wanted to move into this house," he said. "I loved how eclectic the neighborhood was even though the house itself was a money pit for about ten years." Richard sighed. "It was a project. But Vista de Lirio had the most character of any neighborhood in Palm Springs." He pointed to the right. "When we first moved here, there was a couple who lived there, retired college professors from back east. She taught psychology and always read the most interesting books. Amazing library in that little house." He pointed to the left. "And on that side was a couple who were both musicians. Well, one performer and one composer. I think the composer wrote advertising jingles and he was hugely successful. They were so much fun."

"I know what you mean." Vivian nodded. "People know their neighbors here. It's unusual to find that anywhere these days."

"So you wanted to live next to artists and people like that?" Maddy asked. "Why?"

"I'd been around rich, boring people my entire life," Richard said. "That's part of the reason I moved out west." He glanced at Vivian. "Where else was I going to run into a fashion icon, an alpaca rescuer, and a psychic dentist at one party?"

Vivian bit the corner of her lip. "You still haven't asked me about that. You're being very restrained, Richard Putnam."

"Oh my God!" Maddy's eyebrows went up. "It's you? Are you psychic?"

Vivian nodded. "Only recently."

"Wow." Maddy looked fascinated. "Was it when you got pregnant? Did that trigger some ancestral psychic power or something?"

"Ancestral psychic power?" Vivian wasn't too sure about that. "I'm not sure what it was. Evy Landa's aunt Marie might have a better idea since she's the one who was praying to something or someone when she was halfway under anesthesia. The next day? I woke up and could feel my patients' emotions when I put my hands in their mouths." Vivian shuddered. "Thanks, Aunt Marie."

Richard said, "Blessing or curse?"

"I still haven't decided," Vivian said. "Julia was seeing ghosts, so she and Evy came to my office to see Aunt Marie. The next thing I know, a partially anesthetized patient is chanting in Latin, I'm trying to throw Evy out of my exam room, and Julia is arguing with an invisible person. I'm honestly surprised we didn't accidentally summon a demon."

Maddy shook her head, but whether it was in amazement or skepticism, Vivian couldn't tell. "So you can, like, read my thoughts or something?"

"Oh no!" Vivian held up her hands. "I wouldn't want telepathy wished on my worst enemy. Evy can read minds, and it's horribly draining and very confusing."

"I can only imagine," Richard murmured.

"I can sense emotion." Vivian straightened her back and rearranged the edge of her skirt. "Which sounds very overwhelming until you realize that I have to be quite close to anyone to sense it. I'm trying to expand that—"

"How?" Maddy was completely focused on Vivian. "Can you... I don't know, control elements or anything like that?"

"No." Vivian had never felt more famous. "We have a coach to help us, but she hasn't mentioned anything about elements yet. Julia says that ghosts respond to offerings, but that's about as elemental as it gets." Vivian didn't know if there was a ghost still hanging around the glowing portal in the back of Casa de Lirio or whether she'd moved on, but she certainly wasn't going to mention it without talking to Julia first.

"Anyway, Julia—the medium and also the Realtor—is looking for a house around here, preferably ghost-free. I don't know if moving is very feasible when I'm seven months pregnant, but she's looking."

"You need a car first," Richard said. "Do you want to try to move houses before the baby comes? That could be difficult."

"That's what Julia says too." Vivian shrugged. "I'm not in a rush."

Maddy said, "According to the Oliveira-Steward twins, most of the houses in Vista de Lirio never go on the market and are bought by a cabal of evil investors who are trying to keep anyone who tries to thwart them out of the neighborhood."

Vivian bit back a laugh. "Is that the way conspiracy theorists refer to pocket listings?"

"Possibly." Maddy shook her head. "I'm telling you, meeting those girls in the library was an experience. The two of them are hilarious."

"Speaking of the girls..." Vivian looked at Richard. "They have definite opinions about the Booster Club. You heard about Archie Barrett by now, right?"

"Absolutely awful business," Richard said. "I was no fan of Archie, but to die like that? And to not have anyone even realize you're missing for nearly a month makes it that much worse."

"Everyone at the school is in shock," Maddy said. "Mr. Barrett was a huge donor. The science building is named after him."

"Interesting." Vivian tried to poke carefully. "Do you know his kids at all? West Barrett is the Booster Club president, right? Pretty active?"

"Kind of *too* active, if you ask some of the staff and teachers." Maddy rolled her eyes. "All the Desert Prep parents think they own the school a little bit because the board is parent-elected, but West Barrett takes it to the extreme."

"Oh?" Vivian tried to look curious but not ravenous for information. She didn't want Maddy feeling interrogated.

"He was in the office today in fact. Something about his father's legacy donation and setting up some scholarship." Maddy made a face. "I hate being uncharitable—literally in this situation—but I feel like everything that man does is so calculated."

"His wife is the blandest person I have ever met," Richard said. "I feel like that's unkind, but I met her at a club mixer once and had the unfortunate luck to be seated next to her at dinner. She asked all about me at first, which I thought was very polite, but then every time I asked her about herself, she turned the conversation to West or her father-in-law. She seemed to have no personality of her own."

Vivian cringed. "That's horrible."

"It was an incredibly strange dinner."

"They're an odd family," Maddy said. "Their kids seem nice enough, but a little bit like my dad described Mrs. Barrett. Very reserved. Very cautious. Don't talk about themselves much. Talk a lot about 'the family.'"

"I'll be frank: Archie Barrett was a bully," Richard said. "He treated his wife horribly until she died, and I imagine he was an unkind father to his children. I know it's wrong to speak ill of the dead, but I doubt anyone will mourn that man."

Something occurred to Vivian. "Richard, you said the dinner with the Barretts was at the club. You mean Monte Verde?"

"Yes, the Barretts are all members there."

"But his body was found at Desert Oasis."

"Oh, Archie would golf there and do charity events, but he'd never be a member." Richard rolled his eyes. "His money was far too pedigreed for Desert Oasis."

A few things clicked into place. "Oh. So there's an old money, new money thing in Palm Springs?"

"Oh yeah," Maddy said. "It's just as bad as the East Coast where I grew up. The kids at school whose parents belong to Monte Verde are definitely higher in the pecking order than the kids whose parents or grandparents belong to Desert Oasis or any of the other new clubs."

Vivian shook her head. "This is so wild to me. So if West Barrett was good friends with Trent Everett—"

"The Everetts are new money." Richard lifted a hand. "And trust me, I know how it sounds, but I'm trying to give you an idea of how people like the Barretts think."

"Is that why Trent was the pro at Desert Oasis and not Monte Verde?"

"I'm sure he would have *liked* to be the pro at Monte Verde," Richard said. "But yes, I imagine that's why. The club pro at Monte Verde is the grandson of a member. He's not going anywhere, except maybe to manage a hedge fund if he ever gets his degree."

"Do you think there's some resentment there? From people like Trent?"

"It's definitely possible," Richard said. "I don't think a friend of West Barrett is going to be under any illusions about hierarchy."

"West would absolutely be the leader of any club he joined," Maddy said. "You can spot that kind of kid on the playground."

Vivian looked at Richard. "How did West get along with his father?"

"On the surface, they were civil and loyal to each other, but that means nothing." Richard sipped his wine. "Remember, West didn't know his father was missing for three weeks. That says something."

Maybe he knew he was already dead.

Vivian didn't want to say that part out loud, so she sighed and sat back in her chair. "Oh, the wild and crazy world of the rich and the even richer."

Maddy laughed. "Dad's money is so old he could belong to any club he wanted, and if the club was new, they'd call him daring and admire his rebellious streak."

Vivian glanced at Richard, then looked at Maddy with a smile tugging at the corner of her lips. "Rich people are weird."

"So weird."

Richard cleared his throat. "Pardon me, but the Putnams are descended from modest New England stock, and we are—at our most exciting—barely unconventional."

Vivian laughed along with Maddy as Richard checked his phone, then stood and reached for the empty tray of appetizers on the table.

"Give me a minute," he said. "Dinner should be finished."

Richard disappeared into the house, leaving Maddy and Vivian on the back patio alone. Oddly enough, she didn't feel awkward with Richard's daughter. Maddy felt like someone Vivian would meet and be friends with even if she wasn't dating Richard. She was curious, on the other hand, how Maddy felt about the whole situation. She wasn't getting a lot from the cheerful elementary school teacher; Maddy was emotionally reserved in a very similar way to Richard.

"My dad is so happy when you're around."

Vivian felt her cheeks warm. "I was actually just wondering how you felt about the two of us spending time together." She smiled. "That's nice to hear."

"Just..." Maddy smiled. "Woman to woman, I'm going to advise you that he's a fixer."

"Oh. Hmm." Vivian nodded. "Somehow that doesn't surprise me. My dad is the same way."

"He has the biggest heart in the world—even though he's the ultimate quiet guy about it—but if he sees anything in your life he thinks he can fix, he might get a little pushy."

"Consider me warned." Vivian pursed her lips, motioned to her belly, then nodded at the house. "So none of this feels weird to you? Your new dad dating a single pregnant lady who's closer to your age than his?"

"I honestly had not done the math on that, but I guess it is a little different." Maddy shrugged. "If he likes you, I'm happy."

Vivian glanced down at her ever-growing bump. "I admit, when I was your age, this is not something I would have predicted for myself. I had much more conventional ideas about family."

"But what's family these days, right?" Maddy asked. "There's no such thing as normal anymore, which is a relief to someone who was raised by her grandparents and never really knew either parent growing up."

Vivian frowned. "That's hard. I'm sorry."

"Don't be." Maddy smiled. "I had a great childhood, just like I know your son will have a great childhood. The important thing is to be raised by people who love you. Grandparents. Single parents. Two parents. Friends. Family comes in all forms these days."

"Thanks, Maddy." Vivian was feeling a little weepy. "It's so hard to imagine what life is going to be like when he's here, so... thanks."

"And I love seeing my dad happy." Maddy smiled. "And that's all I'll say." She mimed pulling a zipper over her mouth, then tossed the invisible key over her shoulder. "What's your best guess of what we're eating tonight?"

"Whatever the housekeeper made, right?"

"Aha!" Maddy grinned. "You've caught on to his secret of home-cooked meals."

VIVIAN PAGED THROUGH THE CORONER'S REPORT, taking notes in the spiral notebook she'd brought while Julia was on her phone and Evy yawned broadly.

"You guys don't have to hang out here if you don't want to," Vivian said. "So far, everything I'm reading here lines up with what my mom saw. Archie Barrett definitely died violently, and there was a struggle."

Evy blinked slowly. "Were there any defensive wounds?"

"Broken hands, but nothing that would produce evidence. The examiner noted traces of what looked like leather under some of his fingernails" —Vivian kept jotting notes— "so he might have had a glove on. John mentioned they recovered some gloves from the lake, but there were dozens of them and they were all mismatched. There's no way of matching them to Archie."

Julia didn't look up from her phone. "Interesting."

"The body was wrapped in a tarp, and they're still examining that. The bags of sand were wrapped with the body to weigh it down. Honestly, it's amazing a hand even escaped." Vivian continued making notes. "But there are catfish in that pond. They're scavengers."

"Ooooooh, gross." Evy made a face. "Never eating catfish again."

"I wouldn't." Vivian looked up from the report to see where John was in the office. He'd allowed them to look at the report but said they couldn't make a copy and take it home. "There's too much information here."

"We're not in a hurry," Julia muttered. "Take your time."

"I could, or I could..." Vivian grabbed her phone, used a scanner app she used for work, and quickly took pictures of each page of the coroner's report. "There. Now it's on my computer at home."

Evy sat up. "Good, we can go then."

Just as Vivian had tucked her phone away, John poked his head into the conference room. "You ladies done?"

Vivian closed the file and held it up. "Thank you. I took

some notes, but it looks to me like my mom was right. Any leads yet on the golf-club killer?"

"Please don't say that to the papers, they'd run with it." John sighed. "And no. We've questioned everyone who knew Archie Bennett, and no one jumps out. Plenty of people had disagreements with him—"

"Like his son?" Julia glanced up. "I hear rumors, John."

"West Barrett was hosting a table at the benefit that night, and at least six other people who were employees, not friends of his, verified his alibi." John held up a hand. "I think it's suspicious that he didn't report his father missing for weeks too, but he has a solid alibi."

"He could have hired someone," Evy said.

"If he did, there's no evidence of it. He turned over his phone records, and there was nothing suspicious."

Evy, Julia, and Vivian all exchanged a look. It was too neat.

"What about Trent Everett?" Vivian asked. "He was completely panicked about my finding his ring on that tee."

"I checked his alibi too," John said. "It's not quite as solid as West's since he was working that event and was kind of in and out, but I did find out something about the ring he lost."

Vivian perked up. "Oh?" Did they finally have another lead?

"Yeah." John frowned. "He reported it missing on Wednesday."

"Which Wednesday?"

"The Wednesday *before* Archie Barrett's murder," John said. "Sorry, Vivian. But Trent Everett had already lost his ring before that Friday night. Whatever his panic was about, it wasn't about killing Archie."

Chapter Fourteen

There were definite benefits to being friends with your Realtor, like when Julia brought lunch and new residential opportunities to Vivian's office the next day. With any luck, sandwiches and new house listings would assuage their disappointment at not finding any more clues into Archie Barrett's murder.

Julia opened her computer as they started to eat. "Okay, this listing isn't technically in Vista de Lirio, but it's like one block over, so practically speaking you're there, and it's even on the lower end of your price range."

Vivian leaned over to look. "Oh, it's cute!"

"Spanish bungalow—it needs some work because the last owners bought it in the eighties and pretty much haven't updated anything since. But it's just under two thousand square feet. Has three bedrooms and two baths."

"Good size and nice yard!" Vivian saw the bathroom pictures. "Ooh. Yeah, it needs some updating."

"It does, but it's functional. Nothing needs to be done until you want it done. Everything works."

"Okay, good to know." Vivian kept watching the pictures as

they scrolled by. "I'd want to get rid of the carpet before I moved in, but I could probably live with the rest for a while."

Julia nodded. "I think it's worth a visit if you're interested. The owners are motivated and would probably do a short escrow if you wanted one. They're moving to be with grandkids back east, and they've already bought a place in Virginia."

"Okay, let's check it out this week then."

Vivian was feeling optimistic about the house situation, possibly because it gave her an excuse to delay decorating a nursery, but mostly because she loved the idea of moving closer to her friends. "My parents are excited."

"Your sister?"

"Eh." Vivian shrugged. "Less so, but she gets it. She's just not thrilled about having to fly out here for holidays. Her husband's family all live in Chicago."

Julia pointed at Vivian's phone. "Oh, did Michael or Rich call you? They have a friend whose son—"

"Is a brand-new dentist and looking for an associate's position." Vivian nodded. "Michael called me, and I told him to have the young man send his résumé over. He sounds promising."

"Michael mentioned that he's been working at a clinic in the Midwest, but he'd really like to get back out to California."

"As long as he knows what he's getting into with the heat." Vivian stood and wrapped up the second half of her sandwich. "I can't eat any more."

"You hardly had a bite."

"I know, but my stomach is about the size of a tennis ball right now with this little boy getting so big." She patted her belly. "Seriously, I take two bites and I'm full. I'll put it in the fridge and eat later. I just have to eat like a bird."

Julia rose and gave Vivian a hug. "As long as you eat."

"Yes, mom."

"Ha ha." Julia shuddered. "No, thank you. Auntie status

only for me." She patted the side of Vivian's belly. "Be good, Henry. No jumping jacks in there."

"He's starting to run out of room." Vivian felt the little boy slowly roll over. "Only about seven more weeks now. How is that possible?"

Julia's eyes went wide. "So weird!"

They walked out of her office and toward the front desk, where Vivian could hear her secretary Tabitha chatting with a male patient. Tabitha had been at the practice for nearly twenty years and seemed to be friends with everyone.

"Oh!" She spoke to someone just out of sight. "See, I told you she'd be right out. I think she has space in her schedule in about fifteen minutes."

"What's going on?" Vivian didn't love rearranging her schedule like that, but for emergencies she'd always be flexible.

"New patient!" Tabitha smiled. "Well, new old patient."

Vivian turned the corner, spotted the "patient," and froze.

"West Barrett." The man introduced himself with a disarming smile. "I grew up coming to Dr. Sutter, and my back molar is killing me. I was hoping you'd be able to take a look at it."

She felt Julia's fear shoot out, but Vivian forced herself to stay calm. "And Tabitha says that I have room in about fifteen minutes?"

"I'm more than happy to wait." The man had grey eyes. Unusual and striking, they reminded Vivian of a shark.

"Of course," she said. "Just give me a few minutes." She walked Julia out to her car, passing through the hallway where the employee entrance and break room were located.

The afternoon heat washed over them in an oven-like wave.

"You can't be alone with that man," Julia said.

"I'm not going to be alone; I have four dental hygienists working for me."

"You know what I mean."

Vivian wasn't thrilled with the idea of West Barrett in her office—that could not be a coincidence—but she also knew it was an opportunity. "I'll question him while I'm checking his teeth."

"If he knows you think he's a suspect, your mom might be in danger."

"I know." Vivian didn't like that West Barrett even knew who she was, though he'd been questioned by the police and knew there was a witness to his father's murder. "I'll be careful, Julia."

She closed her friend's car door, steeled her emotions, and walked back in her office. She forced herself to act normally and was proud of the fact that when she suited up in a mask and face shield, she felt the barrier of her PPE giving her enough distance to examine West Barrett like any other patient.

He lay reclined on the examination seat. While most people were disarmed by the position, West seemed completely at ease. He had a physicality that told Vivian he was confident in his strength. The muscle tone on his arms told her the man didn't stay in his office after hours. He either worked out or played sports intently enough to build muscle.

"So, Mr. Barrett—"

"Please call me West."

"Sure." Vivian looked at the monitor to see the chart her hygienist had started. West Barrett was still a patient, and she had to treat him as such. "Why don't you tell me a little more about the pain in your molar; then I'll take a look. When was the last time you had X-rays done? Do you know?"

"It's been a couple of years."

"So that might be a good thing to take care of today." She noted his age. "As we age, our teeth change. Not just wear, but our salivary glands change too. That can affect things like how our body breaks down food."

"So I may have a cavity?"

"I'll take a look." Vivian rolled her stool over to West and angled herself to the right. "It might feel a little awkward; I'm getting close to my maternity leave."

"Tabitha said your dad is a dentist too. That he's helping out."

Thanks, Tabitha. "He sure is." Vivian leaned over his mouth, and he opened it. "Did you know Dr. Sutton well?"

"My whole life until I went away to college." His speech was garbled, but Vivian was used to that.

She poked around in his mouth, probing with a pick and trying to absorb everything she could from his emotional signature. "Where did you go to school?"

"Ou-side of Boh-ton."

"Oh?" Vivian might have opened his mouth a little wider. It was always fun to make assholes sound ridiculous. "Tufts? I had a good friend who graduated from there."

"Hah-vahd."

"Oooh, right." She withdrew her probe and rolled away. "Well, there isn't anything visibly wrong with the tooth, so I think we definitely need those X-rays."

West was annoyed; whether it was from the dental probe or her casual questioning, she didn't know.

"Did you want to do that today? I think my X-ray tech has time."

He narrowed his eyes a bit. "Your family lives in Desert Oasis, right?"

"We do. I was sorry to hear about your father. How is your family doing?"

"He was a great man. Many people will miss him horribly."

Well, that was a definite nonanswer.

"There was someone who saw my father's death," West said. "Did you know that?"

"Oh, I'm not a police investigator." Vivian turned to the

computer to enter notes about her examination. "I tend to stay out of those kinds of things."

"According to the police, the witness didn't see the killer, just my father." West watched her with his shark eyes and a neutral expression. "Was it you?"

Vivian looked up. "I don't know why you would think that. Did you want to do those X-rays today?"

West stood and unclipped the bib around his neck, carefully placed it on the seat behind him, then stood towering over Vivian.

She remained seated, looking up at West Barrett with a practiced, neutral expression. "I just need to know about the X-rays."

"I think I'll wait and go to my regular dentist for those."

She didn't waver in her gaze. "Let him know you've been having pain. I wouldn't wait too long."

"I'll remember what you said." West turned toward the door. "Thank you, Vivian. Maybe I'll meet your parents soon."

It was intended as a warning, and Vivian took it as one. She felt a cold finger of dread slither down her spine, but she didn't stand up. "I'm just finishing up your chart; you can talk to Tabitha about how to pay." Then she deliberately turned back to the computer and didn't look at him again.

"Empty." Vivian still felt cold, even in the fullness of the desert evening. "He felt like nothing. A void."

She'd spent half an hour after West left, trying to calm Julia down over the phone, but she still wasn't feeling calm herself. West Barrett's visit had rattled her.

Maud sat across from her at the small patio table in Vivian's back garden. "I've heard that psychopaths and narcissists can read that way, along with various different psychological conditions like detachment disorders, but I'm not a psychologist or an empath. I don't know what you feel when you read a person, but if you suspect he was involved in his own father's death, psychopathy or narcissism would make sense."

It felt strange to talk to Maud—every medical instinct in her rebelled at the idea of revealing anything about a patient—but Maud was the closest thing she had to a psychologist these days. It felt safe to talk to her, and Vivian knew she needed to talk to someone or she'd drive herself into an anxious fit.

"Also, and this is strictly confidential, his teeth were perfect. Like, ridiculously perfect. I think the man actually flosses regularly. Do you know how rare that is?"

Maud raised an eyebrow. "I know I don't do it. Don't tell my dentist."

"If he was actually having molar pain, I'll bite my left toe."

"And you can't even bend that way anymore," Maud said. "So I believe you."

Vivian smiled a little, glad that the older woman felt comfortable joking even while Vivian was in a mild panic. She'd called Maud as soon as she got home. Not only was she rattled by the visit, she was concerned there was something wrong with her empathy when she couldn't read any emotional signature off of West.

"I think what you ladies are trying to do..." Maud shook her head. "Don't get me wrong; I understand it. God knows I've been tempted to get involved in a few police investigations in my time."

"But you didn't?"

"It was a different time and place," Maud said. "I don't think my help would have been welcomed like Chief Marcos has welcomed you."

"Do you think I need to move my parents? Get them to go back to Chicago for a while?"

"I can't tell you that," Maud said. "Maybe talk to John and

see what he says." She glanced at Vivian's belly. "How are you feeling with the little man?"

"I'm starting to get hints from him." Vivian smiled a little. "Just like... little hints. He loves my dad's voice."

"It's deep," Maud said. "And familiar. How does he react to Richard?"

"At first it was nothing, but now it almost feels like when he hears Rich's voice, he's waiting."

"Interesting."

"I'm kind of waiting too." Vivian smiled. "I enjoy spending time with him, but—"

"The empathy isn't a secret, is it?"

"No, he knows. I don't think he quite realized what it meant, but he does know."

"Have you talked about it?"

"Not directly." Vivian bit her lip. "We're still being very... *polite* with each other."

"He's trying to be respectful."

"I think so." Vivian nodded. "I hope that's what it is."

"Are you thinking it may be something else?"

How could Maud ask her questions about this when she avoided them from everyone else? "Maud?"

"Hmm?"

"Are you using some kind of influence on me?"

"Sweetie, I'm a touch-telepath. Psychometry isn't going to give me much to go on when I haven't even shaken your hand skin to skin." Maud usually wore long gloves unless she was meditating. "You feel like you can be honest with me because I'm the closest you girls have to a shrink or a doctor with all the new stuff."

Yeah, that was probably it.

"I'm frustrated that he's being so polite," Vivian said. "I don't know if that means he's not physically attracted to me or whether he's not very physical at all. I hope it's not either of those things."

"Do you consider yourself a physically affectionate person?"

"Yes."

"Have you been as physical with Richard as you normally would be with a man you're attracted to?"

"No, because normally I am not seven months pregnant at the start of a relationship."

"So." Maud spread her hands as if she'd made a discovery.

Vivian was still confused. "So what?"

"So Richard is likely taking his cues from you. You don't feel comfortable in your own body right now. You're disconnected from it. Distant. He's reading your energy and keeping his distance. I suspect he doesn't want you to feel encroached on. He's respecting the boundaries you've set."

"But I didn't set any boundaries."

"Not verbally, no. But he's reading your body language and mirroring it." Maud nodded. "That's actually quite impressive for a man. He was married to his wife for how many years?"

"Like thirty-something. But she was very... out there. Very dramatic, I think."

"And an actress, so he probably became quite intuitive in order to discern the truth." Maud nodded. "You're going to need to be direct with him. He's not going to take any liberties with you, Vivian. Not unless you tell him to."

VIVIAN MANAGED TO STEER HER WAY THROUGH THE winding streets of Vista de Lirio, deliberating passing by the little bungalow she'd be visiting the next day. It was cute, but the trees hid the facade from the street.

She pulled up to the gate of Casa de Lirio and buzzed the intercom. "Richard, it's Vivian."

A crackling voice came back. "Gate's opening."

Richard was waiting on the front walk when she parked her father's car. He ran over to the driver's door to help her to her feet.

"Hi. Is everything all right? Did we make a date and I forgot about it?" He was frowning. "If I did, I am so sorry. Work was hectic and—"

"Shhhh." She put a finger over his lips. "I want you to kiss me."

Richard froze.

"We've been on four dates now, and you've been very respectful, but it's starting to drive me crazy and I need to know—"

He kissed her.

And oh, it was *good*. Richard pressed his full lips to Vivian's, gently at first, then slowly building as he slid his hand to the small of her back. Her belly was pressed between them, but that didn't stop Vivian from placing her hands on Richard's chest to feel the firm muscle beneath his pressed button-down shirt.

He made a low sound in his throat and teased the seam of her mouth with his tongue to demand entrance. His fingers flexed at her side, and she could feel the emotions rebound between them. His desire fed hers, his pleasure stoked the low-burning fire that she'd managed to suppress for months.

God, she wanted sex.

But.

Richard broke off, letting Vivian catch her breath. "Do you want to come inside?"

"Yes," she said. "But also no. But also yes."

Richard smiled and his head fell forward. "It's not a simple thing, is it?"

"You have no idea."

Did she want the first time she had sex with Richard to be when she was very pregnant? No! But did she also want to wait for months until her body had recovered from giving birth?

Also very much no.

"How about you come inside." Richard took her hand in his. "And we can... talk?"

Vivian nodded slowly. "And by talk, you mean kiss some more and maybe some fooling around?"

"Well, I..." He cleared his throat. "Yes, I am fully on board with that definition of talking."

Chapter Fifteen

"You look so happy today." Joan patted Vivian's hand. "You must be sleeping well."

"I am." Vivian had planned lunch with her mother that afternoon, not knowing that she was going to have to fight glowing cheeks from Richard-induced relaxation.

Their talk had been very... illuminating. And she'd been happy to find out Richard was highly dexterous. The hands that wielded a financial sword were also skilled in other areas.

Very excellent areas.

Vivian felt like she was glowing from the inside. "Thanks, Mom. I feel good." No, she felt *great*, but she didn't want to tell her mother why. "How about you?" She reached over and squeezed her mother's hand. "You said this diagnosis was what you were expecting, but now it's confirmed."

"You know? I'm okay. Like you said, it was what I expected, so I feel mentally prepared. And relieved to know what's going on."

The blood work and MRI her new doctor had ordered did indicate that Joan had probably experienced a ministroke sometime in the past month. There was slight damage to her temporal lobe that could have easily affected her memory, and while the damage wasn't necessarily permanent, it was a concern because any stroke could be the prelude to a major event.

"What did Dr. Patil recommend? Does she want to do more tests?"

"Not right now. I'm starting the new blood pressure medication this week, and weekly cocktails at mahjong are going to be a thing of the past. She mainly wanted me to be more intentional about exercise. Walking is good, but I need to step it up."

"Have you thought about swimming? The club's pool is beautiful, and they have lap-swimming hours."

"I'll probably do that. It's too hot out here to do anything else." Joan laughed a little. "Though if I could get invitations to fancy country clubs like Monte Verde like your father, I might take up golf."

Vivian blinked. "Excuse me?"

"Didn't your friend Richard tell you?" Joan started on her salad. "Such a nice man. We ran into him at Jensen's yesterday. Your dad was getting me my favorite cake and your friend walked over. He said he recognized your dad from the practice."

"Oh." Vivian's brain scrambled. "Yes, he's been by the office before." And he knew her mother's favorite cake. "So... what did you say about Monte Verde?"

"He and your father started talking golf, golf, golf." Joan waved a hand. "You know how your he gets. Anyway, Richard mentioned he was looking for a fourth for a round this morning, so that's where your father is today."

"And this was last night that you ran into him at the market?"

"Yes, when you were meeting your hippy friend, remember? We asked you if you wanted anything from Jensen's." Joan took a bite of her chicken salad. "Such a nice man. You've made the loveliest group of friends here in town.

"Uh-huh." So Richard had known he was taking her father

for a round of golf when his hands were doing all sorts of relaxing things to her the night before. "He didn't mention that he'd met you."

"Well, it's not really that big a town, is it?"

"Nope." Vivian sipped her iced tea and wished that weekly cocktails weren't out of bounds for her too. "I told you I was going to go to Dean and Sergio's for dinner tonight, right?" In fact, she'd been thinking she'd take her mother and father to dinner tonight so they could meet Richard.

Not that that was necessary now.

Apparently.

Joan patted her hand. "Are you all right? You look flushed."

Vivian forced a smile. "Just a little warm." She glanced out the window. "I'm ready for it to cool down."

EVY CALLED AT NOON AND TOLD VIVIAN SHE'D PICK her up from work so they could head to Dean and Sergio's together and Vivian could avoid driving. A little after five, Evy pulled up in her vintage 1982 Cadillac Eldorado convertible wearing a sleeveless black pantsuit and giant round sunglasses.

"Hey, sexy. Need a ride?"

Vivian could only sigh in appreciation as she lowered herself into the low-slung, voluminous seats of the classic Cadillac. "I know it's a gas-guzzler, but I love your car."

"I love my car too. It's kick-ass." She pointed to the back. "I'm going to have to get the vinyl repaired before winter though. I just discovered a tear."

"Is it hard to find parts for it?"

"Nah, my cousin knows a guy." Evy had grown up in the valley, and her entire extended family used to live there too. She was half-Mexican and half-Romanian or something like that, and Vivian always sensed a highly chaotic energy, which was both warm and a little nervous, every time she mentioned her family. "He'll find it for me; I just have to take it in."

"How's work been?"

"I got a big booking!" Evy grinned. "Like, kind of a major one after the school fundraiser. I think I may get quite a few gigs off that night. I'm pleased as hell I volunteered to do that."

"You volunteered? The rich people couldn't pay you?"

Evy shrugged. "It was for charity kind of. Sergio asked me. I guess the other option was someone from the sheriff's department, and how depressing is that? Anyway, I've already booked two wedding MC gigs and another paying benefit, so it was worth it. But the big one that I just got called for is the Desert Fancy Dog Show next spring."

Vivian bit her lip to keep from laughing.

"I see the face, Wei! Cut it. This job pays enough that I could skip cleaning pools for a month if I wanted to."

"Are you going to stop cleaning pools?"

"Fuck no," Evy said. "That's easy money, and it keeps my arms toned. But the dog-show crowd is picky as hell and they pay well. I'm gonna MC the shit out of those shih tzus and Pomeranians."

"And I'm going to attend a dog show solely in the hopes that you'll sneak in dirty jokes and disguise them as dog puns."

"Awwww." Evy put a hand over her heart. "You do know me."

"Okay, you've gotten me out of my funk by talking about the dog show, thank you, but now I have to get mad again because Richard is going to be at dinner tonight."

"Why are you mad at Rich? Did something happen?"

"Yes. We fooled around last night, and then I found out at lunch today that he and my dad were golfing this morning. I guess Richard just 'ran into' them at the market and invited my dad for golf."

"Back up to the 'we fooled around last night' part; you are burying the lede here."

"I'm not burying the lede; I'm trying to say that we were fooling around and the whole time, he knew he invited my dad for golf and he didn't tell me."

"Maybe because when you have your hands between a sexy woman's legs—I'm assuming, don't correct me if I'm wrong—that it's not the most opportune time to mention her father."

Okay, that was a decent point. "He could have brought it up later."

"If he knew it was going to make you mad, I totally get why he didn't mention it though. That's a very me move." Evy looked at Vivian. "I would do something like that. I'm highly motivated to avoid conflict. Blame my brothers."

"He can't just avoid telling me he's met my parents though! I was going to bring them here tonight to meet him. I'm not... avoiding them meeting him, I just don't want them to get the wrong idea."

They were pulling into Sergio and Dean's driveway, so Vivian tried to calm down.

"I get why you're pissed," Evy said, "but like, if he'd run into them and pretended to not know who they were, wouldn't that be worse?"

"I don't know. It's not like I think he was stalking them at Jensen's, but couldn't he have just... not said anything?"

"I think he was just being friendly."

"So I'm overreacting?" It was entirely possible. Vivian hardly trusted her own brain these days. It was part of the reason she'd been taking things slowly with Richard.

"I think you should get on him a little about not telling you that he was meeting your dad for golf today when you were actually at his house last night and he had every opportunity to tell you. It definitely caught you off guard hearing it from your mom and not him. I mean, you can make him suffer a little. Just don't go overboard."

Vivian nodded firmly. "Thank you."

They parked beside Julia's white Mercedes and got out, only to be assaulted by the shrill sound of an alpaca squealing in the distance.

"Oh good God!" Evy put her hands over her ears. "Is that Paco?"

"Fisher, you leave that animal alone!" Julia yelled from the patio. "I'll call a priest on you. I am not joking."

Evy and Vivian walked over to the large, flower-bordered patio between the main house and the pool house. Julia was already there, along with Sergio and Dean's neighbor Genevieve, her tall, silent French companion, and Dean, who was serving cocktails.

Evy skipped over to Dean. "Who's my favorite bartender in the world?"

"What would you like to drink?" Dean bopped her on the head with a striped straw. "Ask and I will decide if I want to bless you or not."

"Paloma please? I know you have fresh grapefruit juice."

"You shall be blessed." Dean waved at Vivian. "Hello, gorgeous. What can I get you to drink?"

Vivian lowered herself into a chair next to Genevieve. "Maybe just a ginger ale with ice?"

"You got it. Sergio and Jim will have dinner ready in about a half an hour. Richard isn't here yet."

Vivian tried not to grumble. She was surprised when Genevieve poked her with her cigarette holder. Vivian forced a smile and turned to the tiny, turbaned woman. "Hello, Miss Genevieve. How are you today?"

"How are *you*? That is the question." She pointed at Vivian's belly. "Very smart of you to wait to have children. I firmly believe that a woman should not reproduce until she's in her prime. I had all three of my children after forty, and they're far more intelligent than their cousins."

Vivian blinked. "I didn't know you had children."

"Three. Marcel, Philipe, and Yvonne, who is named after my mother. The boys are from my third husband Luc, but I wanted a girl, so I waited until I was married to Farzaad to have Yvonne. He'd already fathered three girls, so I thought he was a good bet. All three of them live in Europe, but they visit."

"Right."

"Amastan is a good friend of Marcel's. He's here for an upcoming concert in Los Angeles, but he prefers the weather here in Palm Springs, so he's staying with me for the month."

"Who?"

Genevieve motioned to the tall man on her left. "Amastan, of course."

"Oh right." Vivian smiled. "It's very nice to meet you."

The tall man smiled sweetly and nodded at her but remained silent.

Vivian's brain was swirling, but that tended to be her reaction anytime she had a conversation with Genevieve de Winter. She wanted to ask Genevieve how old she was but knew that it would not go over well.

There was another squeal from the alpaca in the background.

Vivian looked over her shoulder. "Is Paco okay?"

"Fisher's ghost seems to be tormenting him." Genevieve waved a careless hand. "I told Julia to threaten an exorcism, but I forgot the man was a Protestant." She muttered something under her breath. "We may be stuck with him unless you can prove he wasn't murdered."

"Well, that's certainly... motivating." If there was one thing Vivian could always say about dinner at Dean and Sergio's, it was never boring. "So Julia is looking for a house for me and Henry in the neighborhood."

"Henry is the baby's name? I approve." She bit down on the cigarette holder, then released it. "And that's excellent, darling. Only Protestants and people from Washington live in those new towns along the highway."

Vivian was pretty sure that wasn't correct since her parents lived there, but she decided to let it be. Amastan watched her with amused eyes, having read her expression, and slowly shook his head.

Not worth it.

Vivian nodded.

"Oh look." Genevieve turned her head. "How lovely. Richard and his daughter are here."

Richard and Maddy had walked from their house a few blocks away; Richard had an insulated bag of some kind over his shoulder, and Maddy was carrying a bunch of flowers. They looked like the quintessential Palm Springs family dressed in loose linen, designer sunglasses, and perfect tans.

And Vivian felt small, bloated, and grumpy.

She forced herself to remember Evy's advice: make him suffer a little bit; don't go overboard.

"Hi." She looked up at the startlingly handsome man who'd made her feel like a goddess the night before. "I heard you had a round of golf this morning."

"Did you?" He looked slightly embarrassed, but not even a little bit sorry. "It was a spur-of-the-moment thing. Your dad is a great golf partner, by the way."

"I've heard that." Vivian decided to poke a little more. "Did you forget about that when I was at your house last night?"

Now he looked a little embarrassed.

Maddy looked at her dad with a smirk. "You're on your own." She wandered over to the bar with Dean and Evy.

"Well, you see..." Richard sat next to Vivian and opened the cooler bag, which contained one bottle of white wine and another bottle that looked like champagne. He held it out to Vivian. "Sparkling cider?"

She could admit it, she was charmed. But she didn't let up. "Did you forget?"

"About the golf thing with your dad?" He raised an eyebrow and lowered his voice. "To be fair, you caught me by surprise last night. I was not thinking about golf."

Okay, that was fair. "Even a text this morning would have been nice."

Richard reached for a wineglass at the center of the table. "Are we doing good-morning texts now? Excellent."

Give him an inch... "Richard."

"Vivian." He handed her a glass of something sparkling, pink, and cold. "Have a drink."

"You really just ran into my parents at Jensen's?"

"I really did. I saw an older Asian couple picking out the exact cake you did that day you wanted to make your mom feel better and they sounded like they were from the Midwest, so I asked if they knew you and the rest was just friendly coincidence. Your dad is an excellent golfer. The guys invited him back next week."

"If he had a good time, I'm happy, but in the future, a heads-up would be appreciated. Did you tell him...?"

"I told him we were friends." Richard poured a glass of white wine and handed it to Genevieve. He looked at Amastan, who shook his head.

"Which is true," he continued. "Though judging from the way you're taking the whole golf-coincidence thing with your dad, you're really going to be mad when you find out what I did this afternoon."

Vivian swallowed the fizzy pink drink and narrowed her eyes. "What did you do?"

Chapter Sixteen

"You bought me a car?" Vivian spun around in Richard's garage to see him, Maddy, Evy, Sergio, and Julia all staring at the luxury SUV with wide eyes and smiles. "Richard, you bought me a car. A whole car. This is not—"

"No." He raised a hand and stepped forward. "I bought *myself* a car, a midsize hybrid SUV with excellent safety ratings and many features that are popular with families who have small children."

Vivian was trying to remain calm. "So this is for you?"

Richard shrugged. "I mean, if you decide that you want to trade your Tesla for a while—or forever—then we can do that." He smiled innocently. "I didn't buy you a car. That would be overstepping."

Maddy raised a hand. "I did warn you about the fixer thing."

Vivian's brain was swirling again. Part of her was massively relieved—she'd been dreading the car-buying process—and part of her knew this was not a fair trade. "This is too nice for my Tesla."

"I think you're undervaluing the appeal of electric vehicles,

Vivian. I don't have one in my garage yet; it's far past time. Think of the gas I'll save when I have to drive to LA."

Vivian looked around the six-car garage at Casa de Lirio, taking in an off-road vehicle, a sleek sports car, a Land Rover, a vintage Jaguar, and a sturdy golf cart. "I guess you don't."

Julia stepped forward. "I think this is a great idea. Richard did all the research for you, so if you don't like it—"

"I can take it back," he said. "The dealership told me it wasn't an issue to try it out for a few days."

"Dealerships don't do that," Vivian said.

Richard shrugged. "I'm a good customer."

She walked to the low-slung SUV, which reminded her of a much fancier version of her parents' old station wagon. She tried to imagine all the things she'd need to pack for a simple trip to the market once Henry was here. Stroller. Diaper bag. Changing table? No, that was ridiculous, that lived at the house.

"This is too much." She ran a hand along the cool green surface of the car. "It's a nice color."

"They had other ones. *If* you wanted to trade."

She looked over her shoulder. "Did my dad say something about the car this morning?"

"He does not mind trading cars with you, but he worried that you were getting uncomfortable driving." Richard rushed to the driver's door and opened it. "This car has adjustable pedals so you can scoot the seat farther back and still reach the gas and brake."

Vivian pursed her lips. "And you thought that would be really useful for you?"

"I think it would be useful for anyone." He smiled. "Trade cars with me. If you like it, keep it for a while or forever. It's one less thing for you to do."

"You know I hate buying cars." She felt herself tearing up and sniffed.

"Are those happy tears or I'm-angry-and-frustrated tears?"

Vivian heard everyone else behind them scurry away, leaving her and Richard alone.

He bent down and wiped a tear away with his thumb. "I was trying to do something to make life simpler for you. I promise, that's all. If you were just a friend, I'd do the same thing. But I do want more than friendship, so I guess I have an ulterior motive."

She turned her face up, stood on her toes, and kissed him. "This is a really great car. I was looking at this model online."

"Your dad maybe clued me in on that one."

She laughed and wiped her tears away. "He would approve of this. I told Maddy the other day, he's a fixer too."

"I'm trying not to be terrified that you and my daughter are conspiring behind my back."

"*Conspiring* is a strong word."

THEY RETURNED TO SERGIO AND DEAN'S HOUSE TO find a taco buffet waiting for them and two irritated fourteen-year-olds who appeared to be drinking Vivian's sparkling cider in champagne flutes.

Aurelia cocked her head and looked at Vivian. "We missed the grand romantic gesture."

Vivian looked at Richard, then back at the twins. "What? It wasn't a grand... I mean, it was a helpful gesture."

Richard cleared his throat. "Girls, we're adults, so it's not really as dramatic as—"

"Tears," Juliana whispered. "She was crying."

"It worked," Aurelia said. "They're a couple now."

"We approve," Juliana said. "We think he's deserving of Vivian's attention, and his teeth aren't perfect, which will secretly irk Vivian, though she will never say anything."

"The underlying tension should be interesting."

Richard frowned. "My teeth are fine."

Juliana and Aurelia looked at Vivian.

"What?" She crossed her arms. "Teeth don't have to be perfect to be healthy."

Richard looked at her. "You think there's something wrong with my teeth?"

"No." Vivian looked back at the two troublemakers. "No, I don't. Thank you."

"On a much more interesting topic than romance," Aurelia said. "We believe there will be another murder soon."

Richard pulled out a chair for Vivian, which was good because her stomach had just fallen to her feet. "Why do you think a murder is going to happen soon?"

Her parents. West Barrett knew one of them had been the witness.

Richard backed away. "I'm going to leave you with the terrible twosome and get us some tacos."

"Sounds good. Surprise me." Vivian didn't take her eyes off the girls. "Why is there going to be another murder soon?"

Juliana held up a wall calendar. "We've tracked it; there is a Booster Club meeting next Wednesday, which means there will be another death within ten days postmeeting."

"Ten days?" Vivian waved Evy over. "West Barrett came to my practice two days ago. I think he knows one of my parents is the witness to his father's murder."

Evy sat down with a plate of tacos and some rice and beans. "Why am I just now hearing about this?"

"Julia was there when he arrived, then I told Maud, then Maud got me thinking about my relationship with Richard, then I found out Richard and my dad met for golf, then Richard bought me a car, and I still haven't talked to John about creepy West Barrett visiting my office."

Vivian was exhausted just recounting the events of the past week.

Evy was frozen. "That's a lot of things."

"Yeah, it's been a busy week." Vivian felt like crying again. She was a bad daughter. West was going to try to murder her parents and she was very pregnant and how was she supposed to defend them? "I don't think I could get them to go back to Chicago at this point."

"Chill." Evy put a hand on Vivian's arm. "Let me call John. I'll tell him that West threatened your parents—"

"He didn't technically threaten them."

"Details." Evy waved a hand. "Fine. No police. I know a guy who's a private investigator and used to be a Marine. I'll call Andre and give him your address. He owes me a couple of months' pool service, so I'll tell him this will square it. He'll keep an eye on your folks."

"Okay, but tell me what his rate is, and I'll pay you back."

"Sure, that'll happen." Evy nodded at the girls. "What's up, ladies?"

"The Booster Club meets next week," Aurelia said.

Juliana added, "They will murder someone within ten days."

Evy blinked. "The fuck?"

Vivian felt like objecting to the language in front of the girls, but she was pretty sure they'd heard worse from Paco. "I know. I feel like that's kind of a leap. What makes you think—?"

"We tracked the last two deaths," Aurelia said. "We're giving Mr. Fisher's ghost the benefit of the doubt even though he's tormenting Paco. The first murder—"

"Heart attack." Vivian exchanged a look with Evy. "I looked at the file and I have to agree with the coroner—it was a heart attack."

"A heart attack that happened seven days after the first Booster Club meeting in July." Aurelia stared at Vivian. "Coincidence?"

"Yes." Vivian nodded. "That is a coincidence."

Evy frowned. "Why ten days?"

"The second murder happened four days after the August Booster Club meeting," Juliana said. "If we account for a three-day variance in the first two murders, then it's logical there could be a three-day variance on the other side, leaving us with a ten-day window after the Booster Club meets. It's science."

"I don't think..." Vivian shook her head. "That's not *science*."

Evy bit her thumbnail, still frowning. "Let me get this straight, you think the Booster Club is planning these murders—"

"There is only one murder," Vivian said. "Fisher Gates died of a heart attack."

"Not according to his ghost." Julia joined them, dropping into her chair with a sigh. "Is it winter yet? I want it to be winter. I'm done with this heat."

"The misters definitely help," Vivian said, "but agreed."

Juliana said, "Auntie, we believe the ghost. Mr. Gates was also a victim of the Booster Club."

"How?" Vivian asked. "And why?"

Juliana slowly shook her head. "Have you never watched Hitchcock?"

Vivian looked at Julia. "What does that mean?"

"Listen." Aurelia leaned forward. "Five chairpersons of the Desert Prep Booster Club, and two of them have lost parents to sudden death in the past two months. We don't believe it's a sad coincidence, though of course that's what they want the world to think."

Juliana tapped her chin. "With the death of Archibald Barrett exposed as a murder, they may take a pause to distract, but we do believe they will continue."

"All the deaths were probably supposed to look accidental," Aurelia said. "We think whoever killed Mr. Barrett made a mistake."

Richard returned with two plates of tacos and set one in front of Vivian. "So girls, how's school these days?"

"Murderous," Juliana said.

"So about the same as when I went there," Richard said. "Not a huge surprise."

"Your daughter should have been a librarian," Aurelia said. "She's wasted in the classroom."

Richard nodded. "I'll be sure to let her know."

"RICHARD BOUGHT YOU A CAR," EVY SAID. "I NEED A boyfriend like that."

"One, he's not my boyfriend." Vivian walked into Evy's house the next night and set her purse on the hallway table. "And two, he bought a car to *trade* with me—if I want to—he didn't buy me a car."

"He totally bought you a car," Evy muttered. "He gave you an orgasm and a car. I think that definitely makes him your boyfriend." She sorted through what looked like photos as Vivian settled. "Oh, did you meet Andre yet?"

"Your private investigator friend?"

"Well, he's kind of being a bodyguard at the moment, but he said he'd checked out your security system and for a home system, it's decent. Just make sure you're using it."

Vivian lowered herself to Evy's couch. "Easier said than done with my parents."

"He's keeping an eye on things. I told him it was West Barrett who threatened them and he smiled, so I think he's familiar with the guy."

"Oh, Vivian, you're here!" Julia walked in from the hallway leading to the kitchen and sat facing the murder board. "How is Richard's new car? The one that you're borrowing for an unspecified period of time."

This again?

"It fits my belly, so it's my favorite thing in the world right now." Vivian stared at all the new faces Evy was posting. "Who are all these new people? Do we know them?"

"We don't." Evy stood and strung yarn between each member of the Booster Club and the new pictures. "Okay, these are the members of the Booster Club that we know, West and Trent."

Julia said, "I know her too; that's Ashley Gates, Fisher's daughter. His ghost followed me here." She turned her face to the corner. "But I'm gonna kick you out if you're not quiet, Fisher. Just..." She raised a hand. "Quiet." Julia turned back to the board. "Okay, so we have West, Trent, and Ashley. Who are the other people?"

Vivian muttered, "Why are murder conspiracies so complicated?"

"Isn't that a good thing though?" Julia asked. "I feel like if they were easy, there would be so many more dead people."

"I'd like to think you're wrong, but you're probably not. There was a third grader this morning that bit my finger." She held up her right forefinger. "Just *bit* it. Full-on, and it was intentional. She laughed afterward like a tiny sociopath."

"Are you saying you felt like murdering a third grader?"

"Yes. For a few minutes? I definitely did."

"Getting back to the murder board!" Evy tapped two pictures along the bottom. "This is Pippa Stanford and Trace Mitchell. Pippa is divorced, and Trace is going through a divorce. There are rumors about them, but nothing public."

"Okay." Vivian stared at the line of thirtysomethings that looked like they'd stepped out of a J.Crew catalog. "And the people below them? Their parents?"

"Yes." Evy pointed to Archie Barrett's picture below West and Fisher Gate's picture below Ashley Gates. "These parents are already dead, so these parents" —Evy pointed to six other pictures below Trent's, Pippa's, and Trace's pictures— "are the next likely victims."

It finally clicked in Vivian's mind. "Okay, so do we think that Trent killed Archie Barrett while West alibied himself at the club, and someone else killed Fisher while Ashley had an alibi?"

"Yes," Evy said. "That's what the girls meant by Hitchcock."

"Of course," Julia said. "*Strangers on a Train.*"

Vivian turned to her. "Fill me in. I have clearly not watched Hitchcock."

"The premise is that two strangers meet on a train and get to talking," Julia said. "They realize they both have someone they hate that they want dead, and the one guy says, 'Hey, so what do you think about exchanging murders? I'll kill your wife if you kill my dad. Since we don't know each other or our victims, the police will never figure it out.' The second guy doesn't think he's serious, so he kind of just nods and walks away, but then the next week or something, his wife is murdered."

"That's horrible and creepy."

"That's Hitchcock." Julia shrugged. "He's my nieces' favorite."

"One problem with this theory," Vivian said. "The Booster Club people *do* know each other."

Evy said, "But if the plan was to make all the deaths look like accidents like Fisher Gates, then you've got another level of deniability."

"It was supposed to be just a horrible coincidence," Julia said. "Whoever killed Archie messed up."

"There was a witness and a body to account for," Vivian said. "But they managed to hide it."

"It had to be West and Trent, right?" Evy looked between them. "I mean, that body was hidden *fast*, and they were at the club that night."

"It couldn't have been West—he was alibied, remember?"

"But I think Trent definitely had help," Evy said. "He had to roll the body up in a tarp with some sand, tie some bungie cords around it, and toss it in the lake."

"That's a hundred-and-fifty-pound man at least—he wasn't a huge guy—and another hundred pounds of sand?" Vivian shook her head. "I don't think Pippa or Ashley would be strong enough."

"Trace Mitchell." Evy pointed at the thick-necked blond man. "I bet you anything, he was Trent's helper."

Chapter Seventeen

Vivian took a deep breath in and released it as Maud walked slowly around the lawn, adjusting people's posture while they breathed.

"And release," the older woman said. "Expel alllll the breath from your lungs. Imagine your tailbone rooted to the earth, and feel the energy rising from the earth below you, up through your spine, and flowing to the very top of your head as you focus on opening your third eye."

It was a week after their last meeting at the murder board; Vivian was back at Morning Club, slightly less stressed but with an even bigger belly, trying not to think about which of her parents the Desert Prep Booster Club had decided to off the night before and focusing on opening her consciousness to *see* her power within.

She was not seeing her power.

Unlike Julia and Evy, who seemed to be progressing in their psychic prowess, Vivian felt like she was in a holding pattern. Her empathy seemed to wax and wane, and so far, the few times she'd tried pushing her own emotions onto others—a technique that Maud said could be very useful—she'd come up with a great big nothing.

If she could learn how to do it though, she could defuse any situation. If she'd been able to do that last winter, a gunman would never have held her and her friends hostage. She'd be able to resolve disputes, even calm patients who were phobic about the dentist. No more bitten fingers!

"If you try too hard" —Maud bent down to speak to her quietly— "you're going to block yourself. It's a flow, Vivian."

"I'm not feeling any flow," she admitted. "I feel *completely* blocked."

Maud settled cross-legged next to her on the lawn. "I suspect that your body and your mind are very focused on your son right now. It may not be reasonable to expect progress in this moment." Maud took off her right glove and settled a hand on Vivian's side, which would normally annoy Vivian, but the woman was so grandmotherly that it felt natural.

Vivian said, "I'm starting to get more and more emotions from him all the time."

"I suspect that you'll be sensing frustration and confusion in these last two months." Maud rubbed Vivian's side as the baby started a slow stretch and roll. "He's approaching a transition, and though he's not aware of it consciously, those deep human instincts are telling him that something is changing. His mind is very active right now."

"Okay." Vivian let out a breath. "So cut myself some slack right now?"

Maud smiled, and the corners of her eyes cheerfully crinkled. "In general, you need to cut yourself some slack. As an empath, the burden of carrying the emotions of those around you will always be a balancing act."

"Oh, I don't think I *carry* anyone."

Maud cocked her head. "Can you tell me who the peacemaker is in your family?"

Vivian pressed her lips together. "Um... me. My sister tends to be much more take-charge, and she and my mom are a lot alike, so they butt heads."

"And you're the calm water that puts out the fire."

Vivian nodded. "My dad sometimes, but mostly me."

"I suspect you've been carrying emotions your whole life on a subconscious level. Now it's more obvious and deliberate because of the supernatural empathy that was triggered when Marie called to the universe."

Is that what she did? Vivian had thought it was a drugged-up accident. "So have you ever heard of someone having psychic power and then getting rid of it?"

"I've heard of people who struggled and tried to deny it," Maud said, "but I've never heard of a person who was psychic suddenly not being psychic anymore."

Great.

Vivian took a deep breath and let it out slowly. "Okay, so this is the rest of my life."

"Probably yes." Maud smiled again. "You and Richard have progressed in your relationship."

"Did Julia or Evy tell you?"

"No, he's on your skin." Maud's hand rested on Vivian's belly. "He's good for you."

"He's..." She thought about Richard buying that car. "He's kind of pushy."

"My sense of this man is that he's a caretaker, which could be very healthy for someone like you, who is a peacemaker."

"I hadn't thought of it like that."

"I think he could be a balance to your psychic energy. You are a planner; you see the wider world and anticipate problems in order to avoid them."

"I wish I avoided them more."

"But that's impossible." Maud rocked back and forth, her hand resting on Vivian's side. "This man is more focused on practicality. He likes to deal with what is, not what will be. It's a good balance for you."

"He bought a car and told me he wanted to trade with mine."

"Did you need a new car?"

"I did. The one I had won't fit a car seat in back, and I really couldn't drive it anymore because my pregnancy is so far along."

"And this car he bought, is it the kind you were thinking about?"

"Yes. I mentioned that I hate buying cars—I find it really stressful—so he bought it and then offered to trade for my old car if I liked it."

"He saw a problem in front of him, he fixed it, but he still left you the choice to trade cars with him or not." Maud nodded. "He's very perceptive. He knew that simply buying you a car would be something your independent nature would reject, but your practical side would appreciate having the option and being free of the task. He respects you very much."

"Huh." Vivian blinked. "I hadn't thought about it like that."

"I suspect he likes the dealing and negotiation that comes with buying a vehicle. He enjoys it and knows you do not. So buying it wasn't presumptuous; it was kind."

"Thank you. That makes me feel better about accepting the trade. I was going to take it anyway, just because I really don't have time to go looking for another car right now, but I was feeling a little strange about it."

"Don't feel strange. I suspect that as much as this man likes you, this is something he would do for any friend or family member he cared about."

"I think you're right." And that just made Vivian like him even more.

VIVIAN SAT ACROSS FROM THE YOUNG MAN SHE WAS interviewing. "University of Michigan is very impressive, Dr. Rasul."

"Thank you, but please call me Hasaan." The young man grinned with the eager enthusiasm of a new recruit. "I'm really excited to be back in California."

"Not going to miss the snow?"

"Not even a little bit."

Vivian smiled. "You grew up here, Michael said. Your dad is a film editor?"

"Yes, he's worked with Michael—Mr. O'Connor—for most of my life."

"And Julia said your mom is like a casting agent or something?" Vivian rested her chin in her hand as she paged through Hasaan's résumé. "I have to ask, what on earth made you want to be a dentist?"

The young man laughed. "A lot of people wonder that, but growing up with parents in the film industry, it can be really hit or miss. I guess it's just my personality, but I always wanted something steadier. I was actually thinking about becoming a medical doctor, but then one of my professors in college was a dentist and I kinda got into it. I love all the new technology."

"The gadgets *are* fun," Vivian said. "Definitely agree on that one."

"And honestly? I love making people feel great about their smile." Hasaan smiled broadly, showing a pair of charming dimples. "I think it's a really cool branch of medicine."

"That makes sense." Vivian read a little more. "I come from a family of doctors, so anything in the movies sounds glamorous to me."

Hasaan's eyebrows went up. "Are there any actors or actresses who are patients here?"

"There are." She looked up. "But remember, when they

come here, they're just ordinary patients and their privacy is superimportant."

"Oh, I get it." He reassured her. "Totally. I guess one thing that I would say would recommend me for your practice is that I'm not wowed by that or anything. I've been around Hollywood people my whole life."

"Oh, I see." Vivian nodded. "Yeah, that's a good point." She tapped the paper. "Not something you can really list on the résumé, so I'm glad you pointed that out."

"Awesome."

"And I see you've passed all your boards and exams..." Vivian looked up. "Are you interviewing anywhere else?"

"I am, but I would say this is my first choice because the other ones are in LA, and if I could move out here and avoid the traffic, that would be great. I don't mind the heat."

"Coming from Detroit, that doesn't surprise me. I moved out here from Chicago a couple of years ago."

"Great city."

"But avoiding the traffic is also a benefit." Vivian stood and stretched out her hand to shake his. "Let me call a few people, check your references, but I feel very good about your résumé, and of course, it was great to meet you." She motioned to her belly. "I have to hire someone pretty quickly, so you'll know fast whether you got the job or not."

"Great." Hasaan shook her hand heartily. "And you said your dad is working here too?"

"Yep." Vivian walked him to the door. "Honestly, working with Dr. Wei Sr. is probably the best perk of this job because my dad has been a dentist for over forty years and he will teach you all the tricks." She dropped her voice. "He's not always great with the computers though."

"I get it. My dad is a total computer guy, so I'm very comfortable with technology, but learning some old-school tricks would be awesome." Hasaan grinned, and Vivian had to admire his gums. They were really healthy. "Thank you, Dr. Wei."

"Thank *you*, Dr. Rasul." She smiled and waved as he walked toward the front door, chatting with Tabitha, who was obviously charmed by the bright young thing.

Just as she sat down at her desk, Inez, one of her most experienced hygienists, popped her head in the office. "New guy seems friendly. How'd it go?"

"I like him." Vivian nodded. "He's young, but he's got really good recommendations. I'm going to call and chat with his old boss in Detroit, but I have a good feeling about him. What's your impression?"

Inez had been the one to show Dr. Rasul around the practice when he showed up early. She was also in her late forties and had been through two owners and three associates. Inez was a gold mine of information. "Smart. Friendly. I think he'd have a really good rapport with patients. He'd probably need some handholding with more complicated procedures, but that's what you and your dad are for."

"You get any sense that he'd have issues with a female boss? I didn't, but I'm curious what you sensed."

Inez shook her head. "I didn't either. He was really respectful of all the girls when I introduced him."

Vivian sighed. "Introducing another man to the mix, Inez. Am I crazy for throwing off our girl-power environment here?"

Her practice was the first place where Vivian had worked in an entirely female office until her dad had come out to California, and it had been really fun and relaxed.

"I'd say your dad broke the streak, but he's such a girl-dad that he almost doesn't count."

"Right?" Vivian smiled. "I think Hasaan said he had three sisters, so there's that."

Inez laughed. "If his references check out, I say go for it. He seems like a sweetheart, and you are running short on time." She tapped the door and leaned back. "I have a biter in fifteen, so I'm going to go wrap bandages under my gloves before he gets here."

"Is it the Braison kid again?"

"The little brother."

Vivian shook her head. "We need to talk to their mom."

"I'll try." Inez turned to go, then turned back. "I almost forgot, I think Tabitha has a message for you in front. Someone named John, and he said you weren't answering your mobile phone."

"Oh!" She pulled it out of her desk drawer. "I had it on silent. Thanks."

"No problem. See you."

Vivian saw three missed calls from John Marcos. She hit his name on the screen and put the phone on speaker while she pulled out the lunch she'd packed from home.

"This is Chief Marcos."

"Do you always answer your personal number that way?" Vivian asked.

"Oh, sorry. I didn't see your name." He sounded flustered. "I'm in the middle of something."

"Bad time? I can call back in a couple of hours."

"No, it's okay." A door closed in the background. "The deputies in Rancho have a suspect in Archie Barrett's murder."

Vivian nearly choked on a cherry tomato. "They do? Trent Everett?"

"No, Oscar Valero."

She stood up at her desk. "They arrested *Oscar*?"

"Not yet, but they're bringing him in for questioning. The DA is looking at the case. They found his prints on the tarp wrapped around Archie's body."

"He's a groundskeeper! Of course his prints were on a tarp they found at the club."

"He has keys to the shed where the sand was taken, Vivian. They did a second sweep of the storage shed and found blood there. It's not that far from the thirteenth tee. They think the body was carried to the shed, wrapped up there, then thrown in the pond before the police came. Barrett was a prominent individual. They're getting a lot of pressure to make an arrest."

"John, I am telling you, Oscar is a giant teddy bear. He loves old people and helps me carry groceries when it's hot. He was not involved with this."

"He doesn't have an alibi, his prints were found on the tarp, and someone heard him threaten Archie Barrett the day of the tournament." John sighed. "I'm sorry, Vivian, but it's not looking good."

Chapter Eighteen

Vivian drove to Julia's office and met her in the parking lot. She rolled down the window and shouted, "Get in, loser; we're going to interrogate a bunch of old ladies."

Julia had been sitting on a bench under a paloverde tree, but she slung her handbag over her shoulder and slowly stood. "You're lucky I'm old enough to get that joke."

"Is Evy at home?"

"She didn't text you back?"

"No."

"She's at Oasis Springs doing a show."

"Oasis Springs?" Vivian shook her head as Julia got in the front seat. "Everything in this damn valley is Desert Springs, Shady Oasis, Desert Oasis Springs, or some combination. What is Oasis Springs?"

"Retirement village in Palm Desert."

"Got it." Vivian put her car in reverse and turned south on Palm Canyon Drive. "Then it should be on the way."

"So where are we going?"

"My mother's Thursday-afternoon mahjong club."

"Do I have to know how to play mahjong? I've always wanted to learn, but judging from the tone of your voice, this might not be the occasion."

"They're trying to arrest Oscar for Archie Barrett's murder." Vivian stopped at the red light. "Tell me where we're going."

"When you get into Palm Desert, it's the second signal, and you're going to turn right. Who is Oscar, and what does he have to do with Archie Barrett's murder?" Julia had her phone out. "I'm texting Evy right now."

"Oscar Valero is the world's sweetest gardener at Desert Oasis, and he also helps out on the course too. He makes special wheelchair ramps for elderly residents. He makes sure to check that the outside walkways are even if someone uses a cane. He fixed up his son's old Spider-Man tricycle and gave it to me for Henry." Vivian felt like crying. "He did not kill Archie Barrett. A bunch of rich assholes killed that man, but the sheriff's department is trying to arrest Oscar."

"What would possibly tie Oscar—?"

"They found his prints on the tarp that Archie Barrett was wrapped in."

"I thought you said he was a groundskeeper. If he worked there, wouldn't his prints be on the club tarps?"

"Exactly!" Vivian took a deep breath. They were going to sort this out. Oscar would not be framed for this murder. "He also had keys to the storage shed where the sandbags were kept. They searched it more thoroughly and found traces of Archie's blood inside."

"That still doesn't seem like enough to—"

"And someone saw him arguing with Mr. Barrett the day of the tournament, hours before the guy was killed. Apparently Oscar doesn't have an alibi; he was home sleeping, and his wife can't even confirm that because she was visiting her mom with all the kids!"

"Shit." Julia tucked her phone away. "Evy's done with her show; she'll meet us in the parking lot with Geoff."

Geoff was Evy's ventriloquist dummy, and he gave Vivian the creeps. She couldn't help it; she'd never liked dolls, and knowing that Geoff was haunted by the ghost of an old vaudeville performer didn't help. "Can we leave Geoff at the retirement home?" She didn't have a fully enclosed trunk in her new car.

"No, we cannot leave Geoff with the old people." Julia looked at Vivian. "Of all the ghosts I have to deal with on a daily basis, Geoffrey is actually one of the less intrusive." She raised her voice. "Unlike you, Mr. Gates; I hear you and I am purposefully ignoring you, so you can be quiet now."

"Oh good, he's with you."

Julia grimaced. "Why is that good?"

"Because here's my thinking—if we can prove that Fisher Gates was also murdered, then Oscar won't be a suspect anymore."

"Why?"

"Because then two murders will be tied to the Booster Club, Julia. Oscar has nothing to do with that circle."

"And what the hell does any of this have to do with your mother's Thursday-afternoon mahjong club?"

"My mom is a retired doctor, which means that like all retired doctors, other physicians are drawn to her on a subconscious level, the same way old dentists tend to congregate."

"Her mahjong group is made up of a bunch of old doctors?"

"One cardiologist, a neurologist, two other pediatricians, and an emergency room lifer. There's also a retired pharmacist and Mrs. Bronstein, but I'm pretty sure Mrs. Bronstein's husband was a doctor and she's a really good baker."

"And every mahjong group needs a good baker?"

Vivian frowned at Julia. "Every group of *anything* needs a good baker."

Julia shrugged. "I can't argue with that. So why do we need to talk to a bunch of old doctors?

"We need to find out the most likely ways to fake a heart attack."

JULIA, EVY, AND VIVIAN PULLED UP CHAIRS surrounding the two card tables set up in the Temple Shalom Senior Center in Palm Springs.

"Faking a heart attack?" Joan said. "You can't really fake a heart attack. If a heart attack happens, there's physical evidence, isn't there, Gabi?"

Gabriela Balvin, the cardiologist of the group, was at the other table. "It depends on the type of event, but if you're talking about *inducing* a heart attack, there are plenty of things that can induce a heart attack."

"Oh, okay." Vivian nodded. "Yes, that's what we're talking about. What circumstances can induce a heart attack?"

"Good Lord, so many." The woman who spoke had a growly voice with a distinct New York accent. She was wearing dark horn-rimmed glasses, and her curly grey hair was cut in a messy shag. "Drug overdoses, cold weather, too much brisket at the holidays. Stress!" She lifted a hand. "Girls, ya gotta narrow it down."

"Fran was an emergency room physician her whole career," Joan said. "But there are also less traumatic conditions that can prompt a heart attack. Drinking and adverse drug interactions are probably the most common. Fran mentioned stress, which is an obvious trigger. Maybe the most common."

Julia raised a hand. "Can attest."

Joan raised her eyebrows. "You've had a heart attack? That's young."

"My God, you're a kid," Fran said.

Gabi piped up again from the other table. "I've seen younger! Was it stress?"

"Yes," Julia said. "That's why I moved out here. Now I sell half the houses I used to and solve murders in my spare time."

Fran snorted. "Yeah, that sounds much less stressful. Good luck with that."

Someone touched Vivian's shoulder and pointed at the corner. It was Shirley Bronstein. "If you girls want some brownies, there are two dozen in the corner."

"Sweet." Evy sprang to her feet. "I haven't eaten since a sad turkey sandwich for lunch."

"What was that?"

"Someone's hungry?"

"Don't fill up on brownies, honey, you need protein."

Unsurprisingly, a chorus of food offers rose in the room. Within minutes, Evy had two granola bars, a package of almonds, a beef empanada, and half a pastrami sandwich shoved in her hands.

Evy sat at a corner of the table and started to munch. "I need to learn mahjong."

Vivian rolled her eyes and leaned closer to Julia. "Can you ask Fisher if he took any regular medications? I know John mentioned the man had a heart condition."

Julia nodded. "Ladies, where would I find the bathroom?"

Three hands pointed down the hallway as tiles continued to clack and the friendly banter of retired-lady shit-talk filled the room.

Vivian decided not to tell her mother about Oscar right then. There was no need to upset her mother if they could prove Oscar wasn't involved. "So this situation is somewhat related to the attack you saw, Mom."

"Archie Barrett's murder?" A woman at Joan's table lifted her head up, leaving her reading glasses low on her nose. "This is related to the Barrett murder?"

"Nasty business," Fran muttered. "Nasty man though, so that's not surprising."

"Did you know the Barretts?" Vivian asked.

"Trudie was their pediatrician," someone at the other table said.

The woman with the reading glasses said, "I can't confirm anything." She shook her head. "But know that I have thoughts."

Vivian understood the pressure of HIPAA and professional ethics, but she was feeling a little desperate. They were going to arrest *Oscar*. "Okay, but what if... you didn't use names?"

Every eye swung toward her.

"Vivian." Her mother's voice was a quiet admonition.

"Mom, we're talking about murder here. People have been *killed*."

Every eye turned toward Trudie, who was frozen, staring at her tiles. "Fuck it. I'm starting chemo next week, and both the parents of... Family X are dead now. What are they going to do? Sue an old lady with brain cancer?"

Fran cackled, and Joan reached out and squeezed the woman's hand. "You're going to be fine, Trudie."

"Mrs. X... I think she was just kind of a Stepford wife. The father?" She shook her head. "A bully. And it rubbed off on the boy. I think the daughter was mostly fine, but I remember treating the boy for a dog bite one time and thinking that I did not blame the dog. I remember thinking..." Trudie looked straight at Vivian. "...maybe the dog was defending itself, if you get my meaning."

Vivian looked at her and mouthed, *Thank you* with every ounce of sincerity she could project. "That sounds like a complicated family."

Trudie said nothing more about her former patients. "Did Archie Barrett have a heart attack? I wouldn't be surprised if an attack like the one your mom saw would induce a cardiac event as well."

"Any kind of trauma," Fran said. "If he had an underlying condition, a heart attack could have happened during his physical attack. It doesn't necessarily make it the cause of death, mind you. In a situation like that, you're talking about multiple levels of trauma in the body."

"At some point," Trudie said, "the body is going to shut down. What causes that final shutdown can be complicated. Many times, a heart attack is listed as the cause of death because that is the final step in a series of events."

"In this case, we're talking about someone in Archie Barrett's circle of friends who died of a heart attack, and it was listed as natural causes."

Trudie and Fran exchanged a look as Julia returned from the bathroom and sat next to Evy. She glanced at Vivian and gave her a slight nod.

"And you think this other death wasn't natural?" Trudie asked Vivian. "Why?"

"We got a tip that it wasn't," Vivian said. "We suspect it was a very clever murder."

"Did he have a heart condition?" Joan asked.

"He did," Julia said. "He'd already survived two heart attacks, and he was on medication for hypertension. But only one."

"You have to know" —Fran shook her head slowly— "the chances of surviving a third attack? Not good."

"We totally understand that," Vivian said. "But that makes it even more clever, you know? Who's going to suspect a heart attack wasn't natural causes when the man had already survived two?"

Shirley Bronstein moved her tiles around her rack. "Did he know anyone who had cancer?"

Fran said, "Shirley, if this man was one of Barrett's friends, he was probably our age. Every person our age knows someone with cancer."

"Well, lots of cancer drugs could cause a heart attack in someone with a previous cardiac condition," Shirley said. "I know Saul always worried about that with his patients who had blood pressure issues."

Joan nodded. "That's a good point. There are any number of cancer drugs that stress the heart and others that are prescribed in conjunction with chemotherapy that could also wreak havoc."

Shirley was still organizing her tiles. "I remember a case that I read about in the papers back in New York before Saul and I moved out here. There was an elderly man who was poisoned by his wife's cancer medication, and the killer got away with it for years because they thought his heart attack was caused by stress."

Fran muttered. "I don't remember that. How did they figure out it was murder?"

Shirley looked up. "Oh, they found his wife's journal after she passed. She confessed the whole thing. Said she wanted everyone to know she'd killed him."

A grim silence fell over the two tables.

Fran finally broke it. "Hard on the kids."

"They didn't seem too broken up about it," Shirley sipped a cup of coffee. "I don't think their father was a very nice man."

Chapter Nineteen

The next day, Vivian and her copilots met at the Desert Oasis Country Club dining room for lunch. Richard was joining them as their guide to Palm Springs society life.

"If I am ever so hated that my own spouse kills me after fifty years of marriage..." Evy narrowed her eyes. "Maybe I shouldn't ever be married."

They were sitting at a round table that overlooked the course; the temperature had dipped into the low nineties that day, so life was beginning to feel tolerable again. In another month, the best weather would arrive.

Julia idly stirred her iced tea. "Even if you got married tomorrow, you'd have to live until ninety-two to be married fifty years."

"Oh right." Evy sipped her Coke. "Just going to pass on that whole thing then."

Vivian was having a hard time relaxing. Not only had Henry decided to sit directly on her bladder that morning, she still had no way to know if Fisher Gate's death was a murder, which would clear Oscar's name and keep him from getting arrested.

She'd finally met Andre, Evy's friend, so she felt a little better about her parents' safety, but then she wondered whether she was feeling too much confidence in a complete stranger because he was a friend of Evy's.

Vivian was bloated, anxious, and confused. She felt like hiding in her house and pretending the rest of the world didn't exist for a year, but if she did that—according to Julia's nieces—she'd have multiple murders on her conscience.

And Vivian couldn't be a good mother with multiple murders on her conscience.

"So Fisher Gates was cremated, right?" She asked Julia, though she already suspected the answer.

"That's what John said. Fisher himself is kind of clueless about what happened to his body after he died." Julia glanced over her shoulder, probably at the ghost that was still following her around. "He's wandering now. He loves it here."

"So the Gateses were members at Desert Oasis," Vivian said. "But Richard said there was kind of a pecking order when it comes to country clubs. That's why we're here today."

Evy raised a glass. "All I know is that I was told that I would get free drinks and two free lunches, so I am game for whatever."

"Ladies." Richard's calm voice immediately soothed Vivian's nerves. She turned when she felt his hand brush her shoulder. "I'm so sorry I'm late."

"Hey." She smiled. "How are you today?"

"How are you?" Richard brushed his fingers along her jaw and sat next to her. Dressed in pressed linen pants and a white polo shirt, he was the picture of aristocratic elegance in the formal dining room. "How's Henry this morning?"

"Getting a little annoyed at the lack of space."

His smile was warm. "Not too much longer, little man."

Okay, why was she tearing up about that? Vivian turned back to her herbal tea and tried to get ahold of her wildly careening emotions.

"Rich, thank you for joining us," Julia said. "You're our Palm Springs social-scene translator."

"Happy to help." He bowed a little. "I'm not sure how I can assist, but I guess I do know most of the people here."

The club server was a sweet girl that Vivian knew; she came over, took their lunch order, then slipped back to the kitchen.

"Did you know Fisher Gates?" Vivian asked. "He was a member here."

"Sure." Richard nodded. "I knew him a little socially. He died of a heart attack a few months ago, correct?"

"Yes but... Let's just say there are questions."

Richard raised an eyebrow. "Questions about his heart attack?"

"Yes."

"I see." Richard shook his head. "Actually I don't see, but for now, how can I help?"

Evy put it bluntly. "We need gossip."

"Fisher Gates was a member here." Julia kept her voice low in the carpeted and greenery-filled dining room. "But his daughter isn't. Her husband's family has their membership over at Monte Verde."

"Okay, if you're looking for the gossip..." Richard kept his voice low. "Gates's daughter is... let's be generous and call her aspirational. She's an ambitious person, and her husband is from a very wealthy family."

"But Fisher Gates was also ridiculously wealthy, right?"

"He was in banking and yes, he did quite well."

Evy leaned forward. "That translates into 'he was a millionaire, but we don't like to talk too much about it.'"

"Why wasn't he at Monte Verde?" Vivian asked. "That's considered the best club, right?"

"I don't believe he had a sponsor there, and he never sought out a membership." Richard looked around the clubhouse. "He was a big fish here, and my impression was that he liked that."

"When I got my social membership at Monte Verde," Julia said, "I had a recommendation from Dean and Sergio, who are full members. But I am a very little fish."

"What's the difference between full members and social members?" Evy asked.

Richard answered, "It varies depending on the club, but social members use the facilities and dining areas. The spa, the swimming pools, tennis courts, things like that. But the golf course is reserved for full members and their guests, and full members can vote on the board."

"It's the same here," Vivian said. "We inherited a full membership from my grandparents, which my parents continue to pay dues on. I'm just a social member because I don't golf."

Evy nodded. "Okay, so maybe Fisher Gates would have been a social member at Monte Verde, but he was a full member here?"

"He was a leader here," Richard said. "And I think his attitude was that it was better to be a big fish in a smaller, newer pond than just an average member at Monte Verde. His daughter didn't feel the same way. She married into a very wealthy family and bought into all of it. Kids at Desert Prep, membership at Monte Verde, family oil painting over the mantel in the house in the estates, kids taking polo lessons."

"She sounds like a peach."

Richard shrugged. "She's very involved at the school according to Maddy. I don't think she works, so she's something of a professional volunteer."

"Got it." Vivian waited as their server brought back two salads and two sandwiches. "And she was friends with West Barrett and Trent Everett?"

"I think she's in that same crowd." Richard dug into his sandwich. "But she's not a leader if I had to guess."

"Why not?"

Vivian was starting to catch on. "Because she wasn't born into it. Not like West Barrett. She married into the crowd."

Richard nodded.

"That's so messed up," Evy said. "I'm kind of relieved to be a non-rich person right now. At least I like all my friends for the right reasons."

"There's a lot of backstabbing in that set," Richard said. "Even when I was with Lily, we didn't get involved in that too much, but it's all very visible."

"Why didn't Lily get involved in that scene?"

"Because she was famous," Julia said. "It's a different standard for famous people like Sergio or Lily because they're rich *and* they're famous."

Richard nodded. "I'm still considered an East Coast snob, so they respect me but they don't pay me much attention. Lily ran our social circle, and to her—and I suspect for Dean and Sergio as well—the people who made money by playing with money weren't very interesting. Monte Verde is more loved by the artistic crowd, probably because there's more history there."

Evy leaned her chin in her hand. "So even among the super-rich, there are still cliques, like in high school, and there are still jocks and theater kids?"

Richard opened his mouth, paused, then nodded. "Yes."

"Wow." Evy dug into her french dip. "That's pathetic."

Richard was still nodding. "It really is."

AFTER A LUNCH OF FRENCH DIPS AND GIN AND TONICS, they left Desert Oasis and drove north on Palm Canyon Drive, turning off the main road and meandering through the winding streets of Vista de Lirio until they came to the historic Monte Verde Country Club at the base of the San Jacinto Mountains.

Unlike most of the newer clubs, Monte Verde had been built

around a natural oasis in the desert, and the towering fan palms created a dense oasis behind the Spanish colonial clubhouse. Tennis courts and crystal-blue pools were shaded by clumps of palms and towering hibiscus trees. The walls were covered in striking pink bougainvillea, and electric golf carts zipped along perfectly groomed cart paths.

Unlike the glossy perfection of Desert Oasis, everything at Monte Verde had the feel of bespoke luxury. They settled into the Oasis Room, a luxurious Art Deco–style bar that overlooked the palm grove and natural pond formed by an ancient spring.

No one asked for their names or seated them; the host nodded discreetly at Richard as they entered and motioned for him to choose a table he liked. Richard selected one near the windows.

"The oasis here actually connects to the one behind Casa de Lirio," he said, pulling out a chair for Vivian to sit. "The stream that runs behind the club starts behind my house in the rainy season."

"How far are we from your house?"

"Here at the clubhouse?" Richard shrugged. "The golf course winds its way along the base of the mountains behind Vista de Lirio, so I'm only a couple of blocks from the course. The clubhouse is maybe a mile or so?"

"And Dean and Sergio's place?"

"All those estates—Dean and Sergio's, Genevieve de Winter's, the Artist's Residence—they all kind of fit in and around the course. That's why there are all those palms on the west side. That's what shields residents from the noise."

Vivian looked around the nearly silent bar. "What noise?"

Richard smiled. "Quiet recreation is encouraged here except for the parties, which are legendary."

Julia nodded. "I've attended a couple." She looked at Evy and Vivian. "Think Sunday Dinner on steroids."

"Yes," Richard said. "Lily loved the parties." He looked a bit uncomfortable. "There's an attitude among the members here that what happens at the club stays at the club, and that goes doubly so for what happens at parties."

"I definitely feel the difference," Vivian said. "This place feels more private than Desert Oasis."

"By far."

Vivian's attention was drawn to a group entering the Oasis Room. "Speak of the devil, and he does appear."

Richard turned his head and raised a single eyebrow. "Well said."

West Barrett and a thick-necked man who looked familiar entered the bar with a dark-haired woman dressed in a tennis costume. West's eyes met Richard's, and his smile faltered for a moment. Then he pushed forward and walked to their table.

Vivian felt silent malevolence fill the air.

"Putnam," West Barrett said. "Good to see you."

"West." Richard stood and held out a hand that West shook vigorously. "I don't think I've seen you since we heard about your father. How are you and your family doing?"

"Broken up, of course. Nasty business." West's eyes fell on Vivian. "But let's not talk about ugly things when you're enjoying such beautiful company." He nodded. "Dr. Wei."

"Mr. Barrett." She motioned to Evy and Julia. "Have you met my friends? Julia Brooks and EV Lane. I think you met Julia at my practice the other day."

"Good to see you again." West pointed at Evy. "And I'll never forget Miss Lane. You were spectacular at the gala."

"Thanks."

"You know, we thought you were a man when we booked you." West hung his hands in his pockets. "Imagine that."

"I get that a lot." Evy smiled. "Aren't you the lucky one to get me instead?"

West's eyes laughed. "Indeed." His gaze swept the table.

"Putnam, old man, you must be living right convincing three gorgeous women to keep you company. What's your secret?"

"Virtuous living." Richard mirrored West's casual posture. "I recommend it."

Vivian felt a crackle of anger disguised by a burst of laughter from West.

"Good God, is that it?" West shook his head. "I'm a hopeless case then." He turned to his companions. "You know Trace Mitchell and Pippa, don't you?"

"I've had the pleasure." Richard nodded at Pippa Stanford. "Miss Stanford, how are your parents?"

"Living well." Pippa Stanford's voice dripped with ennui. "Like always. How's Lily?" She blinked. "Sorry, is that gauche to ask?"

"You'd have to ask her attorney." Richard didn't miss a beat. "My daughter has your oldest in her class this year, I think."

Vivian was surprised by a wave of emotion from Pippa Stanford. Despite her relaxed exterior, the woman was seething with buried anger. The pressure on Vivian's skin was nearly painful.

Trace Mitchell, the thick-necked man, laughed at Richard's comment. "That's something, isn't it? Your daughter teaching at our kids' school, huh?"

Richard turned his eyes on Trace, and Vivian saw the East Coast aristocrat rear its perfectly coiffed head. "I had the same thought, Trace. It's really something that your little prep school has taken this long to attract high-caliber instructors. I suppose it's difficult to tempt experienced academics like Madison to the desert when so many prefer larger cities."

Trace blinked, and Vivian could feel his confusion. The severity of the insult flew high and wide over the man's head. He might be an insider in the Monte Verde crowd, but that did not mean he was a leader.

Trace frowned. "Right. I meant she was a teacher."

West cut his eyes at Trace before he turned his attention back to Richard. "And my wife, among others, is thrilled. I understand she had several offers at institutions back east?"

Vivian tried to feel something from the man, but other than whispers of hostility, she felt the same cold void he'd exhibited at her office.

"Maddy's happy here for now." Richard's posture never changed, but his eyes were laughing at all of them. Vivian felt both his amusement and his vigilance. He trusted none of the three before them. "So West, how's the business handling the loss of your dad?"

West's eyes gleamed. "Oh, you know what they say: a house built on the rocks won't topple. We're doing just fine, Putnam. The old man had a good run, but in the end, it was probably time for new leadership at the helm if you know what I mean. It'll all work out."

"Well, that's a silver lining, I suppose."

Was that the motivation? Vivian felt a cold chill in her chest. Would West Barrett have had his father murdered so he could take over their business?

Just as Vivian was tempted to say something, Evy grabbed her hand under the table and gripped it hard. She felt a wave of panic, fear, confusion... There was too much to take in.

"Evy?" She kept her voice low.

In the background, West and Richard were still chatting. "You have a good afternoon, Putnam."

"Remember, West." Richard sat down. "Virtuous living."

"I'll remember."

Julia watched West and his cronies walk away with a curious expression and a cocked head. Or possibly, she was seeing someone they couldn't.

"Evy, what is going on?" She turned to Richard. "We need to get her out of here. She's panicking."

"If we leave right after we talked to them—"

"Rich, I think she's about to pass out."

He stood and nodded at the demure host by the door. “Come with me.”

Vivian helped Evy to her feet, and the woman would not let loose of her grip on Vivian’s hand. The fear was so great Vivian was starting to feel nauseated.

Richard led them out the door of the Oasis Room and into the lobby. Someone was already bringing his Land Rover around from the valet.

“They’re going to shoot her,” Evy whispered. “I heard him.”

Chapter Twenty

Julia pressed an ice pack to Evy's forehead as Vivian hovered nearby, wishing she could drain some of Evy's fear, at least enough that the woman could think clearly. They were sitting in the immaculate family room off the kitchen at Casa de Lirio, and Richard was pouring them all drinks.

"Here." He brought over a cut-crystal glass with chipped ice and gold soda. "Ginger ale. Always my go-to when I'm not feeling well."

Evy took it and stared at the crystal glass. "No *Star Wars* commemorative glassware for the Putnams, huh?"

Richard frowned. "Commemorative what?"

"Nothing, I'm being obnoxious." Evy tried to sit up. "I have to think. It was all so jumbled when they were there. The three of them—no, it was really Pippa and West, Trace is genuinely a blockhead—said so damn much without saying anything really." She sipped the ginger ale. "Pippa was the clearest, but then not the clearest either. Her thoughts were easy to read but more jumbled if that makes sense."

Richard sat next to Vivian and took her hand. "I can't

imagine hearing people's thoughts. It seems like everywhere you went, it would be like walking into a loud bar with everyone shouting at once."

"It's not unlike that." Evy's color was better after a few sips of the cold drink. "But you'd be surprised how many people don't project their thoughts at all. You, for example, you're very reserved. Not in a bad way; you and Dean are really similar. It makes you easy to hang out with."

Vivian looked at Richard with a smile. "I get the same thing from your emotions. Not cold at all, nothing like West Barrett, but reserved. You don't project a lot; you're very self-contained."

Richard looked at Julia, but the blond woman only shrugged. "You have ghosts outside your house, but not inside?"

He frowned. "I don't find that terribly surprising in a house this age."

"They all seem friendly."

Vivian thought that was an extremely diplomatic way of phrasing things considering Richard's backyard hosted a spiritual portal that attracted ghosts the way flowers attract honeybees.

There was no need to freak the man out needlessly.

"I guess friendly ghosts are fine." Richard shrugged. "The more the merrier? Good to know I'm not actually sixty-two and living alone."

Vivian really wanted to get back to what Evy had said about a woman being shot, but she didn't want to press her.

Evy said, "You'd be amazed how many people don't really think in words at all. I get impressions more than sentences. It seems like a lot of people think visually too, and I can't read that the same way."

Julia asked, "Okay, Vivian said something about a murder though."

Evy's expression was grim. "I don't know who was thinking

it, but I imagine it was West because I wasn't getting many thoughts at all from Blockhead Trace."

"But you don't know for sure?"

"It's not an exact science, Jules." She pressed the heel of her hand to her eyes. "It was more of a picture anyway, so... It's hard to explain. The flavor of the thought seemed male, but it could have been Pippa thinking it. She's a weird one."

"I felt a lot of anger from her," Vivian said. "A lot."

"That's interesting, because she's haunted too," Julia said. "There's a ghost of a young woman that follows her around. I didn't even realize she was attached to Pippa at first because she kept her distance."

"What about Archie's ghost?"

"Oh, he's still stuck like glue to West. He loved the silver lining comment. Drove him absolutely crazy." Julia sat back in the plush sofa. "But the woman attached to Pippa is interesting. I think she's Latina or possibly Native. She couldn't have been more than eighteen or nineteen when she died."

"Why would a ghost be haunting Pippa Stanford?" Richard asked. "Has she killed someone and no one found out?"

"It could be any number of things." Julia shook her head. "There's no way of knowing. She could have been friends with Pippa, though I didn't get that feeling. The young woman probably died violently if she hasn't moved on, but there's no way of knowing what happened unless we talk to Pippa, and I don't know that we want to do that."

"Was the thought you had about a woman being shot...," Vivian started. "Could it have been about this woman haunting Pippa?"

Evy shook her head. "I got an impression of an older woman, and she was driving a very expensive car, and then a mental picture of a gun. It was just a flash, and I don't know cars very well, but it was like... kind of a dark blue color? Or maybe black? I think it was something vintage; it had that look." She huffed. "You know, I have a better impression of the car than I do of the woman."

"That's strange." Richard crossed his arms over his chest. "A dark blue or black luxury car? There are too many of them in the valley to even count."

"But a vintage luxury car?" Vivian shrugged. "That could be something to go on."

"But we have no idea who this person is, what they're going to do, who could be doing it..." Evy groaned. "I hate this so much. If something happens to her, I'm going to feel responsible, and I'm not responsible for this. The damn Booster Club is."

"The Booster Club?" Richard muttered. "Wait, so you think Dean and Sergio's daughters are right?"

Evy, Julia, and Vivian all exchanged glances.

"That's why we wanted the gossip on Fisher Gates," Julia said. "His daughter is in the Booster Club."

"And he died of a heart attack a few months ago," Richard said. "And then last month, Archie Barrett was murdered, and his son is the head of it." He looked at Evy. "Good God, I think those girls are on to something. And now you saw another woman shot?"

Julia nodded. "But how many women in the valley have dark blue or black luxury vehicles?"

"I think you're asking the wrong question," Richard said. "Fisher Gates and Archie Barrett. You don't need to know how many rich women in the valley have black luxury cars; you just need to find out which women related to the Booster Club own them."

JULIA WAS ON HER CELL PHONE IN VIVIAN'S OFFICE, talking to Sergio while Vivian did her charts.

"Okay, but it's white?" She made a face. "You're sure." Julia nodded. "Okay, thanks, Dean. No, it's for something else. I'll be in the office in an hour or so." She picked at her salad from Farm. "Just having lunch with Vivian." She smiled. "Yes, she's looking superadorable. She's wearing this yellow smock thing under her white coat, and it has little flowers on it."

"It's a shirtdress," Vivian said. "It's not a smock." It was also one of the few things that still fit. "Leave me alone."

"She is a little bit grouchy though." Julia winked. "I'll tell her. Bye." She hung up. "Dean says that Sergio wants to decorate your nursery once I find you a house. I guess he had all these ideas left over and a few pieces of art from when the girls were babies."

Vivian blinked. "Really?"

"Yeah. If I were you, I'd just let him. He's really good at knowing what people like; I've loved every room he's ever decorated for me."

"That sounds amazing; I'll call him. Whose car were you asking about?"

"West Barrett's mom is dead; she had a stroke a few years ago. And Pippa Stanford's mother drives a white Lexus. I haven't heard about Trace's or Trent's mothers yet. I called John Marcos, but he hasn't gotten back to me."

Vivian knew the fastest way to check car registrations would be through the police chief, but she also suspected that several of these families had multiple cars and could very well have collections that weren't traditionally registered.

"Evy said she was going to have a session with Maud today," Vivian said. "Have you heard from her?"

"I haven't yet. I know she wanted to see if Maud could hypnotize her. I guess that can help her remember things sometimes?" Julia shrugged. "I mean, if you ask me, we just need to figure out which of the Booster Club's unlucky mothers drives a black car."

"What if it's not a mother though?" Vivian asked. "What if it's an... aunt or a cousin or something."

Julia pursed her lips. "Damn, I hadn't even thought about that." She sighed and jumped on her computer again. "I'm going to call Michael. He knows rich people."

Vivian finished her paperwork and reached for her phone to call her mother.

"Hello?"

"Hey, Mom!" Vivian forced a smile when she heard her mother's voice. "How are you? You sound a little tired."

"Oh, I'm just frustrated with this front flower bed. I checked the drip line and it's not working, but I can't figure out why. It's finally cool enough that I can plant some flowers, and I don't want to have to water them by hand."

"Did you ask Dad?"

"I don't want to bother him when he's golfing."

"Mom, he's always golfing lately."

"Well, that's the joy of retirement, honey. Your dad worked very hard for a lot of years. He's earned the time to—"

"Mom, you do not have to convince me that Dad works hard." She barely kept from rolling her eyes. "Did you call the gardeners? That section of the front flower beds is technically part of the association grounds. If there's something wrong with the drip, they're the ones who need to fix it."

"Oh, that's a good idea; I'll call Oscar." Joan sounded like she was shuffling papers. "Vivian, you said your friend who's following me—"

"Andre's guarding the house, Mom. Just to ease my mind until the police figure out who killed Mr. Barrett."

"I know that, but he's been sitting out in his car for hours now. Do I need to feed him? I can make him a sandwich if he's hungry, but I don't want to intrude."

Only her mother would try to feed the bodyguard. "I think

he's probably okay, Mom. He's a professional, so I imagine he came prepared for an all-day job."

"Okay, but if you talk to him, ask please. I don't want him sitting out in his car hungry."

"I'll check." She heard her phone beep. "I need to get off the phone; can I call you back?"

"Of course, honey. Don't work too late. Is Friday still your light day?"

"It is. I'll see you for dinner." She hung up and answered the other line. "This is Vivian Wei."

"Vivian, it's John."

The chief of police sounded grim, and Vivian snapped her fingers to grab Julia's attention. "Hey John, Julia's here, let me put you on speaker." She motioned to the door and Julia jumped up to close it while she pulled the phone from her ear and pushed the button for the speaker. "Okay, we're both here. Go ahead."

"The Riverside Sheriff's Department just arrested Oscar Valero for the murder of Archie Barrett."

"Dammit!" Vivian couldn't stop the outburst. "You know he didn't do it!"

"I can't give the deputies your theories about West Barrett and the Desert Prep Booster Club as evidence, Vivian. Psychic hunches are not admissible in court."

Julia put her hand on Vivian's shoulder. "What are the charges?"

"Second-degree murder. They're painting it as a crime of passion, and since Oscar doesn't have any kind of alibi and people saw him arguing with the victim the day of the attack, they feel like they can make it stick."

"Was the family putting pressure on them?" Julia asked.

"Oh yeah. There was pressure from all over. You know the Barretts and Judge Stanford are friends."

Vivian was too upset to speak. Oscar, one of the sweetest

people she'd met since she moved from Chicago, was going to jail because she couldn't solve Archie Barrett's murder fast enough.

"Did you manage to get a list of cars registered to the five families?" Julia asked. "We're working on that angle right now. If someone else is a target, we have to do everything we can to prevent it."

"Dark luxury sedan is a tough one," John said. "Basically, all these families own at least one vehicle that would fit the bill."

"So that's superhelpful," Vivian muttered. "West Barrett's mom is dead. Do any of the rest of them have dead mothers?"

"Ashley Gates-Bradley's mother is alive and well, as is Pippa Stanford's. Trent Everett's and Trace Mitchell's mothers are both alive and well, though they're both divorced from their fathers. I'll email you and Julia a list with all the info."

"Do any of them live out of the area?" Vivian asked. "We might be able to rule those out."

"Trent's mother moved to Los Angeles after the divorce, but the other three live in town. I have to go, Vivian. I'll email you."

Vivian looked at Joan. "We have to figure this out. Oscar is a working-class guy; there's no way his family will be able to afford a fancy lawyer."

"Okay." Julia sat down and pulled out her phone to check her email. "I see the list from John. The Gateses, the Mitchells, and the Stanfords all have vehicles that might match, but I can't tell you who drives what."

Vivian sat back in her chair and thought about it. "You said Pippa's mother drives a white Lexus usually."

"Yes, so that's one down."

"No, no, it's more than that." Vivian tried to gather her jumbled thoughts. "Trent Everett's mother lives in LA. She's not out of the woods, but she's not local. West's mother is dead." Vivian wrote down the rest of the names. "Trace's mom, Ashley's mom, and Pippa's mom. We know Pippa's mother drives a white Lexus—"

"But there is a black Jaguar registered to her and Judge Stanford."

"Okay, but that means she's not as likely." Vivian was still jotting notes; she put a question mark next to Pippa's name. "West's mother is gone." She crossed his name out. "Trent's is in LA." She put another question mark. "Ashley... Ashley Gates. Her father already died unexpectedly. What are the chances that the Booster Club would go after *both* her parents?"

"Two dead parents in a matter of months? That would raise some red flags." Julia pointed to the last name left. "Trace Mitchell." Her eyes met Vivian's. "What do we know about Trace's mother?"

"I don't know anything, but Sergio will."

"Call him and tell him we think we found the next victim." Vivian circled Trace Mitchell's name. "We think the Booster Club is going after Blaine Mitchell next."

Chapter Twenty-One

Vivian sat in her driveway, trying to reason with John on the phone. "I'm telling you, it's her. She's the next target."

"How?"

"How do I know or how are they going to kill her? I don't know how they're going to—"

"Do you know where?"

"We don't know that either. Evy just saw a car."

"When?"

Vivian sighed. "We don't know exactly, but they met on Wednesday, and according to Sergio and Dean's girls—"

"You do realize how insane this sounds, right?" The frustration in John's voice was audible. "It's not that I don't believe you, but I can't barge into Blaine Mitchell's law office—"

"Call her then! That's probably a better choice anyway because according to Sergio, she runs that law firm but her husband and her son both work there. So if they know the chief of police visited her, they'd probably ask a lot of questions."

"Vivian, *I* have questions!"

"And I'm trying to answer them, I promise." She turned off

her car and opened her door, feeling the wash of warm air on skin chilled from the new air-conditioning. "John, if no one warns her and something happens, we will be responsible."

"Do you have any idea why Blaine Mitchell's son would want to kill her? Do you have any motive at all?"

"I don't…" She struggled to get out of the car. "John, it's not like I've spent a lot of time with these people. Why would any of them want their parents dead? Money? Inheritance? Control of family businesses? They just plain hate them? I don't know." And she also couldn't get out of her car. Vivian sighed. "I have to hang up and call my dad to come help me right now."

"What's wrong?"

"I can't get out of the car. I think I'm wedged in here and I'll probably pull something if I don't get help."

"I cannot tell you how much I do not like you running around investigating murders when you're two months away from giving birth."

"According to my OB, it's more like four or five weeks actually. I grow babies fast."

"That is even worse! Do you not see how that's worse?"

"Okay." She huffed. "Hanging up now so I can call my dad. Please call Blaine Mitchell and warn her." There had to be a way to get out of the car, she just had to find it. She fiddled with the seat controls on the side.

Oh. Ohhhhhh. She sighed when the seat started to sink and she was able to swing her legs out of the driver's side door. With a little maneuvering and solid arm strength, she hoisted herself up and out of the car.

Somewhat out of breath, she stood in triumph, glaring at the luxury SUV. John was probably right; hunting down murderers on her own was a bad idea.

She'd call Julia and Evy.

Julia was the first to show up at Vivian's house. It made sense to meet there because Mitchell, Armor, and Mitchell, attorneys at law, had their office mere blocks from the Desert Oasis clubhouse. Vivian and Julia waited for Evy in the front garden.

"Your mom got the flowers planted," Julia stared at the colorful beds. "Looks good. Oh! I have another listing for you to check out. We probably want to move on this one too. It'll go fast."

"Does this one have closets?" It had been the only drawback of the adorable bungalow Julia had found for her. Vivian was too practical to live in a house with no closet space.

"Yes, this place is a midcentury, but it still has some really gorgeous trees and a nice lot with lots of space. It's at the end of a cul-de-sac as well."

"Oh, I like those."

"No through traffic, and I think there's at least one other young family on the block."

"Bonus."

They looked up as Evy's land shark of an 1980s sedan drove up to the curb. She rolled down the window and shouted, "The AC is cranked! Let's go scare a lawyer."

"Sounds like fun." Julia opened the door and motioned for Vivian to get in the front seat. "You're in front, mama. I'll hop in back."

They drove away from Vivian's house and through the suburban opulence of the country-club neighborhood.

"So have either of you met this woman before?" Vivian asked. "I know I haven't."

"We were introduced at a lunch a few months ago at the club," Julia said, "but I doubt she remembers me. She struck me as a very focused, busy person."

Evy added, "And according to Dean, she rules the roost over there."

"Maybe that's why Trace wants to get rid of her," Vivian said. "If he feels like his mother has too much control over his career—"

"You're probably right," Evy said, "but that guy is so dense. I cannot even tell you how dull his thoughts are. He is not bright. If his parents didn't own that law firm, he would not have gotten hired."

"That's half the financial and legal firms I've ever encountered though," Julia said. "Nepotism is rampant."

"Trace Mitchell may be the epitome of failing up," Vivian said, "but that doesn't mean he realizes it. I'm sure he thinks he's entitled to more."

Evy had already searched for directions for Mitchell, Armor, and Mitchell. She pulled into a far spot in the parking lot under a bunch of palms and put the car in park before she got out her expandable windshield shade with flamingos on it. She wrangled it onto the dash and opened her car door. "Okay, what's our premise?"

Julia grabbed her purse and opened her door too. "I think we lean into the weird; it's the only thing we can do. If she knows Dean and Sergio at all, Sergio has told him about his psychic Realtor friend. Most people don't realize I only see ghosts, so I'll just tell her I had a vision that she was in danger."

"And you think that might work?" Vivian asked.

"No, the woman is a litigation attorney; she's not going to believe that I'm really psychic or that I had a vision," Julia said. "But, just maybe, something in the back of her mind will make her a little more cautious for the next few weeks, you know?"

Evy nodded. "It's like reading my horoscope. I don't really believe I'm going to have a windfall, but that doesn't mean I'm not going to grab a lottery ticket that day just in case it's right."

Julia shrugged. "It's all we can do. In the absence of any actual proof, all we can do is try."

They walked into the cool, mahogany-paneled lobby and

stopped in front of the large black desk where a secretary was working on a computer.

The secretary answered a ringing phone and raised a single finger for them to wait. "Mitchell, Armor, and Mitchell, how may I direct your call?" She nodded. "One moment please. Can I tell her who is calling?" The secretary transferred the call and turned her attention toward Vivian and her friends. "Good afternoon. Are you here for an appointment?"

"We're here to meet with Blaine Mitchell," Julia said. "We're not on her appointment calendar, but I'm Julia Brooks from Monte Verde Country Club, and she's going to want to see us."

The secretary looked skeptical. "I'll tell her you're here, but Miz Mitchell is a very busy attorney." She nodded to the plush chairs in the waiting room. "Please have a seat."

Vivian lowered herself into the extra plush velvet chair and prayed that she'd be able to stand up again when it was time to leave.

"You think she's going to buy this?" Evy asked under her breath. "I mean, she's not going to charge us just to talk to her, will she?"

"Don't be silly," Julia said. "Besides, the only name she has is mine. If anything, she'll bill me."

A few minutes after they sat, the heard muffled footsteps coming down the hall to their right. A woman in an elegant cream suit stopped near Julia and narrowed her eyes.

"I do recognize you," she said. "We met at the summer mixer that Fred insisted on."

Julia popped to her feet. "I hope we're not bothering you."

"You are." She frowned. "But what is it?" She glanced at Vivian. "If you've had a problem with a fertility clinic, I'm not the right person to speak to, but we do have an associate on staff with some experience—"

"This is not..." Vivian managed to get to her feet without

too much of a struggle. "I'm Dr. Vivian Wei. Can we speak to you privately?"

Blaine Mitchell still looked skeptical, but she was intrigued enough to nod toward the conference room behind them. "Diona, we're taking conference room B."

"Yes, Miz Mitchell," the secretary said.

Blaine led them into the large conference room, which was lined with portraits. A long table dominated the middle of the room, and cut-crystal glasses were grouped in the middle next to a carafe of water.

"Please." Blaine motioned to the chairs. "What is it? Something going on at Monte Verde? I have to tell you, I'm not very involved in the club. My son and my husband are avid golfers, which is why we keep the membership, but I'm hardly the person to solicit for volunteering or anything like—"

"Blaine, I don't want to waste your time because I know you're a very busy woman," Julia broke in with her best I'm-a-busy-professional voice. "As I'm sure you know, I'm a partner at Steward Brooks Luxury Realty, so I know how busy you must be. But if you're familiar at all with Sergio Oliveira, you might also know that I'm a gifted psychic, and it's come to me that your life is in imminent danger."

Blaine Mitchell was frozen and blinking rapidly. "Excuse me, did you say you're psychic?"

"I did. And the vision was related to a dark sedan you were driving and a firearm. I can't say anything more specific than that."

The corner of Blaine's mouth turned up. "Really? Nothing any more than that? I shoot competitively and have for years. I have a target pistol in the trunk of my Mercedes right now. Did you actually pull me away from my desk for this nonsense?" She rolled her eyes and moved to the doorway. "Honestly, do not come to my office again, Miss Brooks. I have lost a great deal of respect for Dean Steward if you're the kind of person—"

"It's your son." Vivian didn't know why she blurted it out, but she couldn't seem to stop herself.

Blaine turned slowly. "Excuse me?"

"That doesn't surprise you, does it?" Vivian moved toward her and reached out, searching for the emotions coming from Blaine Mitchell. "You don't believe Julia, but hearing me accuse Trace didn't surprise you. Why is that?" Vivian moved closer and felt the suspicion and a single, tenuous thread of fear. "Have you sensed his resentment? His disdain for you and his father?"

Blaine narrowed her eyes. "I don't know who you think you are, but—"

"You've felt it. Call it mother's intuition or whatever you want, but you know how he feels about you." Vivian stood calmly, her hands at her sides. "You don't want to believe us, but part of you does. That's your survival instinct; you should listen to it."

Her lip curled up. "You three are ridiculous, and you need to leave."

"Please." Julia tried again. "Just be cautious. It can't hurt, right? Even if you don't believe us, you can be careful. Why would we have come here if we were full of shit?" She spread her hands out. "We knew you wouldn't believe us, but we came anyway. Just please, please be careful. If you can avoid going places alone, then do it. Just be aware."

Blaine Mitchell paused for a second, then let out a breath, shook her head, and turned to the large double doors of the conference room. "See yourselves out," she said. "And please don't waste any more of my or Diona's time. Good day."

Evy stuck her hands in her pockets and watched the solid wood door swing silently closed. "Well, we tried."

A sick feeling hit the pit of Vivian's stomach. "She doesn't believe us."

Julia let out a long breath. "We knew it was a long shot even coming here to warn her. Hopefully something gets through."

Chapter Twenty-Two

Vivian arrived home feeling defeated with sore feet, an aching back, and a sense of dread that wouldn't leave the pit of her stomach. She slipped her shoes off at the door and put on her favorite house slippers that were waiting for her like old friends.

She wanted a glass of wine, but that wasn't an option, so she walked to the kitchen and dumped an herbal tea bag into a mug before she poured hot water in.

She closed her eyes, waiting for the tea to steep, and imagined that she was lying in the cool shade by Richard's pool. The breeze from the mountains swept down and soothed her swollen feet. Silence reigned. In the distance, she heard birds, not golf balls cracking.

"Vivian!"

She opened her eyes and turned toward the living room. "I'm in the kitchen, Mom."

"Oh!" Her mother walked into the kitchen and set her purse and a shopping bag down on the table. "Hannah and I had lunch in El Paseo today. That lovely boutique with the caftans was having a sale, and I found a pretty one."

Vivian smiled. "A caftan? You and Dad are never leaving the desert again, are you?"

Joan smiled. "Did I tell you the Lins and the Ryans have already called and made plans to come visit us?"

Vivian loved that her mother was so happy. "You're going to have the vacation house, Mom. Everyone's going to want to come visit. At least in winter."

"Have you and Julia looked at anything exciting?"

She was having a hard time feeling enthusiastic about anything with a threat against a living, breathing person hanging over her head. She cleared her throat. "Uh... yeah. Julia found a new listing that she wants to show me over in her neighborhood. It's a little more expensive, but it's also a bit newer and sounds like it has better storage."

"That's important." Joan walked over and rubbed Vivian's back. "What's wrong with my daughter?"

Vivian's shoulders fell, and she laid her head on her mother's soft shoulder. "Mom."

Joan enveloped her in a hug. "Vivi, what is wrong? This is more than being tired; something is bothering you."

She wanted to spill the whole ugly story, but she didn't know how her parents would take it. What would they say to their daughter becoming psychic? They were both scientists and had never been prone to imagination or fantasy. When she was a child, they handed her biographies of inspirational historical figures, not books with dragons.

Joan rubbed her back. "Tell me what's bothering you? Is it me and Dad? Are we getting to be too much? I was worried about that. You're used to being on your own and—"

"It's not you and Dad." She straightened and grabbed her tea. "I need to sit down. My feet are screaming."

"Let's sit on the couch." Joan rubbed her back. "Tell me what it is. No matter what—don't be afraid of offending me, okay? Just be honest."

Vivian sat in the most offensively plush seat of her sectional sofa, the one that had the built-in footrest. She kicked it up, set her tea next to her on a nesting side table, and felt relief immediately.

Her mom came and sat next to her. "Okay. Spill, young lady."

She huffed out a laugh between rapidly welling tears. "I'm tired of being pregnant. I just want him to get here already."

"I remember that feeling. That's normal."

"And I'm tired of feeling like my body is this... foreign thing." She looked at her belly and her swollen ankles. Her boobs were too big. Her skin was stretched. "I want to be able to play racquetball again. I miss running."

Joan scooted to the edge of the couch and started rubbing Vivian's calves. "You're going to enjoy all those things again with time, but you also need to remember to allow your body time to heal. Too many women push themselves too quickly and suffer for it. Remember, nine months to grow a baby—"

"Nine months to recover."

"And you are staying home your first month. I may be American, but when it comes to this—"

"I know." Vivian took a deep breath, let it out slowly, and managed to stem her tears. Her mother was adamant about a restful first month, both as a doctor and a Chinese mom. "Bernice said she's happy to help with the housework too, so it won't all be on you and Dad."

Bernice—Bernie, she told Vivian—was the nanny Sergio had found for her, and Vivian had hired her after one interview. She was pleased with the woman's credentials and her cheerful and flexible attitude. Bernie was in her thirties and had been a nanny and a night nurse professionally for over ten years with three different families, one of which was Chinese, which was reassuring.

Joan moved from Vivian's calves to her ankles. "Are you sure you don't want me to coach you? I helped Debra with both her deliveries."

And her sister had warned her. "I want you to relax and focus on being a grandma, okay? You don't need to go into doctor mode."

According to her sister, Joan had nearly kicked the midwife out of the hospital room when Debra had her kids.

Joan mused, "I'm sure I'll like the nanny, but I worry that you might feel like I can't help as much because of my health. And I really feel good, Vivian. I promise you—"

"Mom, no." She reached out and squeezed her mother's strong hand. "I do see a few things, but I don't worry because I know that you see them too. You're aware. Bernie will be here to help with day-to-day care, but she's not Henry's grandmother. He only has one of those."

Joan took a deep breath and let it out slowly. "Now I feel like I made myself feel better instead of talking about what's bothering you."

The conversation with Blaine Mitchell weighed on her no matter how much her mother rubbed her ankles. "I got some information that I believe to be accurate." She had to phrase this carefully. "That a person I know casually is in some danger from someone who wants to harm them."

Joan's eyes went wide. "As in physically harm them?"

"Yes."

"Have you told your friend the policeman?"

"John? Yes. But it's not a direct threat, so there's not really anything he can do."

"And have you talked to this person? The one who is in danger?"

"Yes, but I don't know her that well, and honestly, I don't think she believed me."

Joan wrinkled her eyebrows and frowned. "I'm going to

assume that talking to the person who made the threat isn't a good idea."

"Definitely not."

Joan looked up. "How sure are you?"

"It's not... I mean, nothing is definite. I can't read minds, so there's no way I can be certain of any of this." Of course, she wasn't going to share that Evy *could* read minds. She knew that wouldn't go well.

"If you've warned the person in danger and tried to warn the police, then you've done everything you can do," Joan said. "Ultimately, we are all responsible for our own actions and only those. You've tried to warn these people; you can't make them respond correctly."

She nodded. "I know that."

"But I'm sure it doesn't make you feel any better." Joan leaned over and pressed a kiss to Vivian's cheek. "I'm sorry, honey. That's a horrible burden that you don't deserve."

Aaaaand the tears were back. "Thanks, Mom."

"Maybe we should send your friend who's watching the house to watch this person in danger."

She'd completely forgotten about the bodyguard. "Is Andre still outside?"

"I think so. I took him some soup yesterday. And I saw his car at the end of the block when I got home today."

Thank goodness for Andre. "That's a sweet thought, Mom, but I can't do that without her consent. Andre follows people, so if he tried to follow this woman to protect her without her knowing it, she'd probably just think he was the person after her, and knowing the police around here, Andre would get arrested."

"I suppose you're right. You know, I heard... Well, I probably shouldn't tell you that when you're feeling bad." Joan sat back and curled her hands into fists. "But it makes me so mad."

"What?" She turned to watch her mother. "What did you hear?"

"Did you know the police arrested Oscar for that murder? I don't believe it. That couldn't have been Oscar I saw. I would have recognized him."

"I did know—John told me—and I don't believe it either. It's ridiculous to anyone who knows Oscar."

"He's the most helpful person on this entire golf course, and he's a family man. The thought that he could beat someone like that..." Joan shook her head. "No, it's impossible. Steve and Cathy next door? They said they were keeping Oscar in jail. They don't believe it either. Steve said that someone was pressuring the police to make a quick arrest since that Barrett man was so rich."

"He didn't do it, Mom. Don't believe it for a second." Remembering Oscar put some fire back in her chest. "They are going to have to release him when the truth comes out because he did not do it."

Joan nodded. "You're right. They'll get to the bottom of this, and then they'll have to let him go."

Vivian nodded and gripped her mother's hand.

The truth was going to come out because Vivian and her friends were going to find it.

It was a quiet weekend nearly ten days after the Booster Club meeting, and Vivian was starting to breathe easier. Maybe Archie Barrett's murder had scared the conspirators off their plan. Maybe their warning to Blaine Mitchell had worked.

With no social engagements and no appointments, Vivian and Julia toured the midcentury house for a second time. Vivian loved it. It had beautiful light, a secure wall around the house, and an interior courtyard with mature landscaping.

According to Julia, it hadn't gotten much traction in the market because it only had two bedrooms and no space for a pool, but two bedrooms was perfect for Vivian, and not having to worry about a baby and a pool was a relief.

The house was three blocks from Sergio and Dean's if she wanted to swim, and if her sister wanted to visit, she and her family could stay with her mother and father at the golf course house.

Vivian walked around the adorable single-story house and felt a profound sense of peace. "I love it."

"Do you?" Julia was smiling ear to ear. "I figured you were leaning toward it with a second visit."

"I want to put in an offer."

"Are you sure?"

"It's perfect. It's small, but it has enough room for the two of us. It's close to my friends."

"You are two blocks from Michael in that direction." Julia pointed to the right. "And three from Sergio and Dean in the other direction. You really can't find a better location."

She stared out the windows where the tall paloverde trees lined the inside of the wall. "When the weather is nice, I could ride a bike to work. I can open the back door and Henry could have the run of the outside. I could hang a swing in that tree." She pointed at a large one in the corner with a thick, gnarled trunk. "And no cactuses for a toddler to fall into."

"It is a definite consideration around here." Julia nodded. "Also, I have been informed by one of our younger associates with kids that there's a new Montessori preschool starting next year in this area, so Henry's school could be close too."

"That sounds perfect." Vivian's heart felt like it was floating. "Yes. Everything needs to check out with the inspection, and we definitely need to resurface some things—"

"I agree. This carpet should go before you move in. The main bathroom should be redone, and I imagine you'll want all new wall coverings or paint."

"And maybe new countertops in the kitchen. I don't love the

granite, but that could be a long-term project too. It's totally functional right now."

"Excellent." Julia already had her phone out. "I'm going to advise you to go a little lower than what they're asking to account for the floors, but not too low. I don't think it would be a good idea to..." Julia was staring at her phone, and her expression had gone blank.

The sick feeling returned to the pit of Vivian's stomach, sending the happy, peaceful feelings fleeing for the hills. "What is it?"

"Michael texted me." Julia looked up. "They just found Blaine Mitchell's body on the edge of town. She's been shot; no car in sight. They're calling it a carjacking gone wrong."

Chapter Twenty-Three

"The biggest mistake they've made," John Marcos said, "was killing Blaine Mitchell in my jurisdiction." He was behind his desk at the police department, and Vivian, Julia, and Evy were sitting across from him. "You three tried to warn her?"

Evy nodded. "We even went to her office. She didn't believe us."

Julia cleared her throat. "We were hoping... I mean, even if she didn't believe us, we were hoping she might be more careful."

"Her husband told us she was on her way to meet a friend in Indio yesterday afternoon. I guess they meet once a month or so—she was headed to the highway. He said at the last minute, she decided to take a different car, so she grabbed the keys for his. We have no idea why she pulled over."

"What car was it?"

"Her husband's Aston Martin." John looked at Evy. "Dark blue. 1968. It's a collector's item worth around half a million dollars and it's still missing."

"So they want to make it look like it was a theft," Julia said.

"That stealing the car was the point and Blaine Mitchell just got in the way."

"If I hadn't talked to you ladies before this, that is exactly what I would think." John closed a file on his desk. "Whoever did this? They're not dumb."

"Her phone," Evy said. "Did you find her phone?"

"No. We already requested the records from the phone company, but I'm going to guess whoever killed Blaine Mitchell destroyed it; this is clearly a savvy murderer."

"Was the car tracked?" Julia asked. "Did it have any kind of system for the insurance or...?"

"It did, but it appears that the device installed was taken out at the scene and tossed." He pointed to some people in uniforms who were milling around in a conference room next to them. "I called the sheriff's deputy over in Rancho and asked him to come over. I'm trying to make the case that Archie Barrett's murder and this one are related. That'll allow me to open up some investigative channels."

"Do you want us there?"

John took a deep breath in, then let it out slowly. "I don't think so, but I do think the deputy will go for it; the media is already linking the cases."

"They are?" Vivian hadn't even turned on the news. "What are they saying?"

John turned and reached for his remote, flipping on the television screen in the corner. Immediately the sounds of local news filled the office.

"And this morning, confusion and concern in the Coachella Valley as the second prominent individual has died by violent means in a brief period of time. We go now to Chet Alvarez, who is outside the Palm Springs Police Department right now."

Vivian turned and looked at the front door. "Are we going to have to walk through a bunch of news vans when we leave?"

"So far it's just Channel 9." John motioned at the screen. "But listen."

"—weeks ago. At the time, investigators in Rancho Mirage believed that Archibald Barrett III—president and CEO of Barrett Investment Group—had been the victim of a crime of passion, a dispute gone *wrong*. An arrest was made when a local man, Oscar Valero, was found to have had an argument with Mr. Barrett the day of the attack. Witnesses describe Mr. Valero threatening the victim during a charity golf tournament where Mr. Valero was working and Mr. Barrett was participating. Multiple sources confirm that Oscar Valero had no alibi for the time of the attack, which was witnessed by a local resident."

"Oh shit." Vivian got out her phone. "I need to call my mom."

The news presenter continued, "But now questions arise as another prominent resident of Palm Springs is attacked and killed a little over a month later. While this attack bears the marks of a carjacking, others are beginning to ask: Has class warfare in the valley grown to another level, Amy? Are we beginning to see a war against the rich? And does this mean that sheriff's deputies arrested... the wrong man?"

"It's a shocking prospect, Chet." The blond woman on the screen turned to the camera. "This story is changing by the hour, so stay tuned to your Channel 9 in the valley for more coverage of this sudden and vicious crime spree."

Evy blinked. "Class warfare? So we're blaming this on angry poor people now? The fuck?"

"Crime spree," John muttered. "Crime is down twenty-five percent since last year, which was down from the year before, but two rich people die and all of a sudden we have a crime spree."

"At the very least, it sounds like they might be questioning whether Oscar is innocent," Vivian said. "And that's good. Do you think the sheriff's deputy will agree to link the cases? You'll get access to more information then, right?"

"I should, but my focus has to be on Blaine Mitchell's death. I think the car is the key. She changed cars at the last minute, which means whoever killed her wasn't expecting her to be driving an antique. Now, if this was a real carjacking, the thieves would have been prepared. No random carjacker is going to take a piece like that Aston Martin without having a buyer lined up; it's too rare."

"But this wasn't really a carjacking," Julia said. "This was an execution designed to *look* like a carjacking."

Vivian nodded. "Which means that whoever from the Booster Club killed Blaine Mitchell ended up with a rare car they had to take to keep the illusion of a random crime."

John said, "Exactly. None of them are so rich they're going to dump a half-a-million-dollar car in the desert somewhere, so right now I'll bet they're scrambling. They have a car that could lead back to them, but if they dump it, it'll be obvious that the carjacking wasn't the point."

"So we look for the car," Vivian said.

"No." John held up a hand. "*I* look for the car. You three... just lie low and try not to end up on camera. The last thing I want is these people knowing that you three are onto them."

"Probably too late for that," Evy muttered.

"They suspect right now," John said. "But when we start pulling them in for questioning, they're going to get real nervous and even more deadly. Be *careful.*"

"I'M WITH JOHN." RICHARD WAS STANDING BEHIND the grill, turning steaks as Vivian fulfilled her daydream from the other day about lounging in the shade as the sun went down.

"You think the car is the key too?"

"Yes, but I also really hate the idea of you and your friends investigating any of this." He finished turning the meat, closed the grill, and walked over to sit next to her. "I know the tools you have, the empathy and the telepathy, I know they push you toward solving these kinds of problems because the knowledge is there. I know you can't ignore it."

"We tried to warn Blaine, but she didn't believe us."

"It bothers you, and I understand that. But Vivian, the risk to you and Henry—"

"From all accounts, she was a ferocious litigator." Vivian turned to look at him. "But she was also a wife and a mom; she and her husband had been married for forty years. They had three kids; her two daughters were on the TV talking about how much their mom did, how much she'll be missed. Do you know she was the first lawyer in the valley willing to take on sexual harassment suits? Before her, women around here couldn't even find representation."

"I didn't know that."

"She survived a bout of breast cancer last year and still represented three women in a suit against their employers."

Richard put his hand over hers. "She sounds like she was an incredible woman."

"And because her son is a selfish baby with dangerous friends, she's dead." She turned to look at the mountains. "I think West Barrett killed her himself."

"The leader of the pack?" Richard sat back and stretched out his legs. "Why?"

"The first death was meant to look like an accident and it worked. I think Archie Barrett was a mistake; his death was an obvious murder. But I bet they were all supposed to look like accidents. Or random crimes like Blaine Mitchell's death."

"If that was the plan, it's gone very sideways." Richard rose to check the grill. "Now they have one successful hidden murder and two open ones. It's a mess."

"And I bet they're worried. If West is the ringleader, he'd be the one to take the next step and continue the plan. Their conspiracy only works if everyone is equally guilty, and the others might be on the fence at this point."

"I certainly would be." Richard shrugged. "Then again, I don't think I'd ever be part of a murder conspiracy, so I'm probably the wrong person to ask."

"I really think West did it. He's smart, and Blaine taking a different car didn't trip him up."

"You think he has it somewhere?"

"What John said makes sense. None of them are rich enough to toss a half-a-million-dollar vehicle, but now that they have it, what do they do with it? They're going to have to let it be found at some point, but how to do that without arousing suspicion?"

Richard turned off the grill. "I'm calling a halt to murder-conspiracy speculation for now. The steaks are done, and I'm pretty sure I just heard our company arrive."

Vivian turned. "Our company?"

The corner of his mouth was turned up just a little. "Before Maddy shows them back here, I do want to point out that I have asked multiple times to meet your parents."

Vivian's eyes went wide. "Richard, you didn't."

"I ran into your dad today at the butcher shop, and I was thinking of you and dinner tonight. The invitation just popped out."

"It just *popped out*?" Vivian quickly put on her sandals and tried not to look quite so at home in Richard's house when she heard Maddy's voice in the distance. "Dinner invitations are not dental fillings, Rich. They don't just pop out."

He smiled. "Was that dentist humor? I like it. Oh look, your parents are here." He turned and waved. "Allan! So great to see you. Joan, those flowers are exquisite."

Richard walked over while Vivian ungracefully rose from the lounger. She was going to kill him. Dammit, why did she have to like him so much? It was going to make his death much more tragic. "Hey, Mom." She waved weakly across the patio. "Richard just told me you two were coming over."

"It was such a sweet invitation." Joan walked over, and Vivian immediately knew her mother knew exactly what was happening. "I guess your father was complaining that it was his night to cook when they ran into each other at the market, and Richard mentioned he was having company and why didn't we just come over to his house for dinner since there would be so much food?" Joan leaned over and kissed Vivian's cheek. "I like him," she whispered.

"Mm-hmm." Vivian smiled. "I was wondering why he put six pieces of meat on the grill."

Maddy walked over. "Dr. Wei, can I get you a drink? Do you like rosé? I have a really nice rosé that's chilled right now."

"Call me Joan please. There are too many Dr. Weis here. And a glass of rosé sounds perfect."

"Vivian, I'll make your favorite, okay?" Maddy was so happy her dimples were showing.

"She knows your favorite?"

"Mom, don't—"

"I think your father is still clueless, but this does explain the extra flush the past few weeks. I was wondering what put that healthy color in your cheeks."

"Mom." It was like watching a slow-moving train wreck right in front of her.

"Your father said Rich is in his sixties, but he must have good genes. I would have put him in his fifties maximum."

Her mother was already calling him Rich. She was doomed.

"The only thing I'll mention is that when you do get closer to your due date and you feel like moving things along—we all get there, Vivi—sex can be a great way to stimulate—"

"Okay, stop!" She was going to die and also explode at the same time. "No more, Mom. Richard's and my relationship is very new and we're taking it very slow and I'm glad you're meeting him because he has been wanting to meet you for a while, but if you say anything—and I mean anything—to him that implies marriage or fatherhood or any of the happy motherly thoughts that are swirling around in your head right now, I will force you on a plane back to Chicago and there will be *snow.*" She said it in one breath and nearly passed out.

Joan patted her shoulder. "Relax, honey. It's just dinner."

Richard was already pointing out the putting green he'd installed in a corner of the estate. Her father had stars in his eyes, and her mother and Maddy were chatting about teaching.

Vivian was going to kill him.

Chapter Twenty-Four

"How could you do that?" Vivian finally lost it a few minutes after her parents pulled out of the driveway and Maddy had escaped to her cottage. "Without even asking me?"

"You would have put it off until Henry was starting school." Richard was unrepentant. "I already know your father; we've golfed together. If he was anyone else I'd met and liked as much, I would have already asked him and his wife over for dinner weeks ago. Vivian, you're being unreasonable."

"They're my *parents*. You think my mother didn't know exactly what is going on with us?"

"What is going on with us?" Richard crossed his arms. "I'd really like to know. Because I think I've been very up-front that I want a relationship, and you seem to change your mind on a weekly basis."

It stung because it was true.

Vivian spread her arms. "What do you want from me? You want a relationship with a pregnant lady who's about ready to pop, who got hit with weird psychic powers she's still trying to figure out, and who's juggling her parents moving in with her with her mom recovering from a stroke while also trying to buy a house?" Damn it, she was going to start crying and she was mad! "What do you want, Richard?"

"You, Vivian. I want you." He uncrossed his arms and stepped closer. "Do you realize how extraordinary you are? How amazing? Is the timing ideal? No. I know you have a lot on your plate." He leaned down and looked straight into her eyes. "But if you think I'm going to sit back and let you slip away because the timing isn't exactly what you imagined for a new relationship, then you don't understand how I operate."

She felt the tears starting to well up, which just pissed her off, which just made her tear up more.

Fucking hormones!

"It's too much." She managed to talk through the lump in her throat. "Richard, it's..."

He leaned forward and pressed his lips to hers in a kiss that turned from gentle to bruising in a matter of seconds. The usual wall of reserve he kept around his emotions fell away, and she felt all of him. His affection, his worry, his possession, his desire.

Richard's warm hand was on the back of her neck, and the pressure was delicious. His arm wrapped around her, moving their bodies together, and it didn't feel awkward. It never felt awkward with Richard.

Her mouth opened to his, and he tasted like red wine and the chocolate cake he'd served after dinner. From the back of her throat came a frustrated groan when he pulled away.

"If you tell me you don't want me, I'll back off," he whispered against her lips. "But don't lie to me or yourself."

He was putting himself out there. He had to know she would feel every emotion he was projecting at her, but he held nothing back. It was as if he'd stripped himself bare, and Vivian couldn't step away.

"I want you." She wasn't willing to lie. "I do."

"Then take me," he said. "I'm yours if you want me." He met her gaze in challenge. "I'm yours."

How was she supposed to keep from falling for him when he said things like that?

"You know, when I met you, I thought you were buttoned-up."

He toyed with the buttons on the front of her shirtdress. "You thought *I* was the buttoned-up one?" He slipped the top button free.

"Yes." She looked down, and the lace edge of her only bra that still fit peeked out from her dress. "I do want you, but I don't know about this part."

This part was giving her all the nerves.

Richard sat on the arm of the sofa and looked her in the eye. "We don't have to do anything you don't want to do." He leaned forward and pressed his lips to the sensitive skin of her throat, working his mouth down to her collarbone, spreading her shirt wider and slipping another button loose. "But if it's a matter of your feeling self-conscious or anything like that, please know..." His tongue darted out and licked under the edge of her bra. "I find *everything* about you attractive."

"Everything?"

He leaned back and swept his eyes over her body from her toes to the crown of her head. "Yes, really everything. I know your body is changing by the day at this point—which has to be really disorienting—but I cannot stop thinking about sex with you. I feel like a damn teenager. It's bordering on annoying."

"Really?"

He frowned and looked down. "Vivian, your breasts alone are a revelation."

"Okay, you realize they're not going to stay this way, right? I mean, these are not my boobs." She waved at her bust. "And the newly round butt is going to leave eventually too. I'm just warning you."

He smiled. "All the more reason not to waste time."

Were those butterflies in her chest or heartburn? It was impossible to tell, but if he was into it... "Where's your bedroom? When I'm in my normal shape, I'm a huge fan of wall sex, and you're obviously tall and strong enough to do that, but for this attempt, we're going to need pillows."

His eyes switched from amused to turned on in a heartbeat. "Come with me."

Richard took her hand and led her down the hall and back to a bedroom cast in darkness. The sun had set behind the mountains, and a full moon was rising. He closed the curtains to the french doors, switched on a single light and the tile-lined fireplace on the far wall.

"It's new." He motioned to the four-poster bed. "In case you were wondering. I got all new bedroom furniture after I split from my ex-wife."

"I hadn't even thought about her." She wasn't thinking about anything but finally having sex after far too long and also doing it while she was massively pregnant. "Have you ever had sex with an eight-month-pregnant person before?"

He hung his hands casually in his pockets. "I haven't."

"I want to try this. I *really* want to try this, but I feel like we're going to have to be imaginative and probably have a decent sense of humor."

He walked over and reached for her shirt buttons again. "I think our first step is making you more comfortable." He sat on the edge of the bed and worked on the buttons. "I like this dress."

"It fits, and that's about all I can say for it at the moment."

"It's easy access." He spread the top of the dress and cupped her breasts in his large palms. "So gorgeous." Richard leaned forward and laved kisses along the line of her bra, teasing the bottom curve of her breasts with his fingertips.

Vivian braced herself on his shoulders and gave in to the feeling. It had been too long, and she'd felt so disconnected from her body. It was good to feel like a desirable woman again. Good to feel a man hungry for her.

His hands must have been busy while her head swam because she felt the entire dress fall away from her shoulders, and then Richard's hands were everywhere, skimming along the small of her back, tracing the edge of her panties, cupping her bottom. His fingertips teased the juncture of her thighs, and she felt light-headed.

"I need to lie down."

"Okay." He stood, pulled back the covers, and helped her into the tall bed. "Lie on your side," he whispered.

She watched him unbutton his shirt, get impatient, and tug it over his head. Then he unbuttoned his pants, and Vivian could see that he was just as turned on as she was. He was in incredible shape—clearly the running and the golf were keeping things trim. He had a smattering of silver hair on his chest as well as narrow hips and a very impressive erection.

Richard climbed into bed beside her and propped himself on his elbow. "You stay there and let me make you feel good. Are you warm enough?"

"Getting warmer by the minute." She could feel the flush hitting her neck as she imagined him entering her. "Just so you know, it's been a while."

"Me too." He traced a line of kisses down her shoulder and her arm, then slid his hand around her hip, toying with the lace edge of her panties. He whispered against her skin, "Can I take these off?"

"Yes." It was awkward, but they managed. Richard pulled the covers up, which made Vivian a little less self-conscious. She turned her head and met his mouth as his fingers slid between her thighs.

She was so sensitive she gasped.

"Okay?" he asked.

"More than okay." She twisted a little and felt her body come to life. "Richard, it's so good."

He kissed her again and again. He slid his other hand around her back and cradled her against his chest, brushing her breasts with feather-soft touches that primed her entire body to explode.

She felt him hard at her back and pressed into him as she came, his fingers deep in her as her entire body clenched and released in a convulsive wave.

"Oh *God*, that feels good." The release was so intense she nearly cried.

Relief. Euphoria. *Wow*.

She reached behind her and gripped his erection. "From behind," she said. "If I tilt back...?"

"I get it." He kissed her neck, her cheek. "You're fucking gorgeous when you come."

"In me." She could barely speak she wanted him so much. "Richard—"

"Let me—"

"Yes."

He lifted her thigh, maneuvered her body toward his, and slid inside. It felt as easy and natural as if they'd been lovers for years. The feeling of being full of him was delicious.

"Fuck." He pressed his mouth to her neck and scraped his teeth along her skin as he seated himself to the hilt. "Vivian."

"Move." She needed him to move. She felt him deep inside, but there was no pressure on her side. Her body was supported by the thick mattress and Richard's arms.

The friction was exquisite as he moved in her, the heat of his body covering her back and his long arms wrapped around her, teasing her nipples lightly, brushing against her drenched sex.

They had to go slowly, but he didn't seem to mind. It felt lazy and indulgent, like a glass of sweet wine after dinner.

Her second orgasm surprised her in a sudden wave that stole

her breath. Richard gripped her thigh and spread her legs wider as he moved in her, then groaned against her neck when he came.

"Oh fuck." His voice was rough, muffled against her neck. "I forgot to use a condom. I am so sorry. I have not been with anyone since my divorce, so—"

"I can't believe I didn't even think about that." Vivian was still floating, and she was more than a little drowsy. "Well, you can't get me pregnant because I already am, but you have to clean up the mess."

He laughed, and it was verging on giddy. "That's fair."

"I'm clear though." She turned and met his lips in a long kiss. "They do all sorts of tests at the beginning of your pregnancy."

He met her kiss and took it deeper. His kiss felt different now. Wanting. Hungry. Vivian had the distinct feeling that if she'd thought Richard was protective and possessive before, she had no idea what she was in for from now on.

SHE DECIDED TO STAY AND LET HER PARENTS THINK what they wanted. She was too tired to drive and too comfortable to leave Richard's bed.

He left the fire on to chase the chill in the air, gave her one of his button-down shirts to sleep in, and retrieved her panties from across the room.

She was floating in a happy bubble when she asked the question that had been bothering her for months. "Why did you cheat on your ex-wife?"

Vivian blamed it on the orgasms; it was the kind of question you only asked when you were drunk.

Richard's hand paused for a moment; then he returned to petting the side of her thigh. "I would say that I regretted the affair, but it produced Maddy, so I can't regret it too much. Am

I ashamed of myself? Yes. I *was* ashamed. Lily accused me of cheating on her constantly, but the only affair I ever had was with Kiki, Maddy's mother. And it wasn't..." He sighed. "I was depressed. Looking back, I can see that. Lily and I were both depressed. She was pregnant and lost the baby at five months. It was a little boy. We thought we were past the danger period, so we told most of our family. It had been reported in the papers even. It was horrible, and we were both very depressed. Lily started using drugs to zone out, and I had an affair. There's no excuse for it, but in retrospect, I know it was a reaction to the grief."

She reached for his hand and pulled it around her, weaving their fingers together. "I'm sorry about your child, Richard."

"Thank you." His voice was rough. "He would have been just about a year older than Maddy."

The thought of anything happening to Henry nearly made her heart stop, so she could only imagine how difficult it had been for Richard and his ex-wife. "And I'm sorry I brought it up."

"Don't be. If it's been on your mind, I'm glad you asked. I don't make a habit of cheating on romantic partners. It was a shameful lack of self-control."

Yep, that sounded like Richard, and it did set Vivian's mind at ease. She was falling in love with him, and she needed to know.

"Sweet dreams." He pressed a kiss behind her ear. "I like having you in my bed."

And she liked being there. A lot.

Yep, she was in so much trouble.

Chapter Twenty-Five

Evy slid across from her at Dean and Sergio's house. "A little bird told me that you stayed at Richard's last night, and that little bird was Sergio."

A bread roll went flying through the air and caught Evy on the side of the head. "I told you not to tell her!"

Vivian turned to look at Sergio. "Are you spying on us now?"

"I was out for a run and saw your car there." Sergio shrugged. "I apologize for nothing."

"My car was behind a six-foot wall." Vivian pointed at him. "You were spying."

"And you've been hooking up with Richard." Sergio leaned down and kissed her cheek. "You seem a little less stressed today, Dr. Vivian. Why is that, hmm?"

Evy laughed, and Julia shoved Sergio to the side. "Leave her alone."

"Thank you." Vivian's face had to be on fire.

"But tell me everything." Julia scooted her chair closer. "He looks like he's packing—is he packing?"

"I'm not telling you that."

"What use are girlfriends if you can't tell them torrid details of your sex life?"

Evy sighed. "I remember when I had a sex life. Now I'm afraid of hearing men's thoughts, and I'm fairly sure I'll never have sex again."

"Oh yeah, that would be..." Vivian couldn't even imagine that. Emotions were hard enough deal with.

"That's bad," Julia said. "I don't want anyone hearing my thoughts when I have sex."

"They often don't make much sense."

"Right?" Evy waved a hand. "I mean, you could be totally into it and then just randomly wonder, 'Hey, did I remember to pay the power bill?' And it has nothing to do with how good the sex is."

"It could be great," Vivian offered. "Random thoughts are random."

"Exactly," Julia said. "Michael and I were having sex last week and I blurted out something about a water feature in the backyard. I have no idea why."

"Did it throw him off?" Evy asked.

"A little, but we got back into it. It was more of a pause than a throw."

"The real question is," Vivian said, "are you going to install a water feature?"

"I think a wall fountain would be amazing, right? Just behind where the pool is?"

Evy nodded. "Oh yeah, that would look awesome."

"Agree. Good placement."

"I just mean" —Evy raised her voice— "I know random thoughts are random, but I already have a short attention span, and I just feel like I need better mental walls before I attempt sex with a human being."

"Well, definitely don't attempt it with anything else," Julia said. "Just on principle."

"Toys," Vivian said.

"Other than toys." Julia sipped her drink. "What were we talking about before we started on sex?"

"John started questioning the Booster Club today." Vivian was relieved the conversation finally turned from her and Richard. "And Dean said he's coming over."

"Good, otherwise I was going to call him."

A few minutes later, the gate opened and a sensible brown sedan pulled in behind Evy's land shark. John Marcos got out, and he looked exhausted.

"Do you have a life?" Evy asked. "Wife? Girlfriend? Dog? I feel like all you do is work. You're either at work, you're talking about work, or you're about to go to work."

He collapsed into a chair on the patio. "How can I have a life when I have murder conspiracies and three psychics bugging me?"

Dean walked over and handed him a beer. "Golf next week?"

"Please God, yes." John took the beer and drank half of it in one gulp. "I questioned West Barrett today, and I'm pretty sure he's a psychopath."

Vivian, Julia, and Evy all leaned in.

"Because?" Vivian asked. "And before you say more, I will tell you that he's an emotional void other than random shots of intense anger. The man gives my empathy shivers."

"Yep, that sounds about right." He glanced at Evy. "I wish like hell I could have you in an interview room with him."

"I don't know if it would help; he's very hard to read."

John nodded grimly. "That tracks. Cool as a cucumber. Came in with a lawyer of course. Every time I asked him a question, the lawyer asked what possible motive Mr. Barrett could have for wanting Blaine Mitchell dead."

"To pay Trace Mitchell back for whichever one of the murders he committed or is going to commit," Julia said. "Okay, yes, that sounds like fiction."

"Exactly." John sighed. "I hate to think that these assholes have committed the perfect crimes, but it's starting to feel like it. I'm sitting across from West Barrett, and he's practically daring me to say that he killed Blaine Mitchell. He knows I know, and he doesn't care. He knows I can't pin it to him. He was fucking gloating the entire interview."

"Did you bring up his father's murder?"

"Yep. I believe the lawyer said it was a 'tragic coincidence.' And the thing is, I can't argue with him. On the surface, there's nothing that links the two crimes. Not the means, not a possible motive, nothing."

"Ashley Gates's father, then West Barrett's dad, then Trace Mitchell's mother?" Vivian asked. "All die roughly a month apart and it's a coincidence?"

"The pattern is there, but we have no evidence. As far as Fisher Gates goes, that's been ruled natural causes, and officially Oscar Valero has been arrested for Archie Barrett's death, though I'm really working on the sheriff with that one."

"Thank you." Vivian's heart still felt heavy.

Julia nodded. "So in addition to saying these deaths are only a tragic coincidence, they can blame Archie Barrett's murder on another suspect and there's still no evidence that Fisher Gates was murdered." She glanced to the side. "Mr. Gates, ghosts cannot testify in a court of law! Please calm down."

John glanced to the empty corner where Julia was speaking, then looked back at them. "Which leaves Blaine Mitchell's murder exactly where they wanted people to see it, as a tragic but random street crime."

"Fuck." Evy sighed. "What about the car?"

"The car is my one glimmer of hope. It's the only loose end that I might be able to tug, but I've called every storage place in the valley and I can tell you that none of them—West, Trace, Ashley, Trent, or Pippa—have a storage unit in their name. Could they have one listed under a shell corporation or a business name we don't know about? Yes. Could they own a fucking house and be stashing the car there? Also yes."

"What about a search warrant for their financial stuff?" Julia asked.

"No judge is going to grant a search warrant with the evidence we have." John shook his head. "It won't happen."

Vivian was racking her brain, trying to figure out anything that might shake loose. "John, have you questioned all five of them?"

"No, just Trace and West so far."

"What about the women? You went to school with this whole crowd, right? What do you think about Pippa and Ashley?"

John shook his head. "I only know them a little."

"Pippa or Ashley?" Vivian said. "Who's the weaker link?"

It only took him a moment. "Ashley. Her parents babied her. Pippa is Judge Stanford's daughter, and she'd probably stand up to CIA torture having been raised by that man."

"Ashley Gates and Trent Everett," Vivian said. "On the surface, you have no reason to question either of them. What do you need?"

John huffed. "At this point? A confession. If they're anything like West or Trace, they're not going to give the police the time of day without a fancy lawyer slapping us down."

"They're not going to confess," Vivian said. "But... maybe we can make them nervous and trip them up." She looked at Julia and Evy. "Are you thinking what I am?"

"Some variation of the witches in Macbeth," Evy said. "Excellent. I'll put my theater skills to good use."

MICHAEL DROVE IN FROM LA JUST AS DINNER WAS wrapping up, so he offered to take Vivian home. She climbed in the front seat while Julia sat in the back of the SUV with a large brass-studded wood frame that looked like something off a sailing ship.

"What is it again?" Julia struggled to buckle her seat belt. "A saddle?"

"An antique camel saddle from Mongolia," Michael said. "A director I worked with about six years ago gave it to me when I was making that historical epic, and it's been in storage at a friend's house ever since. But his mom is moving in with them and they need the space, so he told me to come get it."

Yes, it smelled like camel. Vivian's nose twitched. "It's really... unique."

"Thanks. I was thinking if it got cleaned up and refinished a little bit, with the right glass top it could make a really cool coffee table."

"That's... I mean, it's a good idea." Vivian looked over her shoulder to check on Julia, who was looking skeptical. "Where are you going to put it?"

"For now I was going to swing by my hangar and put it there. I know a guy who has a wood shop at the airport and he does custom work."

"At the airport?"

Julia piped up. "A lot of the renters at the municipal airport just use the hangars like very big garages. Some of them don't even have planes." The car went over a bump. "Ouch."

"You okay?" Michael checked the rearview mirror. "How you doing, Jules?"

"I'm fine." Julia's voice was muffled by the large hump that bridged the two brass-studded frames. "My boyfriend is an interesting and internationally traveled individual with very eclectic friends."

"I love and appreciate your understanding." Michael was clearly trying not to laugh. "I promise, by the time Ed finishes with it, you're going to think it's really cool."

They pulled into the residents' entrance and swiped the key card to let themselves in. Michael drove the car past a line of featureless grey industrial buildings that looked like large warehouses.

"These are hangars?"

"Yep." Michael pointed to the third row of warehouses. "I have two units down this lane. One for the plane and my other cars, one for my stuff."

"He has a lot of stuff," Julia said.

"And it's all very cool."

"Someday he's going to have the mother of all garage sales."

"Stop trying to get rid of my stuff," Michael said. "It's cool stuff."

"Honey, you have over twenty rugs and you only have six rooms in your house."

"Oh!" Vivian turned to Michael. "Julia and I put an offer in on that little place a block over from yours."

"That sweet midcentury place at the end of the cul-de-sac?" he asked. "It looks cool; I hope you get it. Do you want a rug?"

"Maybe."

"See?" Michael looked in the rearview mirror as he brought the SUV to a stop. "Vivian is going to need rugs for her new house. Aren't you glad I have extra?"

There were small mailboxes near the doors to each large hangar, and all of them had names and numbers on them.

As they drove by, a name flashed out from the darkness.

Everett.

"Everett?" Vivian thought about Trent Everett, the golf pro. Everett wasn't exactly an unusual name, but something tickled her memory.

Played a lot of sports, I guess that was his claim to fame. Had a lot of expensive hobbies. His dad flies planes—I think he does too —but golf is Trent's thing...

"Michael, do the Everetts have a hangar out here?"

"Jack Everett, the military movie consultant?" Michael nodded. "Oh yeah. I haven't seen old Jack out in ages though; I worked with him on a couple of projects in my blockbuster phase. I don't think he flies anymore—he's getting up there. I see his kid every now and then."

"His kid Trent Everett?"

"I think that's his name. He and his buddies come out drinking on the weekends sometimes. Watch the planes come in and take off. Drive around the place in Mercedes golf carts and slum it with the working folks. They're a bunch of pricks; everyone hates them."

"Do they fly?"

"Not that I know of." Michael pulled up to the door with O'Connell on the mailbox. "They're probably like me. Use it for storage."

You could store all kinds of things in a plane hangar. Vivian watched Michael hop out of the car and raise the massive front door that was at least sixty feet across. The whole of the metal mechanism lifted up and back like a giant garage door, revealing a somewhat organized maze of boxes, chests, and shelves.

Vivian turned to Julia as Michael walked inside to turn on the lights. "Hey, Julia."

"Yeah?"

"Are you thinking what I'm thinking?"

"Are you thinking that a plane hangar at Palm Springs Municipal Airport is a great place to stash an antique car that you pretended to steal so you could murder your friend's mother?"

"Yep. Pretty much."

"Then yes." Julia poked her head over the camel saddle. "We're thinking the same thing."

Chapter Twenty-Six

They waited and debated for over a week, but in the end, they picked Ashley Gates instead of Trent because it was easier for the three of them to snoop on a woman. The investigation was stalled, and John wasn't making any progress prying information out of the Booster Club.

Despite Michael's, Dean's, and Richard's protestations, Vivian, Evy, and Julia decided they needed to spook the conspirators into action.

Julia made a few calls and found out where Ashley Gates had her facial work done. It was an exclusive spa in the middle of the desert that dated back to the 1950s. There were natural hot springs, mud baths, and a top-of-the-line treatment center for aging skin. It wasn't hard to obtain a day pass for the hot springs, so they went a few days later.

Ashley Gates-Bradley might have married into big bucks, but she didn't come from old money. Vivian suspected there was some insecurity there. Vivian had numerous patients in that social circle, and her impression was that most women thought they needed to keep up their youthful looks to keep their husband's interest.

After a certain age, that wasn't going to happen without surgical or chemical intervention.

Vivian, Julia, and Evy all wore the spa's long robes as they strode across the lush grounds of the estate turned day spa. Numerous groups of girlfriends just like them gathered on the grounds, wearing face masks in the shade, sipping green concoctions, or blind from cucumber slices.

Julia watched a group of women a little older than they were as the friends laughed under a clump of palms. "Where do we draw the line between taking care of ourselves and allowing age to happen naturally? Like, I want to take care of my skin, but at what point is it... too much?"

Vivian smiled. "That's the question, isn't it?"

"I don't have the money to grow old as gracefully as these women," Evy said. "Gotta depend on good genes."

"Also a good point," Vivian asked. "So do we know where Ashley Gates is?"

"According to my source—remember Serena?"

"Justin Worthy's ex-girlfriend?"

Julia nodded. "She works here now, and I followed her because I love her facials. She told me that Ashley Gates is getting a microneedling treatment in the Desert Casita."

"Will she be alone?"

"For a good part of it, yes. If we wait outside..." They paused to let a group of older women walk by. All of them were sipping various colored juices. "If we wait outside, we should be able to ambush her."

"While she's naked," Evy said.

"I feel weird about ambushing this woman." Vivian was feeling doubly exposed. They hadn't had maternity robes available, so she was wearing a pair of loose yoga pants under her spa wrap and it kept slipping open over her belly, revealing her stretched skin to the world. "Something about this is really bothering me."

"Vivian, this is not a good person whose privacy we're violating," Julia whispered as they drew closer to the group of private bungalows that could be reserved for spa treatments. "This woman is part of a murder conspiracy that's already killed three people."

"You're right." She needed to get over it. "So we're upping the spooky as much as possible, right?"

Evy jumped in. "I'm the best actress, so just follow my lead. If you feel unsure of anything, just stare at her silently. Silent staring makes innocent people nervous. Someone with a guilty conscience? Her imagination will fill in the blanks."

They perched on three chairs next to a burbling fountain, and Julia kept her eyes on the casita. "Serena said she was working with someone called Eddie today. I don't know if that's a girl or a guy, so we just have to wait."

They waited while a chorus of birds chirped overhead and the fountain tumbled. Vivian had her feet up on a chaise, and the morning was finally cool.

She was drifting off to sleep when Julia said, "I think that's Eddie."

A young man with sandy-blond hair strolled up the walkway from the casita, whistling as he put a pair of sunglasses over his eyes. He adjusted his belt as he walked. As he passed, he spotted Julia, Evy, and Vivian.

"Ladies." His smile was intended to be charming, but something about it made Vivian's skin crawl. The name tag on his shirt said EDWARD.

Evy waited for him to pass. "Did you notice the belt? I wonder if Ashley Gates is getting a treatment that's not on the public spa menu."

"All I'm going to say is that if she is, *microneedling* just got a whole other level of meaning, and it's not one that Eddie should be flattered by." Julia rose. "Ladies?"

Evy held out her hand and helped Vivian to her feet. As

quickly as they could, they walked to the side door of the bungalow where Eddie had exited.

Julia tried the door, nodded, and pushed it open. A curtain blocked everything from view. As Vivian pushed it out of her way, she heard a drowsy voice coming from the room past the window.

"Eddie, did you forget something?"

None of them said a word. Evy looked at both of them, put a finger over her lips, and nodded toward the treatment room.

"We're not Eddie." Her voice was low and ominous. "And don't bother screaming, Ashley Gates." Evy stepped through the doorway into a dimly lit room. "Not unless you want us to tell them everything."

Ashley sat up on the massage table, clutching a sheet to her chest. She was naked under the loose linen. "Who are you?"

"People who know." Evy kept her voice soft. "We know, Ashley. We know about your father. About Trace's mother. About West's father."

Vivian stared at Ashley, pushing down her discomfort. "We know everything."

Sheer panic was radiating from Ashley Gates, but it was hard to tell if it was from what Evy was saying or the fact that three strange women had barged in on her spa treatment when she was naked on a table.

"Your father has spoken to me," Julia said. "His voice haunts me. We know about the poison. We know about the money."

"We know about the car," Vivian said. "We know the hiding place, Ashley."

The color drained from Ashley Gates's face. "Get out of here right now."

Evy leaned toward her. "Do you want your friends knowing your secrets, Ashley? How do you think everyone at the club would react if we told them about the pact?"

The woman started shaking. "There isn't a— Who told you about that? Was it Trent?"

"I told you," Julia continued. "Your father told me everything." She let the silence linger. "Everything."

"What do you want?" Ashley's voice took on a note of hysteria. "You don't know anything!"

"Keep telling yourself that if it makes you feel better." Evy motioned them backward with a hand. "Keep believing it yourself if you want."

Julia and Vivian flanked Evy, both of them staring at the naked woman alone in the dark.

"But we know the truth," Vivian said.

"Remember, Ashley Gates." Evy's voice gave Vivian chills. "A secret only stays a secret…"

Ashley held her breath.

"…if everyone else is dead."

The woman's face was paler than the sheet covering her. "Get out."

"You know what they're capable of." Julia sank back into the shadowed anteroom. "Don't wait for them to hurt you; go to the police now."

Evy backed up even more, pushing Vivian and Julia behind the curtain. "Go before it's too late."

As Evy stepped backward out of the french doors, she shut them behind her, leaving a remnant of the curtain fluttering in the breeze. She motioned Vivian and Julia up the path, following them at a good clip.

"We need to get out of here before she reports us," Julia said. "I don't want Serena to get in trouble."

"She's not going to report us." Evy glanced over her shoulder. "Did you see her? Right now that woman is pissing herself. I couldn't read her thoughts though. Too jumbled. I did get something about the car and lots of impressions of her father."

"She felt guilty every time you mentioned him," Vivian said. "She could definitely be the weak link."

"I say we call John Marcos as soon as we get to the car," Julia said.

They hustled past the pool, the thermal pools, and the mud baths. Vivian felt a small foot pushing against her bladder. "Just letting you know if I don't find a bathroom soon, Ashley Gates won't be the only one peeing her pants."

"'WE KNOW ABOUT THE CAR,'" JULIA SAID AS SHE drove to Vivian's house. "Do you think it's enough? Should we have mentioned the car more?"

"I think it was just right," Vivian said.

Evy said, "Wherever that car is, Ashley getting that warning is going to mean they have to move it. And if Vivian's right—"

"I would still bet you anything that missing Aston Martin is at the airport." Vivian noticed Andre's car sitting in its usual spot as they pulled into her driveway. "I can't read minds, but—"

"I can," Evy said. "Sadly, there wasn't much that made sense. She wasn't thinking clearly."

Julia brought the car to a stop in front of the driveway gate. "Michael said the security cameras by the airport's resident gate are ancient and everyone knows where the security room is, so they've probably already stolen any evidence that the car drove in."

Evy said, "If they move it again, they're going to have to hide it again."

"But honestly? It probably wouldn't be hard," Julia said. "There is a guard, but the one time we went through the gate really late, he was sleeping. I doubt he'd wake up if the gate opened."

"And if the security system is that old," Evy said, "it might even tape over itself."

Julia nodded. "I admit it, Vivian, I didn't think your theory held that much water at first, but I'm starting to change my mind."

"Where else could they have hidden it?" Vivian asked. "One of their own garages? It's far more likely that it's at a private airport instead of at one of their houses where a million security systems and doorbell cameras might capture them bringing it in."

"Oh!" Evy's eyes went wide. "I hadn't even thought about doorbell cameras."

"Every neighborhood the members of the Booster Club live in is packed to the gills with security cameras, guards, and prying eyes," Vivian said. "Even public storage places have recording equipment."

"But the airport has one guard and a security room on the site." Julia's face was grim. "We need to call John."

Vivian pulled a remote control from her purse and opened the driveway gate so Julia could pull her car in. She felt her phone buzz in her pocket, grabbed it, and saw a message from her mother.

Are you almost home?

Just pulled in, she typed back. "Hey guys, I need to go inside. I think my mom needs something." Why was her mother texting her? She hated texting. "I hope she's not stuck in the bathroom or something." She had a sudden vision of her mother fallen somewhere and rushed to the door. "Mom?"

Evy and Julia followed her into the house, but there was no sign of her mother in the living room or kitchen. "Mom?" she called again, starting to panic.

"In the back."

Vivian walked to the kitchen and looked out the sliding doors, only to have her heart nearly stop in her chest.

West Barrett was in her backyard.

She walked to the back, sliding back the screen door, never taking her eyes off West. A cold wave of malevolence enveloped the backyard. It was so potent Vivian half expected the plants around the patio to start wilting. "Mr. Barrett, this is a surprise."

"I was just chatting with your mother." West pointed over the fence. "I spotted her from the thirteenth tee and thought she looked familiar."

Joan looked up, and Vivian felt her discomfort. It was bordering on fear. "West said he was a friend of yours."

And since he'd come in from the golf course, there was no way that Andre would have seen him. She felt Julia and Evy at her back. "West, I see my mother got you some tea."

The steaming cup on the patio table must have been Joan's opportunity to text Vivian.

"She did." West was wearing sunglasses, and his legs were stretched out. Clearly he'd made himself at home. "Beautiful spot here. Such a shame that your mother had to witness something so violent the night my father died."

Vivian sat across from him, keeping her eyes trained on the sociopath who felt like an emotional vacuum. "How is your family? How are your kids?"

"My father was never very involved in my children's lives," West said. "Unlike your family." He glanced at Joan. "I'm sure if anything happened to your parents, it would be a tragedy."

Joan's grip tightened on her armrest. "Mr. Barrett—"

Whatever Joan was going to say, it was interrupted by the doorbell.

Vivian glanced at Evy, who held up her phone and mouthed, *Andre.*

Joan rose. "I supposed I'd better get the door." She looked at West. "If you could excuse me for a moment."

"Of course." West hadn't taken his eyes off Vivian. "So when are you due?"

Joan was out of earshot when Vivian responded. "None of your business. Stay away from my parents."

"Or?" West sipped his tea.

"Accidents happen." Vivian felt like stabbing the man with the gardening clippers sitting on the potting bench. "You know that better than anyone. I heard the police had some questions for you the other day."

"Ridiculous speculation." West smiled. "And a threat from Dr. Wei. That's entertaining."

"Is it?"

"Miss Joan!" A booming male voice echoed from the front door. "I hope you don't mind my interrupting your afternoon, ma'am." A massive Black man the size of a linebacker suddenly filled the patio doors. "And Miss Vivian too. I've been meaning to come by and I got you both." He looked at West. "Good timing, I guess."

"Andre." Vivian smiled. "It's good to see you."

"I was just returning some of your mother's dishes." His eyes never left West Barrett. "You know me, Miss Vivian. My friends take care of me; I'm always going to return the favor."

"And we appreciate that." Vivian looked at West. "I believe Mr. Barrett has a golf game to return to. We don't want to keep you."

"Of course not." West rose from his seat and picked up his tea, taking one last sip before he let the delicate teacup slip from his fingers and shatter on the tiled patio. "Oh dear."

"Don't worry about it," Vivian said. "It's just a teacup."

"Fragile things are so easily damaged." West looked at Andre, spared a glance at Evy and Julia, then looked back at Vivian. "Dr. Wei."

"West." Vivian frowned. "Or do you go by Junior? I wasn't entirely clear on that."

His smile didn't falter, but a muscle under his eye twitched. "I'll be seeing you."

"I'll be watching."

Her eyes followed West as he walked up the pathway leading to the golf course. He opened the gate and left it swinging behind him as he walked toward the cart path.

Andre was at her elbow in seconds. "Vivian, I apologize. I was watching the front and didn't even consider golf course access. I'll get another man over here within the hour."

"Don't worry about it." She put a hand on Andre's arm. "It's not your fault. He's getting bolder. He thinks the police can't touch him, but he's wrong."

"I'm calling Sergio and Dean," Julia said. "How would your parents feel about a sleepover?"

"Richard already offered," Vivian said. "I'll call him right now."

Evy held up her phone. "And I just got off the phone with John Marcos. They're staking out the airport gate."

"When?" Vivian wanted West Barrett locked up. The sooner the better.

"Tonight. I told him we spooked Ashley today," Evy said. "After he got finished yelling at me, he said they'd be out there tonight. If we scared Ashley at all, she'll have called the others. They're not the kind to wait."

Chapter Twenty-Seven

Michael insisted on waiting with them on the back road leading to the airport gate even though Julia warned him they could be there all night.

Vivian sat in the back of Michael's Land Cruiser, drifting in and out of sleep. She was exhausted, her feet were swollen, but there was no way she was sending her friends on a stakeout without her.

"If the police don't stop them, we're going to have to follow them," Julia said.

Michael turned looked over his shoulder at Vivian and Evy in the back of the car. "Absolutely not."

"We can't let him get away with evidence." Julia gestured at the airport. "What if he knows a back road? What if the police give up? What if—?"

"What if Vivian goes into labor while we're chasing down a murderer?" Michael asked. "There are risks I am willing to take with my girlfriend and her two best friends, and there are risks I am not willing to take. Besides, Richard would absolutely kill me if I took Vivian on a car chase."

"Excuse me?" Vivian roused herself at the sound of her

name. "Richard is..." Her mouth stretched in a yawn. "...not my father."

"The only reason he's not here is that you asked him to take care of *your* father and mother," Michael said. "He is about as thrilled with this idea as I am."

"Will all of you shut up?" Evy groaned. "There are too many people in this car." She opened the door. "Too many brains."

She opened the door, slammed it shut, and walked to the back to lean against the rear doors.

"She's tense," Julia said. "I don't think the lessons with Maud are working very well."

"Can you imagine hearing people's thoughts?" Vivian asked. "Feeling their emotions is bad enough, but I can honestly say that's not a huge surprise. Whatever Aunt Marie did to me, I think she just unlocked something I'd always understood by intuition."

"So you were always an empathetic person?" Michael asked. "You just got more?"

"Exactly." Vivian looked at Evy through the window. "But actually reading minds? That's a whole other level. I cannot imagine the stress."

"I confess, I've kind of gotten used to the ghosts," Julia said. "I think I might actually get bored if they suddenly disappear."

"I wouldn't," Michael muttered. "It's been really confusing to try to figure out if you're talking to me or a murdered old guy over the past couple of months."

"I'm hoping that Mr. Gates does take off once his murderer is in jail." Julia yawned. "I'm with you on that one."

Vivian had been staring at the airport and started when she saw lights. She sat up and pressed her nose to the glass. "What's that?"

Michael rolled down the window and said, "Hey, Lane. Get in the car. Stuff's happening."

Evy rushed over and jumped in the seat behind Michael,

who started the car and inched forward as faint lights moved in the distance.

"We can't get too close," Vivian said. "John said they would have two cars watching the gate."

Michael frowned. "Which gate?"

Vivian blinked. "What do you mean, which gate?"

"Well, there's the residents' gate and then the guest gate at the front of the airport over by the main entrance."

"No one told us that," Julia said. "John's probably watching the residents' gate because that's the one we mentioned to him."

Michael frowned. "Well... that's probably the one he'll use anyway."

"Probably?"

A low-slung black vehicle was moving along the line of hangars, heading toward the gate where a yellow light flickered over the guardhouse. Michael kept the car in gear, his foot on the brake, as a dark sports car approached the exit.

"Is that it?"

"What other car could it be?" Julia asked. "How many people are driving around vintage cars at three in the morning?"

Michael inched forward, his lights turned off.

"Is it safe to drive without light?" Vivian asked.

"If we start driving, I'm going to have to turn them on, but for now I think we can assume that everyone else would have theirs on, so we'll at least see if any other cars are coming." Michael crept forward a little more, edging the Land Cruiser toward the road. "He's heading toward the gate."

"I don't see any police cars," Vivian said. "But that's definitely a black or dark blue car."

Michael pulled onto the road, still moving slowly with his lights off. He leaned forward with a frown creasing his eyebrows. "What make did you say the stolen car was?"

"An Aston Martin," Julia said.

"I don't remember the exact year," Evy said, "but I think

Michael is noticing what I am." Evy leaned forward, poking her head between the front seats. "That's a dark vintage car, but it is *not* an Aston Martin."

"I think it's a Jaguar," Michael said. "Same era, similar coloring, but not an Aston."

"The profile is pretty close," Evy said, "but the front end is wrong." She leaned back. "That's not the right car."

Just as she leaned back, the car drove through the gate, and two red and blue lights flashed in the distance.

"Dammit," Julia said. "They're pulling over the wrong car."

"Because it's the wrong gate." Vivian blinked. "Michael, where does the other gate leave the airport?"

He didn't wait to answer but flipped on the lights, spun a U-turn, and headed in the opposite direction.

"They sent one car out the obvious exit," Julia said. "The real one is leaving from the public entrance."

"West Barrett is too careful to do the obvious thing," Vivian said.

Michael pushed down the gas. "One of you better be calling John Marcos right now."

"Just find the gate," Julia said. "Evy will call John."

"Why do you all assume I have the man's number on speed dial?" Evy said.

"Because you kind of have the hots for him," Julia said. "We noticed."

"I do not!"

Vivian said, "He's interested in you, so it would make sense."

"Wait, he is?" Evy's voice softened.

"Evy, call the police!" Michael was definitely not in the mood for chatting. "Talk about your love lives when we are not chasing a murderer." He cursed under his breath. "Richard warned me this was going to happen."

He ran a red light at the empty intersection, turning left onto the road leading to the front of the municipal airport.

There was a line of old fighter jets between palms and multiple signs advertising an old-time diner.

There were no cars visible on the road, but just as they approached the entrance, a moving van with dark sides pulled up to the light.

Michael turned left into the airport, and Vivian caught sight of the driver in the dim streetlights.

"It's West!" She pointed at the truck. "West Barrett was driving that truck. He's moving the Aston Martin in the truck!"

Evy was speaking into her phone. "No, we're at the front of the... Yeah, I know it's not the right car, John! That's what I'm trying to tell you. West Barrett is pulling a moving van out of the front of the airport right now. The car is in the truck."

"We're following him!" Julia shouted. "Michael, follow him."

"I'm trying." Michael turned and jumped the Land Cruiser over the median, rolling over the landscaping as he tried to follow the truck. "Tell John he better not give me a fucking ticket."

"We're following the truck; it just turned south on El Cielo," Evy said. "Come find us because it's West Barrett driving this truck." Evy covered her phone. "It was Trent Everett in the Jaguar. Claimed it belonged to a friend and he was just storing it."

"Is John coming?" Vivian leaned toward the center. Michael had caught up with the truck but was following it at a distance as it headed south.

"He's turning on Ramon Road," Michael said. "Probably headed toward the highway."

It was three in the morning, and the truck had little use for traffic lights. It slowed down before each intersection but blew through lights as soon as the driver determined they were clear.

Vivian felt the nervous energy bouncing around the car, and

it made her a little nauseated. "If everyone could just calm down, I'd appreciate it."

"I'm following a murderer," Michael muttered. "I am literally in a car chase with a man who's probably responsible for three deaths. Does that make him a serial killer? Fuck, Richard is going to kill me. This can't be legal."

"Michael, you're making me stressed out," Vivian said. "Just keep West in your sights and wait for John to catch up with us. He's got to be on the way by now."

The driver of the truck must have been feeling something similar because just after the Los Alamos turnoff, the moving truck swung to the right down a dusty dirt road before it reached the highway.

Michael was barely able to follow it, but as the truck moved away from the streetlights, it abruptly stopped in a massive cloud of dust. All the lights shut off, and as Michael's car approached the stopped truck, a figure in black emerged from the billowing dust with a ski mask over his face and a gun pointed at the Land Cruiser.

"Gun!" Michael shouted. "Get down!"

Evy was shouting on the phone. "John, he pulled off the road and he has a gun!"

Vivian screamed when a shot went off.

Michael spun the car around to face the main road, hit the emergency lights, and reached in the center console to pull a black pistol from the compartment. "Stay down," he shouted. "Do not pop your head out of this car no matter what."

"You have a gun?" Julia shouted. "When did you get a—?"

"I told you to stay down!"

"John's coming!" Evy said.

Not fast enough. Vivian felt her heart racing, and her abdomen clenched. It wouldn't be fast enough. Michael was going to get hurt, and it would be their fault.

Vivian tried to grab for him, but he was out of reach.

Michael cracked the door open as another shot rang out, and something struck the vehicle. "Barrett, you bastard, it's Mick O'Connor and I've got a nine millimeter!" Michael edged along the side of the Land Cruiser. "Put the gun down; the police are already on the way."

Silence.

Would his bravado work?

Michael waited, but no sound came back. "I swear to God, if you fire on my car, I *will* fire back. That gun better be on the ground."

Vivian heard nothing outside the car but the sound of wind and the faint and glorious echo of police sirens in the distance.

Michael stayed outside shouting threats, his gun drawn, but no more shots rang out.

Chapter Twenty-Eight

"I ran out of interview rooms; can you believe it?" John sat across from Vivian in the break room while Michael and Julia gave statements to an officer and Evy crashed on the small couch. He slid a paper cup toward her. "Herbal tea. I didn't know if you're drinking caffeine or not."

"Not much, and at this time of the night, it would probably just make me sick."

"How you doing otherwise?"

Vivian shrugged. "I'm okay. Not loving my track record of having guns pointed at me in Palm Springs, I can tell you that."

"I'm not loving that either, but I can't seem to stop you ladies. You talk to your parents yet?"

"I talked to Richard and filled him in. My parents are staying at his place since West came to our house yesterday afternoon. They're fine; hopefully back to sleep now. Though knowing my mother, she'll be up for the next three nights on principle."

"Barrett's claiming—well, his lawyer is claiming—that was a *friendly* visit to your house."

"It wasn't. It was a threat." She sipped the herbal tea. "Thanks. So how is he trying to explain firing on Michael's car?"

"He's trying to convince us that he thought you were the same carjackers who shot Blaine Mitchell trying to get him too. Said as soon as he realized it was Michael, he put the gun down and waited for the police."

"So it was all a big misunderstanding?"

"That's what the fancy lawyer says." John raised an eyebrow. "He hasn't explained the car yet."

"I was wondering about that."

They'd all been taken to the police department in different cars, some as witnesses, some as suspects—including Michael, though his gun and carry license checked out—and all exhausted.

It had been hours, and Vivian watched as, one by one, the members of the Booster Club trickled in. First West Barrett and Trent Everett from the airport, then Ashley Gates, Trace Mitchell, and Pippa Stanford.

John looked as exhausted as Vivian felt.

"I'd love to be in those interview rooms," she said. "Ashley Gates is the weak link."

"She may be—she's certainly crying enough for it—but I have a feeling that Pippa Stanford is going to be the key."

Vivian raised an eyebrow. "Pippa?"

"She's a judge's daughter, remember? She knows how the system works." John stretched his arms over his head. "She who snitches first gets the best deal from the DA."

Vivian nodded slowly. "Right." She took a deep breath. "So at least one of them is going to get away with it."

"There are five of them and three people dead. If your theory is correct, that means two of them never killed anyone. I'd bet money that Pippa has kept her hands clean and her father is still alive. No murder on her hands, no parent dead. That makes her the likeliest candidate for a deal."

"I know you're right, but it still feels wrong." Vivian shook her head. "I've met both of them; Pippa was cold as ice. I think Ashley actually feels some guilt."

"You think it feels wrong to you?" John rose. "Imagine being Pippa Stanford's parents right now, bailing their daughter out when they know she was probably plotting to kill one of them."

Vivian stretched her arms up and felt her sides twinge. "That's going to make for an awkward holiday season."

"Ashley might get a deal too. Her lawyer keeps trying to shut her up, but she keeps talking. According to her, she thought it was a joke. It was all supposed to be a big joke. Then her father died and she didn't know what to do. She felt trapped. She's talking around real details, but it's obvious she wants to save her skin."

"Does she know who killed her father?"

"She's not saying yet, but she suspects it was some kind of poison, like you ladies thought. She says she doesn't know for sure."

Vivian felt nothing but disdain. "How do you even…? She thought it was a *joke*?"

"Again, her lawyer kept trying to talk over her, but it sounds like they were all in a meeting last fall before school started and every one of them started bitching about their parents. How they were too controlling, wouldn't give up the reins on the family businesses, were spending all the family money on themselves, and so forth."

"So they deserved to die?" Vivian shook her head. "Horrible people. Is Oscar out of jail yet?"

"In the process," John said. "I already called the sheriff's office and let them know what was going down."

"West Barrett killed Blaine Mitchell, didn't he?"

"I suspect that's going to be what we find because I can't see Ashley or Pippa pulling the trigger, and I suspect it was Trent Everett who killed Archie Barrett. He's the strongest of the three, and that was a very violent attack."

Vivian nodded. "That makes sense to me. You found the Aston Martin in the moving truck, right?"

John nodded. "The truck was rented in the name of West Barrett's gardener. Poor guy probably had no idea what was going on. I suspect they were going to go dump the car in the desert. They may not have liked to lose a car that valuable, but at the end of the day, it was too much of a liability."

"She was never supposed to take the Aston Martin," Vivian said. "She was supposed to take the Mercedes that was like a hundred other cars in the valley."

"Exactly." The corner of his mouth turned up. "You know, Blaine Mitchell did pay attention to your warning. She took a different car. Probably thought if anyone was aiming for her, they'd be looking for her personal vehicle."

"And if she'd taken that one, the Booster Club probably would have gotten away with her murder."

"More than likely, they had a plan in place to get rid of a newish Mercedes, not an antique Aston Martin." John reached over and patted her hand. "Her taking that car pointed right at them in the end. At least, in a small way, your warning worked."

"She's still dead." And Vivian was exhausted. "When can we go home?"

"Soon."

VIVIAN WOKE UP IN RICHARD'S BEDROOM. SHE HADN'T had the energy the night before to make it up to the second floor of his house, and the other guest room on the first floor was occupied by her parents.

They could think what they wanted to think.

She rolled over to see Richard watching the television in the corner, which was flashing subtitles as pictures of the Booster

Club filled the screen and animated news journalists stood in front of the Palm Springs Police Department.

"Hey." He smiled and reached over to smooth her hair back from her forehead. "How are you feeling?"

"Exhausted, but better now that West Barrett looks like he's being arrested."

"I wish it moved that fast, but right now they're still just saying that they're being questioned." Richard nodded at the TV. "The one name they're not mentioning much is Pippa Stanford. I think she's probably the one cutting a deal."

"John thought that was going to happen."

Richard shook his head and took a deep breath. "You know, my father passed when I was in my forties. Heart attack, very sudden." He shifted lower in bed so he could put his arm around her. "I would give anything to have another day with him. Even another hour. He wasn't a warm man, but he was a *good* man. He taught me about honor and taking care of the people you love. What kind of families did these people have?"

"Clearly not healthy ones."

"Your parents were really worried about you." He kept his voice soft. "When John called me and told me you'd been involved in a shooting, I was terrified. I tried to reassure them, but I don't know if it worked."

She put a hand on his cheek and felt the beginnings of stubble. "I'm fine. Henry is fine. I think he enjoyed the excitement."

"You know, I would not have pegged you as an adrenaline junkie."

"I'm really not. Promise."

He leaned over and placed a gentle kiss on her lips. "Spare a thought for my heart, okay? Try to avoid any more guns pointed in your direction."

"I promise I'll do my best." She shifted when she felt a twinge in her side. "He's making me pay for it today though. I'm aching everywhere."

"Want me to run you a bath? You're probably sore from Michael's car going over those rough roads. You know, the Land Cruiser is a good vehicle, but—"

"Whoa." Vivian held her side and her breath as her abdomen tightened, as if it had been pulled by a giant rubber band. She gripped Richard's hand and squeezed hard. "Ahhhh, ha. Oh."

"Vivian?"

"I think..." The pressure eased gradually, like a balloon slowly losing air. "That was a contraction."

"A contraction?" Richard sat up in bed and reached for his phone. "I'm calling an ambulance. It's too early. You're not due for another three weeks."

"What?" Her eyes went wide. "No, don't call an ambulance. I'm fine. My last appointment, my doctor said that Henry was big for his gestational age. She thought I might go early, and she didn't seem worried. Besides, this probably isn't even real labor."

Richard looked utterly confused. He already had his robe on and was heading for the door. "Are you telling me there's fake labor?"

"There is something called false labor, but there are also things called Braxton-Hicks— Just relax. Even when I do go into real labor, having a baby is nothing like the movies. Nothing happens quickly, I promise. That was probably, like, a practice contraction. Just my uterus getting ready for the main event."

"Are you sure?" Richard looked wary. "I have a doctor that will come to the house if you want. You had a shock; could that lead to early labor?"

"Richard." She tried to pull him back down to the bed. "Relax. I know this is my first baby, but I promise there is nothing to worry about. I was stressed last night, but there is no reason to think that any of this would lead to Henry coming early. Trust me, my sister and my mom have both quizzed me extensively."

He gradually eased back onto the bed. "If you're sure."

"I'm sure." She patted his arm and tried to get him to slide back into bed with her. "Let's just relax and I'll try to get a little more sleep, okay?"

THREE HOURS LATER...

VIVIAN PANTED AS EVY HELD HER HAND. "I KNOW nothing. I never should have said I was sure."

Julia stood on her other side, imitating the breathing techniques they'd practiced in her prebirth class. "Just do what I'm doing." She did the rhythmic breathing designed for the last stage of labor.

"And squeeze my hand as hard as you want." Evy ran a piece of ice over Vivian's forehead. "Besides, admitting you know nothing is probably a great starting point to being a successful mother."

Vivian felt like crying. "This was the worst idea ever."

"I mean, it's definitely not making me sorry that I never wanted kids," Evy muttered, "but there's really only one way out of this now, so... You can do it!"

"You are going to be great." Julia rubbed her back. "Just breathe with me, and focus on Henry finally stepping off your bladder."

"And hey! Your water broke in the shower and didn't ruin Richard's ten-thousand-dollar bed, so that's excellent news."

"It's too early. Is he going to be okay?" Vivian was crying again. "I think my doctor was wrong; make it stop."

Julia wrapped her hand in hers. "Focus on your breathing. Your doctor said everything looked fine, remember? You just grow babies faster than average."

Evy said, "And since you're the world's biggest overachiever, this completely makes sense."

The labor nurse was looking between the three of them like they were insane.

Vivian nodded at Evy. "Her assignment was to entertain me because we thought this was going to take a lot longer."

The nurse shrugged. "Sometimes it does, sometimes it doesn't. You almost ready to push?"

"Yes?" Vivian couldn't think straight. Where were the drugs she'd so carefully planned for? She looked at Evy. "Wait, Richard's bed cost ten thousand dollars?"

"I mean, probably. Isn't that what rich people pay for beds?" Evy shrugged. "Either way, better that you didn't ruin it, right?"

"Right." Vivian felt one contraction recede just as another started to build. "Oh my God, this really was the worst idea ever."

"Best!" Julia said. "Totally the best. You're going to be a mother soon, and you're going to crush it."

"Crush my *hand*, you mean," Evy said.

Julia gave her a dirty look.

"I had two hours of material written, and she only labored for forty minutes! I don't want it to go to waste."

"Time to push," the labor nurse said. "Tell your friends this isn't the entertaining part."

"If this isn't the entertaining part, then why is there a whole tray of drugs in the corner?"

"Evy!"

"Okay, okay, I'll shut up now."

Chapter Twenty-Nine

Vivian opened her eyes to see her mother on the far side of the room, rocking Henry while her father and Richard stared at the baby like the tiny, adorable alien he was.

"I'd forgotten how small newborns are," Allan said. "Debra's kids were all bigger than he is though."

"She had big babies," her mother said. "Early, just like Vivian. But Henry is perfect. Six pounds and perfect. I already checked him over."

"This kid is going to be the healthiest kid and have the best teeth with you for grandparents," Richard said. "I can't imagine growing up with a doctor for a grandmother."

Vivian smiled and cleared her throat. "It mostly means she ignores your whining unless there's blood."

"Hey, you." Richard walked over and brushed a kiss over her forehead. "How are you feeling?"

"Tired. Sore." She glanced down. "Very sore."

"I can imagine."

Vivian stared at him. "Really?"

Richard shook his head. "I *cannot* imagine, but I can sympathize and commit to bringing you as many ice packs as you want."

"I'll take it."

His emotions were all over the place, but the one that kept washing over her again and again was tenderness. Richard was feeling very protective and very sentimental right now.

"Are you thinking of Maddy?" she whispered.

He frowned a little. "I missed so much."

"But you have now." She squeezed his hand. "Do you think there's any way I can wrestle my son away from my mother?"

My son.

She couldn't believe her own ears. She had a son.

A son.

Henry.

Joan heard her and stood, walking over to the bed with the tiny swaddled baby who had entered the world three weeks early with a shout and an impatience that reminded Vivian of herself. He was a little bit light, so they'd have to monitor his weight carefully, but other than that, he was completely healthy.

"Here he is." Joan laid Henry gently in her arms. "He's perfect, Vivi. Absolutely beautiful."

And he's mine.

She looked at Richard, looked at her mother and father. "I did it. Well, with Evy and Julia's help. Where are they?"

Richard was staring at Henry. "I think they said something about finding margaritas."

Vivian had no idea what time it was, but that tracked. Her two best friends had stayed with her through the delivery, watched over her in recovery when she was completely out of it, and been ready to bully the nurses around when she needed something.

If they were ready for margaritas, she could take it from there.

"He's so beautiful, Vivian."

"I know." She stared at Henry. His lips were a perfect little bow, and he had so much hair. His cheeks were already round, and his eyes darted beneath delicate lids as he dreamed. "What do you think babies dream about?"

"Right now? Probably milk." Joan was beaming. "All his tests look good, but you should try to nurse soon. It's been about two hours, and they'll be keeping an eye on his weight."

"Sure thing." She started to untie her gown, completely forgetting about her father and Richard. She felt high and exhausted all at the same time. She wanted to lay Henry on her chest and sleep for a week.

Allan cleared his throat. "Rich, I think this is our cue to go get some decent food for the new mom. Sound like a plan?"

"There's a noodle place Vivian likes about a block away." He tucked her hair behind her ear. "How does that sound?"

"Right now any food sounds good."

Henry was starting to make fussy sounds. He was ready to eat too.

"We're starving here, aren't we, Henry?"

The men ducked out of the hospital room, and Joan pulled her chair up to Vivian's bed. "At this stage, it's better for them to take care of you while you take care of Henry."

"If I get noodles out of the deal, I'm not going to complain."

Four weeks later...

VIVIAN STARTED AWAKE WHEN SHE HEARD THE doorbell at the gate. A burp cloth fell from her eyes and landed in her lap. Her gaze darted to Henry, who was still sleeping in his swing.

The chime came again, this time a little louder. Vivian struggled up from the couch and walked to the door. It was Sunday,

Bernie's day off, and Vivian was catching a nap while Henry slept.

She cracked the door open to see John Marcos waving from beyond the garden gate.

"Hey! I hope I'm not disturbing you." His hand shot up, and it held a bright orange bag filled with blue tissue paper. "I come bearing gifts."

Vivian smiled, glanced at Henry, then slid on a pair of sandals and walked to the garden gate. "Hey, you. I haven't seen you since Henry was born. How's it going?"

"Well, Sergio and Dean threatened me within an inch of my life if I came too early asking any questions about the case." He gave her shoulders a squeeze when he walked inside. "They're both convinced West Barrett's stunt with the gun and the truck is what made you go into labor."

Vivian waved a hand and straightened her shirt. "I asked my sister, and she didn't seem to think it would have done any harm. I wasn't shot or anything. Just had a little scare. Henry was ready to make his entrance."

"Yeah?" John grinned. "How is the little guy? Is he sleeping or...?"

"He's great! He's in the front room. Come on in." She waved him in and pointed to the shoe rack by the door as she slid off her sandals. "Don't tell my mom I went outside. She'll get all weird about it."

"Being outside?"

Vivian was going stir-crazy in her house, but she had to agree with her mom on one thing about staying a full month at home: she was better rested than she expected. Between Bernie, her mother, and her dad, she was sleeping enough and nursing had become routine.

She could not imagine doing this alone.

John handed her the bag. "My sister picked it out when I

told her my friend just had a baby. She has three boys, so I figured she'd know what to get you."

"That's so sweet." Vivian sat on the couch. "Thank you." She waved at Henry. "Well, here he is. Pretty quiet right now. That can and will change at three in the morning though."

John bent down over the swing, peering at Henry with the curiosity of a single man. "He's a cute little dude. Gotta love those cheeks."

"You should see him without his hat." Vivian held her hands out from her head. "So much hair. He looks like one of those little troll dolls. I love it."

John looked around the house. "No nanny?"

"I have one, and she's great. Her name is Bernie, but it's her day off. She's a godsend." Vivian leaned back as soon as she was sure Henry was going to continue sleeping.

"Not Julia and Evy?"

"They're the most hilarious and annoying aunties in the world, but they have limited usefulness when it comes to stuff like changing diapers."

"Ah." John nodded. "Got it."

"But Henry is completely in love with Evy. I think it's all the funny faces she makes." The baby was out like a light. Even with all the conversation, he was passed out in a milk-drunk haze. "Sorry he's not more awake for your visit. He just ate a big lunch, so he's gonna sleep for a couple of hours. He's pretty funny when he's awake."

John perched on her dad's favorite recliner. "My sister says babies are like campfires; you can watch them for no reason and they're still entertaining."

Vivian smiled. "Yeah, that's pretty accurate. I definitely lose track of time sometimes."

"And how's Richard keeping up?"

She laughed a little. "Let's just say that Richard is the king of takeout delivery, and it's a very good thing he's an easygoing guy with the way my mom orders him around."

"He is a good one. I'm glad the two of you..." John nodded. "Yeah. It's good."

Well, that was darn near effusive coming from John Marcos. Vivian felt quiet happiness with something more complicated bubbling under the surface. John wasn't just at her house to visit. "How's the case?"

He nodded slowly. "It's coming together."

"Pippa take a deal?"

"Yeah." He let out a long breath. "Her lawyers have been negotiating with the DA for weeks. Not going to lie—it feels wrong, but the lawyers seem to think that Pippa's cooperation means they'll be able to put West Barrett, Trace Mitchell, and Trent Everett in jail for a long time."

The local and national news had been an endless loop of breathless coverage of what the news had dubbed the "PTA Murders" in Palm Springs. A joint task force from Palm Springs and Rancho Mirage regularly offered updates, and West Barrett and Trent Everett had already been arrested.

"So Pippa's willing to testify against all of them?"

John nodded. "Can you believe they drew straws?"

"They *what*?"

"They drew straws at a Booster Club meeting, like playing a game in school or something. Each person held the straws to choose their own parent's murderer, that way no one could trace it back to them."

"Ashley Gates said she thought it was a joke."

"Yeah, she's still claiming that, I think."

"Unbelievable."

"All the deaths were supposed to look like accidents or random acts of violence. Archie Barrett was the big fuckup."

"Because my mother saw the attack?"

John's face was grim. "There was never supposed to be an

attack. Archie was supposed to get drunk and fall in the water. It was supposed to look like he drowned, but Trent Everett screwed up. Archie wasn't cooperating even when he was drunk, and Everett panicked. Hit him with a golf club to keep him from going back to the party."

Vivian's mouth fell open. "Is that when he lost his wedding ring? All this time I wondered—"

"Your first instinct was correct." John bowed a little. "My apologies to the psychic. The girl at the club, the secretary? She admitted that he lied about reporting it stolen a few days before. Thought she was just helping a friend avoid unnecessary questions from the police."

"What is the DA saying about Ashley Gates? She didn't kill anyone, but she obviously knew her father's death wasn't natural."

"Not sure. Since she didn't kill Judge Stanford like she was supposed to, she might be able to get a deal."

"But she knew that one of her friends killed her dad."

"She knew, but Pippa was the one who told us who."

Vivian raised her eyebrows. "Trace Mitchell?"

He nodded. "According to Pippa, he used some of his mother's old medication from when she had cancer and dosed Gates's drink. The old man's death was ruled natural causes though, so not an easy hurdle to jump. Since he was cremated, there's no body to exhume. It'll be a harder case to try."

"But they think Pippa's testimony will be enough?"

"In the context of a conspiracy, his role makes sense. Plus..." John smiled a little. "Did you see the news this morning?"

"I've been doing laundry and sleeping," Vivian said. "I don't know how this tiny person makes so many dirty clothes, but I have not caught the news in days."

"Trace Mitchell tried to flee to Mexico last night," John said. "Bunch of cash in the car. No wife or kids. We think his dad helped him out, but he was stopped at the border. Trying to flee makes him look extra guilty. I imagine he'll be the next arrest."

"Dumb."

"He is." John nodded. "West was the mastermind, but I suspect Pippa was right after him. They're the two smartest in that group. We've found a lot of calls between the two, especially right after Archie Barrett's murder. I think that spooked them all, but I think Pippa and West were the ones egging the others on."

Vivian could tell that was what was bothering John. Pippa was a ringleader, but she'd be escaping the most serious consequences. "The DA is doing the right thing, John. At the end of the day, she didn't kill anyone, and a deal with Pippa puts the others in prison for sure."

He looked up. "You think? Their parents weren't the only victims. How's your mom?"

"My mom is fine. She's feeling much safer now that West Barrett is behind bars, though I do think she misses Andre. She's invited him for dinner like three times now." Vivian took a deep breath. "But she's sleeping well. Her doctors are saying good things about her stroke rehab, and she's responding well to her medication." She reached across and squeezed his hand. "My parents are safe. Pippa's parents are alive; she didn't commit any murders. They're doing the right thing."

"Thanks." He cleared his throat. "I don't really have a say in it, you know. I'm just a cop at the end of the day, but hearing you say that... It helps."

"Wow, what a group." Vivian shook her head. "Makes me grateful for my own friends. They're not nearly that murdery."

John closed his eyes and laughed. "Not many people are."

"Hey, you coming to Sunday Dinner at Sergio and Dean's tonight?" She wiggled her eyebrows. "I think Evy's going to be there."

"Is this how it's going to be now?" John's smile was wry.

"You and Richard are happily coupled up, so are Julia and Michael, now Evy needs a boyfriend?"

"You should be flattered. We're very picky. Not murdery, but picky."

"Please, no more murders." He closed his eyes. "I've had enough to keep me busy for a decade. I took this job because I thought the worst I'd have to deal with was drunk festival kids, you know? Maybe the odd screaming match over a nasty divorce."

"Don't worry about me," Vivian said. "I can't speak for Evy and Julia, but after Henry, I think I'm definitely retired from crime fighting."

Mostly.

That was... hardly at all.

After all, she'd be moving to Vista de Lirio within a few weeks since the owners of the adorable midcentury house had accepted her offer for the place on the cul-de-sac, and she'd be just another boring neighbor in the most eccentric neighborhood in Palm Springs.

"Yeah." She nodded. "I'm totally retired. Nothing but tooth fillings and mom stuff for me from here on out."

She didn't have to hear his skepticism, she could feel it.

"Seriously." Vivian smiled. "My life right now? It's about as close to perfect as I could imagine. No way am I going to let anything mess that up."

She had a family now. She had Henry and her parents. Evy and Julia. Dean, Sergio, and their daughters. Even Richard and Maddy were inching closer every week.

She'd left Chicago with professional ambitions and a loathing of snow, only to find a wealth of the unexpected that couldn't have made her happier. Absolutely nothing had turned out the way Vivian had planned.

It was so much better.

Can't get enough Vista de Lirio? Keep your eyes open for
TROUBLE PLAY
Coming October 2022!

COMEDIAN EV LANE THOUGHT SHE'D DONE IT ALL, but taking on the role of mistress of ceremonies for the Desert Fancy Dog Show may be her most challenging gig yet. The locals are a menagerie of high-strung prima donnas, nervous Nelsons, and she's not talking about the dogs. When high stakes competition leads to gruesome murder, she's going to need every telepathic power at her disposal—and every psychic she knows—to make the show go on.

For more information about TROUBLE PLAY or other titles, please visit ElizabethHunterWrites.com!

Looking for more?

Whether you're a fan of contemporary fantasy, fantasy romance, or paranormal women's fiction, Elizabeth Hunter has a series for you!

The Elemental Mysteries

Discover the series that has millions of vampire fans raving! Immortal book dealer Giovanni Vecchio thought he'd left the bloody world of vampire politics behind when he retired as an assassin, but a chance meeting at a university pulls student librarian Beatrice De Novo into his orbit. Now temptation lurks behind every dark corner as Vecchio's growing attachment to Beatrice competes with a series of clues that could lead to a library lost in time, and a powerful secret that could reshape the immortal world.

The Cambio Springs Mysteries

Welcome to the desert town of Cambio Springs where the water is cool, the summers sizzle, and all the residents wear fur, feathers, or snakeskin on full moon nights. In a world of cookie-cutter shifter romance, discover a series that has reviewers raving. Five friends find themselves at a crossroads in life; will the tangled ties of community and shared secrets be their salvation or their end?

The Irin Chronicles

"A brilliant and addictive romantic fantasy series." Hidden at the crossroads of the world, an ancient race battles to protect humanity, even as it dies from within. A photojournalist tumbles into a world of supernatural guardians protecting humanity from the predatory sons of fallen angels, but will Ava and Malachi's attraction to each other be their salvation or their undoing?

Glimmer Lake

Delightfully different paranormal women's fiction! Robin, Val, and Monica were average forty-something moms when a sudden accident leaves all three of them with psychic abilities they never could have predicted! Now all three are seeing things that belong in a fantasy novel, not their small mountain town. Ghosts, visions, omens of doom. These friends need to stick together if they're going to solve the mystery at the heart of Glimmer Lake.

And there's more! Please visit ElizabethHunterWrites.com to sign up for her newsletter or read more about her work.

Acknowledgments

Once again, nothing happens in book world without the tireless work of my publishing team. Without their help, I'd be much more stressed and much less coherent.

Many thanks to my personal team:

Genevieve Johnson, my extraordinary assistant and favorite sister. If I couldn't work with you, I'd be calling you all the time to complain about having a subpar assistant, so I guess you're kind of doing yourself a favor there.

Nina and the entire team at Valentine PR. You gals rock! I am so happy that your spreadsheets found my sister's. It is a romance for the ages, and I am grateful.

All the excellent staff at Dystel, Goderich, and Bourett Literary Agency. Thank you for all you do to represent me and my work.

Melissa, Kaitlyn, and Angi, thank you for doing what you do! Cause that allows me to do what I do instead of what you do, and we all know that you don't want me doing what you're doing because you do it better. MUAH!

To my editorial team:

Amy Cissell, I still haven't figured out how you're both an amazing writer AND an amazing content editor. Like, that seems like too many superpowers, and I'm wondering if you're going to take over the world now. I love you, but I'll be watching. I'll be watching.

Anne Victory, I love that you know my comma issues, my internal may/might conflict, and my addiction to the passive voice, yet you still allow me to send you things. I am very grateful for that.

And to Linda, proofreader of mystery, thank you for catching as many of those typos as you possibly can. If there are any left, it's most likely my own darn fault.

And to my Hunters!

You're the only thing that makes me happy to go on Facebook anymore. I can't wait to get back to book signings so I can see your smiling faces again and you can see my awkward affection.

Thanks everyone. I hope you enjoyed Vivian and her story.

About the Author

ELIZABETH HUNTER is a seven-time *USA Today* and international best-selling author of romance, contemporary fantasy, and paranormal mystery. Based in Central California and Addis Ababa, she travels extensively to write fantasy fiction exploring world mythologies, history, and the universal bonds of love, friendship, and family. She has published over forty works of fiction and sold over a million books worldwide. She is the author of the Glimmer Lake series, Love Stories on 7th and Main, the Elemental Legacy series, the Irin Chronicles, the Cambio Springs Mysteries, and other works of fiction.

Also by Elizabeth Hunter

Vista de Lirio

Double Vision

Mirror Obscure

Trouble Play

(October 2022)

Glimmer Lake

Suddenly Psychic

Semi-Psychic Life

Psychic Dreams

Moonstone Cove

Runaway Fate

Fate Actually

Fate Interrupted

The Cambio Springs Series

Long Ride Home

Shifting Dreams

Five Mornings

Desert Bound

Waking Hearts

The Elemental Mysteries

A Hidden Fire

This Same Earth

The Force of Wind

A Fall of Water

The Stars Afire

The Elemental World

Building From Ashes

Waterlocked

Blood and Sand

The Bronze Blade

The Scarlet Deep

A Very Proper Monster

A Stone-Kissed Sea

Valley of the Shadow

The Elemental Legacy

Shadows and Gold

Imitation and Alchemy

Omens and Artifacts

Obsidian's Edge (anthology)

Midnight Labyrinth

Blood Apprentice

The Devil and the Dancer

Night's Reckoning

Dawn Caravan

The Bone Scroll

The Elemental Covenant

Saint's Passage

Martyr's Promise

Paladin's Kiss

(August 2022)

The Irin Chronicles

The Scribe

The Singer

The Secret

The Staff and the Blade

The Silent

The Storm

The Seeker

Linx & Bogie Mysteries

A Ghost in the Glamour

A Bogie in the Boat

Contemporary Romance

The Genius and the Muse

7th and Main

Ink

Hooked

Grit

Sweet

Printed in Great Britain
by Amazon